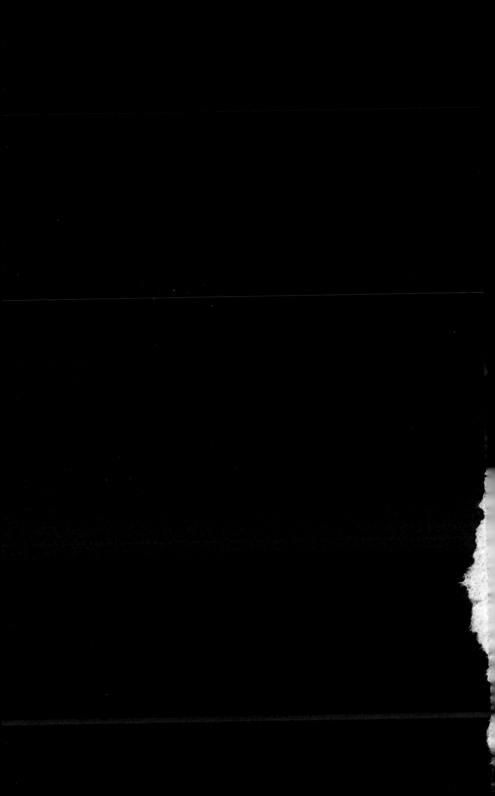

Tangled Webs

Lee Bross

HYPERION

First Edition, June 2015
1 3 5 7 9 10 8 6 4 2
G475-5664-5-15091
Printed in the United States of America

This book is set in Baskerville
Designed by Whitney Manger

ISBN 978-1-4231-8423-2

Reinforced binding

Visit www.hyperionteens.com

SUSTAINABLE FORESTRY INITIATIVE Certified Sourcing
www.sfiprogram.org
SFI-00993

THIS LABEL APPLIES TO TEXT STOCK

06 15

TO MY DAD, WHO SHOWED ME
THAT LIFE IS TOO SHORT NOT
TO CHASE YOUR DREAMS.

I MISS YOU EVERY DAY.

CHAPTER 1

LONDON, 1725

*L*ord Huntington made his way through the crowded ballroom with the poise and elegance of an over-fattened Christmas goose.

Arista watched, in no hurry to reveal her presence. She smiled, a languid movement that did not betray the way her heart thumped in her chest. The element of surprise worked in her favor on nights like these. She could almost hear his heart pounding from across the room. Every few seconds he tugged on the edge of his cravat, an outward sign of his agitation.

Masked people spun by in a rainbow of dizzying colors. Excitement filled the air of the ballroom, causing bursts of laughter to erupt spontaneously around her. It did not matter if you were rich or poor, as long as you could afford the price of admission. Only at the public masquerades did the aristocracy mix with commoners without care; here, the rich dressed as milkmaids and the poor as queens.

For Arista, it was the perfect opportunity to conduct business.

Dressed in black silk, she blended into the background, unremarkable. Adorned only with a simple black mask, among all the other masquerade characters, she garnered little interest. No one ever approached her for a dance. Curious glances were met with a frosty stare or folded arms. With so many willing partners, she was soon forgotten.

The ones who'd had previous dealings with Bones knew her, though they pretended otherwise. They stayed far away. And if they happened too close, or met her stare by chance, Arista never missed the contempt in their eyes. She was good enough when they wanted something, but otherwise she meant nothing to them.

Arista's gaze never lingered on any one person for too long, either, even as she kept the nobleman in question within view. Her clients didn't often try to run, but when they did, she needed to be ready.

This part, the predatory rush of stalking her prey across a crowded ballroom, was most satisfying. Anticipation buzzed in her head. She glanced casually over the masked guests until she spotted him again.

The nobleman moved cautiously along the outer edges of the crowd, away from the throng of people. If he was planning to try and sneak out, he should have chosen a less obvious costume for the evening. The bobbling points of his bright jester hat made it easy to keep him in sight.

Moments earlier, a servant had delivered a discreet note to Lord Huntington with only two words written on the small card.

Library. Midnight.

A quick glance at the enormous grandfather clock to her left told her it was only a quarter till. Lord Huntington still had fifteen minutes to try and do something stupid.

You make a deal with the devil, you pay the price.

They always seemed to forget that part.

Arista ran her fingers over the familiar shape of her knife, safely strapped to the outside of her thigh and hidden under yards of satin. It gave her comfort. Courage. Sometimes all it took was the threat of the blade to encourage compliance. But there had been a few times, unfortunate as they were, when Arista had been forced to use it. That fact alone made her a target. Powerful men did not like to have their control stripped away, especially by a woman in a mask. They would not hesitate to stick a blade in her gut if they knew her face beneath the mask. If they ever found her alone.

Desperate aristocrats dealt with Bones out of necessity, not choice. They dealt with her, with the infamous Lady A, who collected payment for the poor choices they'd already made.

Bones was a "fixer," a trader of information—or more often, secrets—in exchange for money. Now seventeen, Arista was the face of his operation, a pawn he had molded and groomed to use in a society he could not navigate. If they knew she was merely a marionette, they would not be so wary of her.

In the past year alone, Bones had obtained more than enough secrets from the London aristocracy to bring them to their knees. But that wasn't all he wanted. He wanted their indebtedness.

Bones wanted to own them all.

And when he did, his need for Lady A would end—something she tried not to consider. The future was an abstract place to Arista, though she often spent hours at the docks, watching the ships come and go and wishing she could change her own life. She found it safer to exist only in the present. That mindset had kept her alive so far.

Lord Huntington glanced around furtively, then made a sudden move toward a set of open patio doors. Arista sighed. So it was going to be like that, then.

She caught Nic's ever-watchful eye and tilted her head in the direction of Lord Huntington. He understood right away and disappeared into the crowd.

Nic would not harm him. The nobleman simply needed a reminder of his obligation. Of what he now owed, in return for using the services of her employer. Arista had practically delivered the title of earl to him, along with all that went with it, just one month ago. Thanks to Bones's information—that the previous Earl of Huntington, cousin of Arista's current quarry, was illegitimate— Huntington had been elevated beyond his wildest dreams. He had secured the earldom for his own, as the only *rightful* male heir still alive.

And now he expected her to chase him down for payment? It was damned near impossible to run in a dress and heeled slippers.

Nonetheless, she would chase him all over London if necessary.

Arista had almost reached the open doors when a surly Lord Huntington reappeared. Right behind him was Nic. The earl shot a venomous glance over his shoulder, then pushed his way back into the crowd. Arista moved away from the doors, to a spot where she could see the earl and also the clock. They had only five more minutes to wait.

Nic wouldn't let Lord Huntington out of his sight now, but she still glanced back at Huntington every few seconds. In crowded spaces like the ballroom, it became harder to keep a watchful eye on the nearly unnoticeable tics that gave away a person's intentions. Most people gave off small clues—tensed muscles, a slight shift in movement, a subtle glance—that indicated what they were about to do. Body language told her what people were thinking before they even knew it themselves.

When she was a child, sent to the market to pick pockets, Arista had spent hours watching people. The way they held their heads; what their hands were doing; the way they walked or stood. All were useful clues. This skill showed her the best people to steal from: the ones who were thinking about something else, who were distracted or daydreaming. It also made Arista one of the best thieves Bones had.

Her abilities had saved her life on more than one occasion. Just last week, the Duke of Conley—a thin, vapid man who sniffed into a perfumed handkerchief the entire time Arista waited for payment—had thought to use several hired men to attack her to get out of his obligation. Unfortunately for him, Arista had seen the flicker of the duke's gaze, the merest nod of his head, and the shine of victory in his eyes—all of which gave away his lackeys' location.

"Behind me. Left," she'd said, without breaking eye contact with the duke. Nic had sprung into action. The hired men were disarmed and unconscious before the duke could even blink.

Nic was powerful, fast, and deadly accurate.

The look of disbelief on the duke's face had almost been payment enough. Arista had smiled during the rest of the transaction, even when the duke hissed out a new threat before disappearing into his carriage. "I love it when they think they're gonna outsmart you," Nic had said with a wide grin. He lived for the fight. The scars on his knuckles proved it.

But Arista already knew Lord Huntington would not fight. He was entirely too soft to have ever gotten physical with anything more than an oversized roast duck.

A couple swept by, and Arista could not help but notice the way the woman tilted her head back, just enough to let the gentleman sneak a kiss where her neck and bared shoulder met. For one fleeting moment, Arista wondered what it would be like to be that woman. To lean in close, her hands on a man's chest, and smile coyly up at him. To see the flare of desire make his eyes dilate in the candlelight.

Arista met Nic's dark stare between the dancers. Did he wonder the same thing?

He had dressed as a pirate for the masquerade, and looked as dark and dangerous as the real thing. His clothes were not of the finest materials, but they hugged his lean body like a glove. The mask he wore was a simple eye patch that covered his left eye.

Arista's chest tightened, and for a moment, she could picture them as guests, dancing to the soft strains of the orchestra. Nic would brush his lips over hers, whispering in her ear, like he did with the girls at the docks. Those unknown words that made the girls smile flirtatiously as they slipped their hands into his, leading him up the scarred wooden steps to the floor above.

Heat pooled in her stomach and she pressed her fists against it to try and physically force the feeling back down. When had she started to see Nic as more than just her bodyguard? He was the only person in the world that she trusted with her life on a nightly basis. She wouldn't be alive if not for him. He was her friend. That was all.

And still . . .

The restlessness had been growing stronger lately. The urge to get away from everything; to have a different life without fear hanging over their heads. More often than not, when they left a party, she had to fight the urge to keep going. To simply disappear. But they had nowhere to go. No means to afford even a cheap hackney to the outskirts of London. Bones owned them both.

They were stuck in this life, but at least she had Nic.

The brow over Nic's eye patch rose, and a knowing grin tipped one corner of his mouth. Wisps of black hair curled around the strings of his disguise. Damn him. He knew what he did to her. He always played the rakish flirt when they were working. He made her blood do crazy things inside her veins, yet he reverted to acting like her friend the moment the masks came off. It frustrated the hell out of her.

As she watched, a woman sidled up to him and he turned his attention to her. She leaned in and said something as he reached up to trace a lazy circle on her shoulder. When she leaned against his arm, fiery jealousy exploded inside Arista. He should be paying attention to the job, not to some barely dressed woman. She pushed through the crowd, hand on the knife hidden under her dress. A knife that Nic had given to her.

He had not yet noticed Arista getting closer. The woman held all of his attention. She wore a costume of shimmering blue satin. The bodice dipped down very low in front, and the entire costume rippled like waves when she moved. A swan's mask obscured the features of her face, but Arista could see the hungry gleam in her eyes as she looked up at Nic.

The woman could have been a street-corner flower girl or a princess, and every man there would still want her. The anger fell away from Arista like a discarded cloak. There was no comparison between her and the radiant girl that held Nic's gaze.

Arista stopped before she reached them. What was she thinking—was she going to pull her knife and demand the woman leave Nic alone? He didn't belong to Arista. He didn't belong to anyone except Bones. None of them did.

The fire in her gut turned to ice.

It did no good to wish things were different. Arista knew that. And even though Nic appeared engaged with his companion, his awareness was focused solely on Arista. If she gave him the signal, he'd abandon the woman without a single glance back.

She met his gaze and raised one eyebrow at him. Nic only grinned back at her, his finger now sliding down over the woman's collarbone. Arista turned away, her long dark curls brushing her back. The curls were an unfamiliar and heavy presence, even now. The wig had become a perfect accomplice to her charade, but she preferred the feel of her own much shorter hair, tucked safely under a wool cap.

After all this time, Arista still had not gotten used to playing the role of Lady A. There was a certain vulnerability in wearing a dress—shoulders bared, breasts accentuated to the point of indecency—that she could not get used to. Even after Becky had raised the neckline, Arista complained it was still too low. By the end of nights like these, she only wanted to retreat back into her normal disguise. As a boy, no one bothered her, apart from an absent swipe or two from a disgruntled workman.

Lord Huntington now stood at the buffet stuffing delicate pastries into his mouth as if this were his last meal. Only a few more minutes, and their business could be started. A dull throb had started at the base of her neck. She wanted to end the evening and go back to the quiet of her room. Absently, Arista rubbed at the source of the pain, and her knuckles brushed against the silk scarf wound around her hair.

"You've been to India?" a deep voice from behind her asked.

Arista half turned her head, enough to look up, and found herself face-to-face with a highwayman. A black silk scarf obscured the lower half of his face. He had an equally black hat pulled so low, she could only see a glimpse of his eyes, which were reflecting the flickering candlelight. It might have been a masquerade, but she could almost believe he was an *actual* outlaw. "Excuse me?" she asked, unable to look away from him.

He fingered her scarf, his touch grazing the back of her neck. Tension coiled just under her skin. Should she stay? Run? The urge to do both overwhelmed her.

"This scarf is from India, if I'm not mistaken. I only wondered if you'd traveled there." She found herself mesmerized by his rich voice.

"No," she whispered. "Have you been?"

"Yes."

His one-word answer sent a thrill of anticipation over her skin.

How often had she visited the docks and watched the ships sail in and out? How many times had she wished she were on one of them, on her way to India? The men at the docks told stories of people who rode elephants and wore colors so bright you had to look away; of air full of the pungent aroma of spices.

The scarf in her hair had been a gift from Nalia, the Indian laundress at the orphanage, the only woman there who'd showed any kindness toward Arista. When Arista had left, Nalia had given the scarf to her as a reminder that a whole other world existed out there. India became the refuge that Arista clung to on cold, dark nights. One day, she vowed, she would escape from London and go.

Now she was closer than she'd ever been before. "Where did you go? What did you see?" she begged. The party around them faded as she focused on his answer. He leaned in close, and her pulse leapt in an unfamiliar way. She took a quick step back. Her instincts had saved her more than once, but this didn't feel unsafe. In fact, the feeling in her veins excited her.

"We traveled to the West Indies, then to the islands, then to Fort St. George. My father owns a fleet of merchant ships, and I am working my way up to captain." Pride shone from his eyes as he again leaned in close, as if he were going to share a secret with her. "This next trip, I hope, will be under my command."

"You don't seem old enough to be a captain."

He laughed. He had a very nice laugh. It sank under her skin and made her want to hear it again and again.

"I'm nineteen, so yes, maybe a little bit young. But I've been aboard ships since I could walk. I love the freedom; open ocean as far as the eye can see. Away from the rules of society, it doesn't matter who you are. London is stifling. I hate coming back here. Well, until now, that is." Light danced in his eyes. Their bodies were almost pressed against each other, so close she could feel the heat radiating from him. Distracted by his words, she hadn't noticed right away. People never got this close without her sensing it. Arista swallowed but didn't move.

"That sounds so perfect," she whispered.

More questions danced on her tongue. She wanted to know everything—what the air smelled like when no land could be seen; what kind of people he had met; what cities looked like across thousands of miles of ocean.

"It is perfect." His expression was so open; she kept waiting for his disguise to crack. It had to be an act. No one could be this . . . nice. Everyone wanted something from her. Yet he was talking to her as if they were equals. Maybe he thought they were. People

of dancers passed by, she dove among them, putting the crowd between her and the man who had nearly destroyed her defenses. She stood on the outskirts of the room, forcing the errant feelings back inside, where she hoped they would eventually die.

Grae. Like his eyes. Like the thunderclouds that filled the sky before a storm.

She pressed her gloved fingers to her lips to keep from saying it out loud.

A hand appeared on her arm, and another at her back. For a moment she thought Grae had followed her, and an unexpected rush of anticipation made her skin tingle.

"You okay, gypsy? Thought I lost you there for a minute." Nic stood in front of her, partially shielding her from the crowd. Always the protector. Always looking out for her, like he'd promised to do so many years ago.

Arista closed her eyes and took several deep breaths. Not Grae. Nic.

"You know I hate when you call me gypsy." The words came out rough, betraying her still-fragile control. Where had the highwayman gone? She could not see him over Nic's shoulder, which meant he had not followed her. The bitter sting of disappointment made her close her eyes.

"Well, we still have work to do—*gypsy.* You feeling up to it?" Though Nic asked, she knew there was no choice. It didn't matter that her composure had slipped dangerously out of her control. She had a debt to collect. A job to do.

She cleared her throat, took a deep breath to clear her thoughts, and nodded. "Where is Lord Huntington now?"

Nic flicked his eyes toward an archway where Lord Huntington stood. Arista already knew it led to the library, just as she knew every exit in the house. The first few minutes of each job were spent getting the feel for their surroundings. Unless they had been there before. "It's time, then."

They walked side by side around the edge of the room. Little by little, her composure returned. Each step took her away from what had happened on the dance floor.

Lady A had regained control once more.

Just steps away from Lord Huntington, Nic stopped her with a slight touch on her arm. She could not help the immediate comparison to how Graeden's fingers had affected her.

Arista stared at Nic's hand, waiting, hoping for something more, but there was only the familiar feeling of safety, not excitement.

"Really, is everything okay, gypsy?" He stared at her, his eyebrows drawn with concern. No trace of humor remained in his eyes.

For the briefest second, she had an overwhelming urge to cry. She had not cried since she was six years old, and it had been in Nic's gangly eight-year-old arms. She'd sworn it would never happen again. Tears were for the weak—the powerless. She was neither.

"I'm fine. Let's go."

Nic looked as though he wanted to say something more, but Arista turned away before he could. No more distractions.

Lord Huntington saw them coming and quickly disappeared down the hall. After they entered behind the earl, Nic checked to be sure they were not followed. He switched to bodyguard mode seamlessly.

An enormous pair of carved-oak doors took up most of the wall at the end of the hallway. Nic pushed them open soundlessly and locked the doors behind them after they entered.

Arista's skirts rustled in the quiet of the room.

Lord Huntington stood in front of the large mantelpiece, his back to them. Arista waited several long seconds before he turned and acknowledged her—a tiny play for control on his part. She gave it to him. She let him think he had a choice, at least for the moment.

Lord Huntington's mask had been carelessly tossed aside on a polished side table next to his ridiculous hat. The seams of his silk jacket were even more strained up close, and it seemed as if the buttons would fly off at any moment. It took him three tries to clear his throat enough to speak.

"Lady A." His voice sounded hoarse, like he'd only just started using it.

She inclined her head slightly. He took a long swallow from the glass of brandy clutched in his fat fingers. Just like that, she had the power again.

His gaze shifted over her shoulder to Nic, who stood with his back against the door. Arista glanced back and smiled. Nic's arms were folded across his chest, his black jacket pulled tight across lean muscles. Though he looked almost casual standing there, no one could mistake his deadliness.

Lord Huntington cleared his throat again. "I trust, after this, I won't see you again." He handed her a thick envelope with a red wax seal. It bore the insignia of his family crest: an open-mouthed lion, crossed by a sword and spear. He seemed to relax enough to swallow the last of the brandy in several hasty mouthfuls.

The envelope was thicker than the normal payment. It appeared that Bones had set a much higher price on Huntington's request. The going rate for a seat in Parliament, and a very powerful position at that, was indeed high.

Now it only remained to be seen who would eventually pay an even higher price to lay Huntington low. Every secret could be sold.

Bones played no favorites. And those who had a secret and wished it to be kept—well, they would be forced to pay even more to keep it safe.

They never quite thought that part through—that someone else, someone more desperate, might be willing to pay dearly for *their* secrets to gain an advantage. Bones's services went to the highest bidder, plain and simple.

Those prices grew higher every day.

"Lord Huntington." Her voice came out perfectly manicured and a tad bored. It was all part of the aristocratic image she had to convey—her elaborate deception. "Whether you've fulfilled your side of the bargain remains to be seen. Bones will decide after he receives this. Until then, consider your obligation outstanding."

Lord Huntington's face turned beet red. He threw the crystal glass, and it flew past her head to shatter on the stone hearth. Arista did not flinch. She'd seen it coming. Nic, however, immediately started across the room.

"You've gotten your bloody secret from me as down payment, and now a small fortune to keep it quiet. If you think for one second you're not done with me . . . I could snap you in half, girl." The words exploded from his mouth and spittle flecked his chin.

He took a single menacing step toward her, and Nic growled a soft warning. Arista saw the surprise on Huntington's face, and then something else. A tic began in his right eye. The fingers on his right hand flexed, and he shifted his weight to his right foot.

He would fight after all.

She knew he had a knife under his vest. The earl really should have chosen a more relaxed fit of clothing if he'd wished to use the element of surprise.

"He has a weapon."

Lord Huntington shoved his hand into his pocket, but Nic was faster. He twisted the earl's right arm behind his back. The buttons that had been on the verge of exploding flew across the room as Nic ripped open Huntington's vest and disarmed him. Disbelief filled Lord Huntington's eyes and he stumbled away from them. Arista chuckled.

The sound seemed to shock Lord Huntington. He pressed against the wooden doors as if trying to disappear through them. They thought they were so much better than her, men like Huntington, but in moments like these, she held all the power. Arista walked toward the sputtering man until she stood close enough to smell his overindulgence of cologne. It did little to mask the odor of sour sweat and hard liquor.

"You would do well to remember . . ." She lifted her booted foot and rested it against the door by his leg. Slowly, she raised her skirt well past the curve of her knee with a sly smile. "Cooperation would be in everyone's best interest, and much less . . . messy."

His eyes ran down the length of her exposed flesh, and he visibly balked at the sight of the knife strapped to her thigh. He swallowed nervously, and his Adam's apple bobbed up and down like a dinghy adrift on the Thames.

"You're mad." Lord Huntington fumbled behind him, his cheeks getting redder as he struggled to find the lock. "I don't know who you think you are, but you stay away from me or I'll put a reward on your head the size of the palace, and *then* we'll see who pays."

He sneered at her, but his lips trembled.

Arista slipped the knife from its sheath. The earl's gaze darted from the blade to her face as she lifted the knife and slowly ran the tip down his cheek. Not hard enough to draw blood, but enough for him to know that she was deadly serious.

"Are you threatening me, sir?" Her voice lowered and turned deceptively soft, coating the steel lurking just beneath the surface. If he thought he could scare her, he would be disappointed. She did not cower at the raised voice of a man like him. "You made a deal, and you *will* honor it. Are you not a gentleman of your word, Lord Huntington?" She lifted one eyebrow and let her words, and the blade, trail off.

He sputtered but did not reply.

"Good evening, then, my lord." Arista sheathed the knife and sank into an exaggerated curtsy. Lord Huntington remained silent. With a dismissive turn, he clicked the lock and swept out the door in a flourish of peacock green.

As soon as the door shut, Arista leaned her forehead against the cool wood. She closed her eyes and exhaled.

"That went well." Nic's wry chuckle sounded very close. "Thought we'd have a real fight on our hands for a second. Ready to head back to the palace, princess?" Arista lifted her head. He stood no closer than a foot away, and held out his arm like a gentleman would.

With a relieved smile, she took it without hesitation. Now that their business was done, the high from being in charge faded instantly. Exhaustion set in and her body felt heavy. His arm was strong and solid under her hand.

Nic was her rock, the wall between Arista and Bones. He made sure that no matter what, she remained safe from their brutal guardian. There had been opportunities over the years when she might have slipped away—away from Bones and her life on the streets. But she had never taken them. She had nowhere to go. Not without Nic.

Once, she'd had the childish dream that they might get away

from London together. But as Nic grew into a man, Arista saw the reality of the situation. He liked this life.

Nic liked the power that came with controlling those better than them. Lately, Arista had started seeing traces of Bones in Nic, and it scared her. Maybe there was a way to convince him to leave with her before it was too late.

"This way if you please, my lady." Nic led her through a set of doors hidden by heavy drapes, and they slipped out onto a brick courtyard, away from the partygoers. Thick fog had rolled in as it did most nights, creating an almost dreamlike atmosphere. Buildings rose up into the dark shadows above them.

Away from the stifling heat of the crowded ballroom, the air chilled her flushed skin, making her shiver involuntarily.

A lady of quality always has a shawl.

Becky's admonition sounded as clearly as if the girl were there with them. The damned gentry had a rule for everything, and it exhausted Arista to remember them all—but tonight, a shawl would be welcome.

Not that she was a lady of quality, by any stretch of the imagination.

Sensing her need, Nic shrugged out of his jacket and slipped it around her bare shoulders. He brushed his fingers over her skin, and this time, warmth quickly spread from the spot he had touched. Nic tucked her arm in his and led her through the heavy front gate. They passed by several couples too engrossed in each other to even lift their heads. Arista pretended not to see them.

A sleek black carriage rolled by, the wheels rattling on the cobbled street, hooves clopping a steady rhythm as it passed. The sounds of the orchestra faded as they walked farther from Dover Street.

Tonight's task had been completed; the thick package was tucked securely in Nic's jacket. It pressed into her ribs as they walked. Exactly how much money was she carrying right at that moment? Enough to buy passage on a ship for all three of them—her, Nic, and Becky? The thought came and went quickly.

She would not look. Not ever again. Only once before, when Bones first sent her out as Lady A, had she dared to peek inside an aristocrat's envelope. She hadn't thought Bones would miss just one shilling from the package. It had taken weeks for the bruising to heal. Of course he knew, to the halfpence, how much to expect.

"Do you think he'll ever have enough?" Arista asked softly.

Each time Lady A made an appearance, the risk to Arista grew. At first, she'd only collected secrets and delivered information back to the clients. Then Bones had started sending Lady A to collect the actual money as well. That's where the real danger came into play for Arista.

Bones used the aristocracy's own secrets to blackmail them: they paid up or risked having their secrets sold to a higher bidder. Bones often left out that part of the deal until he had what he wanted *and* his client had what he or she needed. Only the most desperate or devious people resorted to the service Bones offered—ones who would lose big if their truths ever came to light. So they always paid. Only one had ever refused.

He'd hung himself from the London Bridge when his secrets had been exposed in the *Spectator*. A powerful message to all who thought to double-cross Bones; it also put a larger target on Lady A.

They might pay for silence now, but none would hesitate to kill her if given the chance. It was why she never went out in public as herself. If anyone found out what she looked like under the disguise, she would never be safe.

Nic never worried about his own safety, though he, too, wore a mask when they met with clients.

"I doubt it," Nic replied. "He's greedy, and he enjoys the power more than the money, I think." He expertly whisked her down another maze of alleyways filled with dark shadows, where the light from the street lamps didn't reach. There was no need to illuminate this part of London. No one cared what happened in the dark there. Her skirt swished in the silence.

None of the people who used Bones's services really understood what they had done—the true ramifications of trading their darkest secrets for more power and money. At some point, there would be no more secrets, but it wouldn't matter. Bones would have the means for a lifetime's worth of blackmail, if not multiple lifetimes—generations of noble families. No, these people who thought themselves so clever had become pawns in a game only Bones would win.

After several minutes, she stopped and looked up at Nic. "He could destroy every single one of them, if he wanted to."

Though she couldn't see his face in the shadows, Arista could hear the smile in Nic's voice. His words chilled her even more.

"Aye. Whoever controls the secrets controls those rich bastards."

CHAPTER 2

*T*he walk back to their "home" only took a short half hour. Taking shortcuts through alleys was second nature to Arista and Nic, and few dared maneuver them in the darkness of night. Nic gripped her arm, and his muscles tightened and released at her touch. Always in a constant state of alertness. To be mistaken for gentry in this part of London would not end well.

In her usual attire she wouldn't have attracted a second glance, but clothed in silk and paste jewelry, she was a walking target. Thankfully, Nic's dark jacket covered most of the skin exposed by the cut of the dress, and the black silk blended with the shadows. Still, she would not be completely safe until she made it back to her room.

Arista felt no pleasure, no rush of warmth, upon seeing the run-down tenement buildings she called home. Off Fleet Street a row of gutted buildings stood, so badly damaged from the fires that no one had bothered to rebuild them.

That's where the worst of the worst made their homes. The murderers, thieves, and those hiding from the Watch. The rest of London could pretend people like Arista didn't exist if they remained cloistered away from sight, but they were there, waiting in the shadows for some unsuspecting fool to stagger by after a night at the alehouse.

It was the perfect place to live unnoticed. And the worst place to grow up.

At the orphanage where Arista had been dumped at barely three, all had treated her as the devil's own daughter, except for one woman. While the rest called her a gypsy, spat in her face, and made her do the most menial tasks like scrubbing the floors and emptying the chamber pots, Nalia wrapped Arista in her arms and told her thrilling stories about her home country of India.

Her lilting accent became Arista's safe place. The exotic smell of Nalia's tea soothed Arista's spirit after days of scrubbing until her tiny hands were raw. The laundress would rub salve on the blisters and distract Arista with tales of monkeys riding elephants; she'd let Arista wrap herself up in the brightly colored scarf that Nalia wore over her head.

For two long years, Arista had endured life at the orphanage, sure that everyone except Nalia wanted her to die. Indeed, after her refusal to climb inside the huge kitchen chimney to dislodge an obstruction, she'd been banished to a dark broom closet. If not for Bones, she might have starved to death in there, alone.

The old memories swept over her.

"You, get your sorry arse out here. You're leaving." Agnes, the old kitchen woman, yanked open the door and pulled Arista out of the closet. "And good riddance to you, too." Agnes shoved Arista at Sister Beatrice, who sidestepped to avoid touching Arista. None of the other women ever touched her, except Agnes, and her hands were never kind.

The nun led Arista to a group of two dozen other children huddled in the

cold foyer, clutching each other. None of them were older than seven. The young-
est looked three. Some wept; others stood with their fists at their sides. That
was Arista.

Even at five, she knew what was happening. Twice a year, the crooked old
man with the cruel eyes came. Bones. He took the children away. No one knew
why, only that the transaction happened on the darkest, moonless nights. None
ever returned.

Arista was pushed against the wall, and Bones went down the line, giving
each child the once-over. He barked questions at Sister Ann about disease and
fortitude. He forced their mouths open with sharp fingers and looked at their
teeth. One by one, they were chosen or cast aside. The ones overlooked disap-
peared back into the orphanage without a backward glance.

Arista found herself among the chosen that moonless night.

As she waited her turn to climb into the wagon, movement caught her eye.
Nalia stood in the shadows, her hand pressed to her mouth. Her cheeks were
shining with tears. Without thinking, Arista broke free from the group and ran
to the woman, her only friend, and threw herself into her arms.

Bones shouted and came after her, but before he got to them, Nalia unwound
the scarf from her head and tucked it under Arista's jacket.

"Never give up, little one. There is a great big world out there, and in it you
can find anything your heart desires."

Before Nalia could say anything more, Arista was ripped from her arms.
She screamed and kicked all the way to the wagon, and Bones threw her in. She
landed so hard it knocked the wind out of her.

The supply wagon carried over a dozen children away from the orphanage
that night. Arista curled into a ball and tucked her face under her jacket, where
the scarf's familiar smell helped calm her quaking nerves. They traveled several
hours, cramped and wedged together, until they finally pulled up to a door.
When Bones prodded them all out, Arista looked up. The building seemed to
loom upward forever, a charred black silhouette against the sky.

She wished she could fly. Push off from the ground and never touch down again.

A tiny girl, no older than three, fell out of the wagon and began to cry. No one moved to help her. Bones lifted her by the scruff of her neck, and she dangled like a rag doll, softly mewling in fear. Rage curled Arista's fingers into fists, but there was nothing she could do.

No one else made a sound as they were herded into the house, down a dark, narrow hallway to a room with no windows. He tossed the little girl in, and she hit the wall hard and landed in an unmoving heap in the corner. Then without a word, he shut the door. The grating sound of the lock clicking into place was a sound Arista would never forget.

They sat, huddled together for warmth, for two days. No food was brought, and only a trough with murky water unfit for animals sat in one corner. The time spent in the blackness was filled with quiet crying and fitful moans of pain.

The smell of urine, and worse, permeated the air until it choked Arista. When Bones finally opened the door, only eight children staggered out into the light. Four small, unmoving bodies were illuminated by the lamplight. Arista saw the tangle of dirty hair that belonged to the small girl, still lying where she had landed in the corner.

Two men walked toward them and threw a bucket of ice-cold water over each of them. Arista clenched her teeth tightly to keep them from chattering.

"You want to eat, you bring back something worth a scrap of food. If you come back empty handed, you will go right back in there. If I'm feeling benevolent. Ain't that right, boy?"

A boy, only a year or two older than Arista, swaggered up next to Bones. "Aye. He ain't likely ever feeling that way, tho. So you best be bringing sumpthin back what's worth his time." The boy's gaze ran over the ragtag group, and he sneered at them. "Follow me, you lazy arses. It's time to earn your keep."

They spent all day on the street, learning to beg and steal. When they returned, Bones lined them up in the hallway just inside the door, and they presented him with what they had found. Arista kept her hands behind her back, fingers clenched around nothing.

The first child, the oldest of the girls, held out her hand. A few pennies tumbled from them. Bones grunted, gave the girl a small piece of bread, and moved on to the next one. The second child, a boy, had nothing. He glared up at the old man in defiance, his chin lifted, though Arista could see the slight quiver in his jaw. Bones grabbed him by the hair and dragged him down the hall to the filthy room where they had been kept, and threw him inside. The click-tap of alternating shoe and cane echoed as Bones came back to the group.

Arista was last in line. The dreadful boy who led them out and back again stood right next to her, his arms crossed over his chest, staring straight ahead. In the light of the lamp, Arista could see his jaw flexing as if he were clenching his teeth as hard as he could. He'd barely said a word to her all day, except to bark an order or tell her to get to work.

Sweat beaded on her lip as Bones got closer. When a child gave him something, he in turn gave them a piece of bread. They fell on it like rats, hunched down and devouring their scraps as if they were nothing more than animals. Arista's stomach growled and she clenched her fists tighter, pressing her body so hard against the rough wood wall that her knuckles ached. The boy glanced at her, his expression unreadable.

There were just two children between her and Bones. The thought of spending another second in that black room made her want to scream as loud as she could and tear her own hair out. A tiny whimper escaped before she could stop it.

Bones stood in front of the girl next to her. Silent tears streamed down the child's dirty face as she presented her open, empty hands to him. "Please," the girl whispered. "I'm so hungry."

The silence stretched out for several long seconds before Bones grabbed her hair and dragged her down the hallway as she screamed and pleaded with him to stop.

Arista held her knuckles against her lips to keep from crying out. With sickening dread, she knew she was next. Her legs went weak, as if she would fall to the floor any second. If she went into the dark room again, she knew with certainty she would not come back out.

As Bones started back down the hall toward her, something brushed against her hand. The boy next to her still looked straight ahead, but his arm stretched behind her. She opened her fist and something was pressed into her palm.

Then Bones was standing in front of her.

"Do you eat or starve?" Bones asked. His eyes narrowed, and he was just about to grab her when she pulled her hand out from behind her back and shoved it at him. Arista had no idea what she was giving the man. What if the boy had set her up? He'd been treating them badly all day, yelling and ridiculing them when they failed to beg successfully for even a halfpence. What if he'd given her a rock?

But Bones growled out a warning, and she had to open her fingers. Two shillings gleamed in the lamplight. Arista had never seen so much money before, much less held it in her hand.

The boy had given that to her?

Why?

"This, my wee bits o' baggage, is how it's done. Mighty fine work on your first day, gypsy. You earned yourself an extra ration." Bones shoved a chunk of bread twice the size of his hand at her and she grabbed it without thinking. She sank her teeth into the stale crust even before Bones stepped away.

"What about you, boy—where's your offerin'?"

The boy shrugged nonchalantly, though Arista noticed that his fingers were curled tightly at his side. "Looking after these good-for-nothings all day took all me time."

Bones backhanded the boy before Arista could swallow. She tried to protest, but her words were muffled by the chunk of dry bread clogging her throat. The boy lay panting on the floor, his gaze downcast.

"Show 'em where they're sleeping." Bones was halfway down the hall when he stopped and turned. "And Nic, my boy, next time you'll be in the dungeon with the rest o' the worthless ones."

Arista met Nic's gaze, and in that moment something happened. She offered him a hand up, and half her bread, while the other children looked on wide-eyed.

Nic led them to the room where they would sleep for the next ten years.

That night had only been the beginning. . . .

A drunken shriek too close for comfort jerked Arista back to reality. Nic's hand tightened on her arm.

He stared at her curiously. "Where'd ya go, gypsy? Not like you to be so quiet."

Arista couldn't meet his eyes. Unconsciously, she lifted her hand to touch the scarf she had wound around her wig. She never went out as Lady A without it.

Have you been to India? The phantom voice filled her head. How could she explain that she was not herself because she'd been so close to her dreams of escape?

"Nerves," she answered. "I didn't think that fat arse would fight."

He seemed to accept her explanation. He stopped them in front of a familiar locked door. Though she was older now and not returning empty handed, the sick, strangling feeling from that first night never quite went away.

Nic squeezed her hand in understanding, then gave a series of knocks. After a moment, the door swung open. Becky stood just inside the door. Her eyes darted around like a frightened rabbit's, but she opened the door wide enough to allow them inside.

Arista stepped back into her personal hell, leaving behind the brief illusion of freedom.

Becky held out a lantern and hurried them down the same narrow hallway where Arista had been led that first night. Somewhere on the other side of the wall, the sounds of men's voices rumbled. Arista drew Nic's jacket tighter around her shoulders.

No one outside these thin walls knew that the infamous Lady A lived only a few feet away.

At the end of the hall, Becky stopped in front of two doors and pulled out a ring of keys. She unlocked the door on the right, pushed it open, and disappeared inside the room she and Arista shared, taking the light with her. Arista blinked against the sudden darkness.

"Until we meet again, Lady A." There was more than a hint of laughter in Nic's voice.

"Parting is such sweet sorrow." Arista used her best aristocratic vowels as she quoted a line from a Shakespeare play Nic had once taken her to see.

They had stood in the very back at the Haymarket Theatre, and Arista held her breath until the very last line echoed in the hushed room. The tale of doomed love had been unlike anything she'd ever seen before. Her heart had ached for days.

Nic had just shrugged. "Neither of them needed to die."

Still, his words had done nothing to diminish the emotion running through her. *Was it worth it, Juliet?* Arista still yearned to know the answer, but what did it matter? She would live and die without ever knowing love.

"Gypsy," Nic whispered into the darkness. He wrapped his fingers around hers, and for a second, her heart stopped. They were warm and calloused. Familiar. She started to tell him about earlier, about the errant thoughts flying around in her head, but he stepped closer and she forgot everything. The warmth of his breath caressed her cheek.

This was *not* part of their usual routine. Not at all.

In the dark, where no one could see them, anything could happen.

"I have something to tell you, but this is not the place. Meet me later, at the spot—you know." He left before she could exhale. A key turned in a lock, a door opened and closed, leaving Arista alone. Nic had gone down a short flight of steps that would take him into the main living area, where Bones would be waiting for the packet. Arista pushed into the shared room and closed the door behind her. The lock clicked as it slid into place. What did Nic want to tell her? Arista tugged at the ribbon holding her mask in place. Cool air washed over her skin.

"Oh, Miss. A feather is missing," Becky fussed. "I'll have to have Mr. Nic find me another before you go out again."

She vaguely heard Becky chattering, but was too distracted to pay much attention. What did Nic want to tell her? The look in his eyes had been strange. A sort of excitement mixed with pride. His meeting with Bones would not take long. She had to hurry. Filled with a sudden urgency, Arista began pulling the pins from her hair to loosen the wig. Becky swiftly pushed Arista's hands away to do it for her. Arista fidgeted under Becky's ministrations. She hated to be tended to, but didn't protest.

When Bones had taken Becky in when Arista was thirteen, Arista hadn't expected the scared, beaten-down girl to last more than a few weeks in Bones's household.

She would never forget the night Nic had told her that Bones planned to sell her and Becky to the brothels. Arista would have died first, but to her shock, Becky had come up with the idea that had saved them both. What if she could turn Arista into a proper lady who could attend the parties where jewels and money were ripe for the picking? Bones's greed had become their savior. He'd agreed, and from that moment on, Arista's life was full of reminders about good posture and refined speech. Some days, Nic would sit in on these lessons and twist his mouth to form proper vowels. It became a game, much to Becky's displeasure at having her lessons interrupted. His accent diminished somewhat, but he would always have that roughness that defined where they came from.

One night, soon after they began their new charade, Nic noticed that Arista had avoided one particular gentleman, a portly slobbering fool too drunk to stand. Instead she went for the tall, stately man who stood on the outskirts of the crowd.

Nic would have gone for the drunk, but Arista had noticed the way the man's eyes darted around and he fidgeted with his hands. Signs that he was nervous about something. Sure enough, only moments after Arista walked away, he had been caught stealing a watch from the Duke of Rochester. In the commotion, Arista had taken a very nice pair of diamond cufflinks from the man who appeared focused, but was in fact high on opium.

Arista's success at the balls had given Bones the inroad he'd needed to begin blackmailing the aristocracy. She had been his pawn for the last two years.

Becky took her duties very seriously. From the start, she had insisted that Arista look and act like a lady, as if they actually lived in some countryside manor house and Becky was in charge of preparing Arista to enter high society. The fact that their *home* was a twelve-by-twelve room—made of rough boards, with a lock on both sides of the door and no windows—seemed to escape the maid's grasp.

Arista often wondered if the treatment Becky received from her last employer had somehow addled her sense of reality. Surely no one in their right mind would mistake how they lived as acceptable, yet Becky went about her daily duties with nary a complaint about their living conditions—or about the fact that they were virtually prisoners.

If not for Becky's amazing skills as a seamstress, Arista would have been forced to wear whatever clothing Nic outgrew, or could find, tossed aside as unserviceable. As it was, Becky could construct beautiful costumes with hardly any resources. Lady A always went out looking like an aristocrat, though her costumes were always the color of night. Each year as Arista outgrew them, Becky had sewn something new, fancier most times, but always in black to allow Arista to hide in the shadows of the ballrooms.

At first Arista had protested. She didn't need fancy clothing to do what Bones needed done. She could conduct business in the shadows, dressed like a boy as usual.

Only once had Arista refused to let Becky dress her—Lady A's first meeting. Bones got wind of Arista's complaints, and Becky still bore the scars from that act of defiance. It had been a dark warning to Arista, and she had listened. Now she let Becky do what she must, if only to keep her safe from Bones's heavy hand.

Lady A became a familiar shadow at the masquerades with her raven-feather mask, but though people knew who she was, no one dared to think of turning her in to the Watch. Not with so many of society's best indebted to Bones. Their secrets gave her a small measure of safety, and Nic watched her back.

And so far, Arista had avoided harm.

"Did you dance, miss?" Becky's nimble fingers made short work of the task, and soon the blessedly cool air caressed Arista's hot, itchy scalp.

Becky's question abruptly brought back images of a highwayman. Specifically, his eyes. Had she really let a stranger put his hands on her like that? As Becky unlaced her stays, Arista reached for the spot on her neck that the highwayman had touched. Her own fingers traced the path from her shoulder to just below her ear.

It wasn't the same. It wasn't even the same feeling as when Nic had touched her in the hallway.

Arista's mind flew in a million directions. She wanted to get her trousers on, pull the dark wool cap down over her head, and go for a walk. She needed to try and sort out what had happened at the masquerade so it wouldn't happen again.

"Did you remember everything I taught you, then?" Becky interrupted her thoughts, and a prickle of irritation swept over Arista. The girl loved to talk, especially after Arista had gone to a party.

Arista wanted to snap back that yes, she had remembered her rehearsed dialect and subdued graces after they'd been pounded into her head for years, but she held her tongue. Becky didn't deserve abuse for her show of concern.

Arista glanced over at the girl who had become her friend. She flitted about the room, seemingly wrapped up in her own thoughts. Becky might have been pretty once, but now she walked with her head down and turned away from anyone who might look too closely. From the left, she appeared normal; but on the right, her skin was misshapen and lumpy from her temple to her chin.

The deep burns had not been tended to properly, and as the skin healed, that whole side of her face had been left horribly disfigured. No one but Arista knew the circumstances behind the injury. After two years of teaching Arista the finer graces, Becky had reluctantly told Arista the story.

Becky had worked as a lady's maid for a family in Piccadilly. Becky and the lord of the house had had a disagreement over her young charge's future husband, and he had beaten her. As she lay on the floor cowering from him, he had taken a candelabra and tipped the hot wax over her face. There were smaller, matching scars on her arms where she'd tried to protect herself from the burning wax, but her sleeves usually hid those.

Her employer had then turned her out with nothing. Arista wanted to gut the bastard, but Becky refused to name who had done it.

"Yes, I remembered everything you taught me."

Becky beamed as she shook out the black silk dress and carefully hung it away, to be brushed down later for the next time it would be needed.

Arista exhaled, her first real breath without the constraint of the corset, and pulled a ratty, stained chemise over her head, followed by a plain brown shirt. It had grown threadbare in several spots, but Becky's nimble fingers had patched the holes as if they were never there. Not that it mattered. Arista always wore the shirt under an even darker brown coat that hid it, and her shape, effectively.

Black wool trousers covered her legs, rough and familiar. She strapped her knife to the outside of her thigh, in plain view now for anyone thinking of trying his luck. She slipped bare feet into an old pair of Nic's boots that now fit her perfectly.

"I'll be back by morning." Arista grabbed her wool cap off a peg that was wedged into the cracked wall and clicked the lock to their room open.

Before she left the room, her glance slid to the crude charcoal drawing on the boards lining the far wall. Nic had made it for her when she was barely eleven. They were supposed to be picking pockets at the market, but instead, Nic had wanted to show her something. They'd spent an entire day at the docks watching the ships arrive and depart.

There had been a ship there unloading goods from India. She recognized the same smells that used to come from Nalia's tea. A man in a turban and clothes unlike anything she'd ever seen before stepped off the ship, and when he reached the dock Arista saw a monkey perched on his shoulder. A real, live monkey. He must have seen her staring, because he smiled and approached them.

"A pence to carry your bags, sir?" Nic asked.

Instead, the man handed them each a shilling and told them both stories while the monkey wound around his head and chattered as if he, too, were telling tales.

It had been the best day of her life, that afternoon on the docks.

When the ship finally emptied, the man bowed and thanked them for their time. She had never met anyone so kind, except for Nalia. Arista watched him walk away, his words still conjuring vivid images in her head.

"I *will* go there someday," she told Nic.

When they returned that evening, Nic had drawn the ship and a crude monkey on the wall, so she could see it from her pallet on the floor. Every night before she closed her eyes she imagined herself on board that ship, sailing far away from this life.

Except six years later, they were still here.

Arista quietly made her way down the hallway to the door they'd come in through, the one that led outside to the alley, with Becky close behind. "Open it for me," Arista said.

"But, miss . . ." Becky always protested when Arista went out at night. The seediest of characters came out under the cloak of darkness, but that meant little to Arista. She knew the shortcuts through the alleys and the blind spots where a thief was likely to hide in wait. She knew because she was one of them.

"I'll be fine. I just need some air." Arista cracked open the door and peered up and down the alley. When she saw no one, she exited and waited until the click of the lock sounded before she turned and sprinted off down the alley.

This was as close to freedom as Arista would ever get.

There was a spot by the river that she'd found years ago, hidden from view in the recesses of a burned-out warehouse. She could think freely there. Already she had outlived the lifespan of an orphan, but only because Bones saw her as a commodity he could exploit for his own purposes. If he ever decided he no longer needed her, she'd be on her own. Or worse.

Noxious scents wafted from the blackest corners of the alleys, where garbage and refuse and decaying animal carcasses piled up. The night soil men, the ones who kept the main streets clean, rarely ventured this close to the river to clean up. The comfort of the working class was not a priority to anyone. The rich simply pretended that they didn't exist; or if they thought of them, it was as just another kind of garbage.

Arista wrinkled her nose and hurried on, past the dark window of the bookmaker's shop, until she finally came out on Fleet Street. The sounds changed, and in the pools of the streetlights, girls of all ages milled around, waiting for an intoxicated man to proposition them.

"Aye, there, sweetie." A woman twice her age stepped into the glow of the oil-lit streetlamp and grinned at Arista. Her black-stained teeth were visible even at that distance, and her face was framed with a mop of unwashed dark hair.

The whores on Fleet Street were the lowest of the low. Rarely would a real gentleman make use of their services, as the girls at

Covent Garden were much prettier and cleaner, though more expensive as well. These ones gave away their bodies for mere pennies to the scurvy-addled sailors who passed through in a constant flow.

"Fancy a little bit o' fun, do ya?" The woman grabbed her breasts and jiggled them.

"Bugger off, you pox-ridden whore." The deep-voiced retort slid off her tongue, and she kept walking. Dressed as she was, she'd come to expect this from the street girls. She watched them out of the corner of her eye. Their emotionless faces were painted thick with rouge, eyes lined heavily with kohl.

The woman, the one who'd called out to Arista, had on a dirty, torn shift that barely came to her knees. Her stays were laced tight enough to cause ample exposure of what she sold. "Think yer too good for the likes of us, then, li'l guvnor?" The woman extended her pinky finger and waggled it at Arista. Another woman snickered loudly.

That could have been her—very well *would* be her, if Bones ever decided that Arista was no longer useful to him. It would be a far worse hell to sell her body for a shilling than anything she had endured so far.

The woman's attention shifted and Arista saw a man staggering down the street. A chorus of high-pitched voices called out to the man as the group began shouting prices and services at him. Wretched.

I'd sooner die than peddle myself on a corner.

The voices grew fainter and Arista pulled her coat closer to her body. In the dim light, from a distance, she could easily pass for a boy—a slight boy, perhaps, but clearly one with a knife strapped to his thigh.

No one else bothered her. She made it to where the unused

warehouse stood, its tattered edges outlined against the sky. The spot where she liked to go was just past the dilapidated building, through the overgrown path leading to the river's edge. Though it was completely hidden from view, if she was spotted, she'd have nowhere to run but into the Thames. As she could not swim, it would be a certain death for her. She had to be careful.

Footsteps came faintly from the right, growing louder with each breath she took. A stack of empty crates gave her enough cover to hide behind, and she forced her lungs to quiet as the Watchman made his rounds. In only moments, he turned and ambled away, taking the faint lamplight with him. Next to the river, the night was even darker. The working dock sat much farther upriver. There was no need for anyone to be around at this hour except the occasional Watchman.

The air grew damper as she moved closer to the river. In the stillness, she could hear faint whispers of the water lapping against the riverbanks. She exhaled softly and straightened. Though her boots were heavy, she barely made a sound as she hurried around the corner of the long building.

There had been a fire years before and the old building had been destroyed. The only thing left of the loading dock was a small bit of wood jutting out a few feet into the river. Weeds grew up along the bank, effectively hiding it, and giving Arista the perfect place to sit and watch the lights reflect off the water. The cool air there didn't reek of refuse and deadness so much during the night. Only under the thick midday fog did the stench test the stomachs of even the most hardened of seamen.

Arista pushed through the dense brush and carefully stepped over the spot with a missing plank. Water lapped gently against the wood supports, and the tension gripping her shoulders finally melted away. The hopes and fears of a seventeen-year-old bubbled to the surface, finally free from the constraints she kept them under. Every minute of the day, her movements were calculated, as either a gypsy beggar boy or the notorious Lady A. Neither role fit. She wore someone else's skin all the time, except in rare moments like these, when she could escape both and just be Arista.

At the ball earlier, when she'd lost sight of herself for a moment in a stranger's arms, a slight breeze had swept over her from an open courtyard door, beckoning to her. An indescribable urge to run away had overtaken her. An urge to go someplace like where the man described; where she could be completely free. She'd never been so close to running.

Bones owned her, and he made sure she never forgot it, but something stubborn inside Arista refused to give up. She wanted freedom. Wanted to make her own choices and have a future, away from the streets of London. Maybe even find love.

She yearned for something pure and beautiful in her life. When she looked at Nic, she could sometimes see a ray of hope. Oftentimes it was clouded beneath the darkness that had been lately creeping into his eyes, but when she remembered everything he'd done for her, she tried to ignore it. She could see the faint hints of a future she hardly dared to imagine.

Lately though, trying to find hope in these short moments of solitude had become harder. As if she were fading away from herself. How long would it take before she only existed as a beggar or Lady A? What would happen when she forgot who she *really* was?

Across the river, a light pulled away from the glittering reflections, and a barely discernible boat glided across the water. Oars dipped down and cut through the water, and Arista saw the lamp-lit face of an old man staring earnestly down at the river.

Goose bumps spread up her arms. Bodyfinders. They skirted the river's edge in the dark, dredging for bodies with a long, hooked pole. Once found, they would pull them onto the boat, rummage through the pockets for valuables, then take their clothes and dump the naked corpse back into the river.

There were no proper burials for the forgotten.

The thought made Arista tremble harder. How different was she from a body floating in the river? Who would care if she ceased to breathe? She had no past and no future, no family to lay claim to her.

"Daydreaming again, gypsy?" Nic's amused voice came from behind her. He settled down on the rickety dock without a sound, his arm brushing against her. The familiar ache started again, and she looked up at him from the corner of her eyes.

"If I ended up like that . . ." She swept her hand out over the river, where the old man in the boat was now fishing something out of the water with his hooked pole. The words lodged in her throat and she had to force them out. "Would you care?"

She'd never been closer to asking Nic if she meant something to him. Her breath hitched on the exhale, waiting for his answer.

He waited so long that heat burned a path from her neck to her cheeks. *Stupid. Of course not. We don't care about anything, right?* She turned away, pretending to be engrossed in what the man on the river did, and that Nic's silence meant nothing to her.

"When Bones brought you to us, I thought you looked like a drowned kitten."

She could feel him smiling, and she let herself relax enough to exhale. He was still talking to her as he always had.

"You were a spitting, angry, scared kitten who scratched any-one who came near. You were so small—five, I think. I know you still think about the first night every time we go back through that door."

"Yes." Her pulse thumped dully in her ears. She didn't know that he knew that.

Nic reached out and slowly twined his fingers through hers. "I remember the panic when I realized you had not brought anything back that first day. I tried to keep an eye on you in the square. I half expected to find you trampled at the end of the day."

Arista hated the memories that slammed into her head. She'd been so helpless and scared.

"I remember you gave me what you'd taken and then got hit for it." Emotion swelled inside her throat. "I thought you were just a mean boy, but you weren't. You saved me that night. I would have died if I'd been put inside that room for one more day."

"I know." He grew quiet again, but he kept his fingers wound through hers. "I thought you were the prettiest thing I'd ever seen."

Arista glanced over at Nic, but he looked out across the water now, as if back in that moment. A small smile played over his lips. He wasn't just toying with her, feeding her a line like he did with the brothel girls. Heat pooled in her stomach. She had never dared to ask him.

"I hated the idea of him putting his hands on you." His grip tightened painfully around her fingers, but then slowly relaxed. "I begged him to let me teach you how to steal. I was the best at it, you know. I've always looked out for you, gypsy—not because I had to, but because I *wanted* to." His voice lowered and grew thick with the rough accent of the streets. The warmth of it sank deep into her bones. He was familiar; with him, she felt safe. Her fingers tingled where he touched them. His thumb stroked the back of her hand in lazy circles, and a shock of heat raced up her arm.

They'd never had a conversation like this before. He'd never touched her so deliberately before. Her pulse leapt. "Do you think we'll ever get away from this?" Neither of the orphans had ever spoken of escape.

Instead of answering, Nic scooted back until he leaned against a mooring pole, then pulled her back to rest against his side. One arm curled lazily around her shoulders. "Where would you go, gypsy?" His finger danced up her arm, leaving a wake of goose bumps. She liked this side of Nic. A lot.

Though she spent almost all her free time at the docks, watching the ships come in and out of the harbor, she knew very little of the world outside London. Only the bits and pieces of talk bantered about by the sailors that constantly filled the docks. India. China. The Caribbean. America, even. They sounded so exotic and wild.

But going anywhere, even getting to the outskirts of London, took money. It was nice to dream about running away, but without the means, she would not get far. Plus, she was a commodity that Bones would kill to keep. Becky and Nic, not so much. She could not risk their lives for frivolous thoughts of escape.

This was her life.

She shook her head. "There is nowhere."

Nic leaned down until his lips brushed across her ear. "What would you say if I told you that Bones has grown so afraid of the Thief Taker General's ever-expanding reach that he has cut ties with most of the men in his employ for fear of betrayal? What if I told you I am one of Bones's last confidants, and I know where he now hides his money? That I can get to it? Where would you want to go then?"

Icy fear sliced along her spine. Was he really thinking about stealing from Bones? If he got caught, he'd be killed without a second thought. Bones was swift and cruel with retribution; Arista had seen it firsthand many times. It was how he ensured complete loyalty among his men.

"There's a board in his office, under the chair by the stove. If you pry it up . . ."

Arista spun around and covered his mouth with her hand. "Stop." Her plea came out as a whisper, like Bones himself might hear them talking. Men had been gutted and left to bleed for far less.

Nic gently pried her hand away. A glint of excitement shone in his eyes. His lips turned up into an eager grin. "I'm serious, gypsy, I have a plan. We can use Bones's paranoia to take what we want right from under his nose. We can do this. Imagine if we took Bones out of the equation. We could have enough money to be one of them. *We* would own them. No one would ever dare to cross Lady A."

A cold breeze blew in off the river, but Arista shivered for a different reason. She had always known that Nic had ambition—he'd risen in Bones's ranks until he was the old man's trusted right hand—but to hear him talk like that, say such things, only solidified what Arista feared. Nic would never give up this life. He loved bringing the rich to their knees, and he wanted Arista—no, *Lady A*—to help him. She tried to pull away, but he held her fingers in a tight grip. Almost too tight. Arista ground her teeth together and stopped fighting.

"Really, gypsy, what do you want the most? Anything. Don't you want what they have? To go to a party as a real guest? To have a grand home? And carriages and dresses and people to take care of you? What about your freedom, gypsy? I know how you long for that."

She shook her head in denial, but for just a second she had allowed herself to imagine it. The taste was bittersweet on her tongue, because it would never happen. Nic huffed and looked out at the water. "Why should Bones get everything, when we're the ones doing the dirty work? We are exposed to the danger and yet we get nothing. It has to stop."

If anyone heard what he'd implied . . . Panic licked at her skin like fire. She glanced around, wide-eyed, afraid someone might hear them.

The man on the boat seemed closer than before. Could he be in Bones's employ?

"Nic." She tugged desperately against his grip, but he held her firmly. The man in the boat drifted away again, intent on another spot in the water.

"We can do this, gypsy, together. I've been thinking about it for years, and Bones trusts me now. I've been talking with someone who can help us, too. It's the perfect time."

He actually wanted her to help him take over Bones's operation.

"Don't worry, gypsy, I'll still keep you safe." Nic ran his free hand up her arm and slid it behind her neck. Instead of the familiar heat of his touch, there was only dull, thumping discomfort. He urged her head closer, and she stared up into his eyes.

He was going to kiss her.

She'd wanted it for so long, and yet could not push away her unease. It was as if the kiss would seal a bargain she hadn't yet agreed to. But when his lips brushed across her cheek, so soft that they barely touched her skin, she leaned in closer. This *was* what she wanted. Yet there was still hesitation in her movements.

Part of her uncertainty stemmed from inexperience. What if she did it wrong? Almost all her knowledge of what happened between men and women came from watching the girls at the docks. The rest came from the masquerades she attended as Lady A. Neither were exactly places of virtue.

Nic, on the other hand, had plenty of experience. He cradled her neck gently in his fingers while stroking his thumb over her jaw. The simple feeling of being touched like that, like she was finally wanted by someone, took her breath away. Arista closed her eyes and shushed the voices in her head. A gentle nudge was all it took to move her face toward Nic. All that stood between them now was a whisper.

When his lips finally pressed against hers, he was gentle and slow, and Arista found herself leaning closer, deepening the kiss. This was it. Finally, she was kissing Nic. Her Nic.

After several long moments, he pulled back with a sigh and cradled her face against his chest. "I promise I'll give you the life that you deserve, gypsy." He pressed another kiss against her temple and Arista leaned back in his arms to look up at him.

In the dim light, she studied his profile. A bump rose up in the middle of his nose from a fight many years ago. His jaw was square and hard and clenched in determination as he stared out across the river. Arista finally had proof that Nic cared for her, that she was more than just an obligation.

The kiss should have fixed everything she thought was wrong inside her. Pieces should have fallen into place. Damaged parts should now be miraculously fixed. Instead, the hollowness remained and it only added to her confusion.

What did this mean?

Was she so broken that nothing could heal her anymore?

Could she not feel anything?

Yes, she could feel something—*had*, in fact, earlier in the evening. Only it wasn't her longtime friend, the boy she thought herself in love with, who made her body tingle with awareness. It wasn't Nic's promise that made her heart pound erratically as she sat in the darkness.

It was the memory of a dark-eyed stranger in a highwayman's disguise that made her yearn for so much more than this life.

CHAPTER 3

One night later, Arista stood alone at the entrance to Lady Carstair's opulent mansion. The three-story home towered over the street, and every single window shone with light. Through the wrought-iron fence, Arista could see a pair of ornately carved lions sitting sentry on each side of the enormous front steps.

Even from the street, the soft strains of music drifted through a thick row of hedges, adding to the exclusivity of the event. This affair was anything but a typical public masquerade.

Arista gnawed nervously at her bottom lip. The strings to her mask seemed too tight suddenly. Around her, people moved toward a lone, gloved servant standing sentry. Only those with the correct invitation were allowed in.

Bones's newest client must be someone very important if they frequented a party of this caliber. Typically, the information was passed to Nic, who then brought Arista to the planned rendezvous; but this time, Arista had been handed a card directly from Becky. And Nic had not yet joined her.

After the kiss last night, Nic had taken her hand and led her

back to the house. Not a word had passed between them. She knew
with a sinking clarity that Nic thought she had accepted his offer.
She had not tried to persuade him otherwise, either. In truth, she
still couldn't quite believe what he had proposed. Surely he didn't
really mean to betray Bones?

All the next day, Arista waited for Nic to come to her room.
She waited until Becky told her she had another task, a last-minute
meeting. Arista figured Nic would be there waiting to escort her,
just like always. But he wasn't. Arista had walked to the address
alone. Maybe he would meet her here.

"Your card, miss?" The butler had turned to her; it was her turn.

Arista gripped the card as tightly as possible, and took one last
look over her shoulder for Nic before moving toward the man. The
black card in her hand simply had an address in gold foil on the
back. She waited to be called out as a fraud and turned away, but
the butler took the card from Arista and ushered her through to
the magical world that lay hidden behind those stone walls. Behind
her, a vocal woman dressed as a queen was denied entrance.

Arista followed a wide path edged with glass-encased candles. It
wound through shrubs and aromatic flowers, opening into a small
garden. She walked around the edge, fighting the growing apprehension in her stomach. Without Nic at her side, she felt vulnerable.
A few heads turned to watch her as she made her way down a second walkway.

Arista had always skirted the edges of crowds, blending in to
remain anonymous, but tonight, she felt noticed. Rarely did she
attend such intimate gatherings with so few people. The crowds of
a public masquerade helped her to blend in. Here, every swish of
her dress could be heard as she tried to keep from running back out
through the gates. Her neck prickled.

Only the weight of her knife against her thigh kept her on task.

Arista moved on; her chin lifted. Enormous crystal vases of lilacs and roses had been placed along the crushed-shell walkway, and the heady scent brushed over her skin like a gentle caress. Everywhere she looked, couples were hidden away in the darkness. Soft chuckles and long sighs pierced her head like arrows. The party had a decidedly different atmosphere than any other masked ball she had attended. The others were full of gaiety and fun, but this party had a distinctly indulgent air—and with good reason.

Lady Carstair was well known for the exclusivity of her guest list for her masquerades. The King himself could be in attendance, though Arista had heard a rumor that he had been excluded on purpose after a particularly rancorous evening. She could not imagine how one would enforce such a restriction if the King showed up at the gates.

There were unspoken rules about not revealing what went on at these private events—or who attended—and to speak of it would ensure permanent removal from the list. A punishment worse than death to those who craved excitement. Arista had only heard about these parties, had never been invited until now.

The pathway opened up to an even larger, more opulently decorated garden. On a raised dais, backlit by enormous floor-to-ceiling glass doors, sat a string quartet. All of the players were dressed as fairy folk. Soft strains of cello and violin drifted past her, adding to the decadent feeling that hung thick in the night air. The music did not encourage dancing, but instead created a sultry mood. A woman drew her bow across the strings of a violin as light reflected off the blue crystals that adorned her eyelids.

Why had Bones acted so out of character by sending her here alone? If any meeting required a diligent chaperone, it was this one.

Arista could not stand still, so she walked along the outside edge of the garden again. A couple sat partially hidden by ornamental shrubs. When Arista turned her head away, the feathers on her mask swayed gently. Even *they* seemed invitingly sensual in their movements.

Her dress swished softly as she moved toward the elaborate display of food and drink on huge tables in front of a gurgling fountain. A crystal bowl held some sort of punch. Arista took one of the delicate cups and filled it herself.

At Lady Carstair's balls, there were no servants—only the butler who took the tickets. People were completely on their own in the gardens, free to pursue any pleasure, limited only by their own imaginations. Away from gossiping mouths and curious eyes, any manner of things could happen.

The punch tasted sweet, full of exotic fruits that Arista could not name, and with an undertone of rum that should have eased the tension in her shoulders. Instead, prickling heat climbed the back of her neck. She turned her head slowly, and found the highwayman only a couple of steps behind her. A rush of warmth flooded her face. He made no move to get closer, but his stare pinned her in place as firmly as if he held her. She could not mistake him. He wore the same black silk scarf around his face, the same dark hat pulled low. Arista turned completely to face him, and if she'd had any doubt about his identity, his eyes proved it without a doubt. Grae.

He had filled her thoughts constantly over the past several nights, despite her best efforts to push him away. She stared up at him, waiting, fighting the breathlessness that had made it difficult to inhale normally.

He stood tall, hands clasped behind his back as he watched

her. His confidence was almost palpable. He had to be someone important under that mask, if he had procured an invitation to this particular event. But he had told her before that he was working toward becoming a ship captain. Surely merchants would not have the means or status to attend a masquerade at Lady Carstair's home.

Had he lied to her? And if so, why?

She should turn away, move, before he took her silence as an invitation. She shivered at the thought of being close to him again. As if he'd read her mind, he started toward her. His steps were confident and determined. If she were going to run, it had to be now.

But Arista remained caught in his stare until the highwayman closed the short distance between them and stopped much too close. She tilted her head back to look up at him. He brushed his fingers along her arm and goose bumps broke out over her bare skin.

The same wave of longing swept over her again. Half for Grae himself, and half because of the ache their previous conversation had unleashed. She wanted to know so much more about the places he'd traveled, and thought she'd never have the opportunity to do so. Now, here he stood, right in front of her. Questions burned on her tongue.

"Good evening, my lady." He slid his fingers down and took her gloved hand, then raised it to his lips. "I had hoped I would find you again."

A touch of unease made her hand tremble. Did he wish to strike a deal with Lady A, then? Was he her client tonight? No one ever approached her directly. Everything went through Bones.

"If you wish to do business, sir, I'm afraid you must start with my boss. Good evening to you." Arista started to turn away, but his touch held her there. Even in the dim light, she saw the confusion in his eyes.

"I have no business that needs attending to this evening, milady. Unless you count convincing you to dance. Then I cannot deny you're correct."

Arista studied him. There was no tension around his shoulders or mouth; his arms hung loosely at his sides, and his gaze never wavered from hers. All signs that he spoke truthfully. She let out a small sigh of relief. The idea that he had charmed her simply to get to Bones had made her feel ill. She didn't want this man to be seeking Lady A. She wanted him to be looking for her: Arista.

"So, will you dance with me tonight?" He held out his hand and waited for her response. Around them, only a handful of couples were moving to the soft music. None paid any attention to the others.

You're here to do a job, she reminded herself.

As if sensing the reason for her hesitation, he leaned in close. A fresh aroma of cedar and something spicy, exotic, made her head feel cloudy and light. "I'm not really a guest here tonight. The truth is that I snuck past the butler when I saw you arrive at the gate."

"You were spying on me?"

"No. Only hoping that you would be in attendance tonight."

Again, she saw no signs of deception. And if he had indeed sneaked into the masquerade, that would explain how a merchant had gotten into the party. If anyone there knew they were in the company of a merchant and a beggar . . . It almost made her laugh out loud.

"You realize if anyone finds out, you will be escorted off the grounds?"

He leaned in even closer. "It's a risk I'm willing to take. Are *you* going to tell them?"

A shiver danced down her spine. Not from apprehension or fear, but anticipation. She held her breath until he moved away again. The intensity of his stare made her heart beat faster. She heard the way his breath hitched slightly as he waited for her reaction. He'd come to see her. Arista was unprepared for his honesty.

"No, I will not." Her reply came out on her exhaled breath. Duty and her reason for being there vanished. Despite all her years of training to be aloof and unapproachable, her thoughts scattered and she was left unsure. Her gaze dropped to his lips without her consent.

He inhaled sharply and closed the distance between them in two steps. When he touched her bare shoulder, Arista forgot how to breathe. The warmth she remembered so well spiraled outward from his touch. When he curled his fingers around the back of her neck and inched her head closer, a frantic beat began in her chest.

The indulgent nature of the party wound around them as the strains of music drifted through the air. Fire burned in his eyes, and it made her feel wild and reckless. It made her forget who she was supposed to be. She was not Lady A now. She was only Arista. And this highwayman wanted *her*.

This was a masquerade, after all—why shouldn't she indulge, just a little? It might be her only chance to let go for one time in her life and just *feel*. No Nic. No Bones. No Lady A. Just the two of them.

His eyes grew darker. Holding her so her head was almost pressed against his chest, he took her hand and led her into the first steps of a waltz. Her feet followed automatically. Grae held her tightly and much closer than propriety would have allowed under normal circumstances. She could hear his heart beating. His breath brushed over the sensitive slope of her ear, causing her to forget everything. When she stumbled, he pulled her completely against him, never missing a step.

Arista had never danced at a party. She didn't attend them for fun, and had never indulged in the frivolity that went on as she conducted business. And yet, Becky had insisted Arista learn to dance as part of her training. Right that moment, Arista had never been more grateful that her friend hadn't listened to her complaints that it was an unnecessary skill. Nothing in her life had ever felt better than being in Grae's arms. The ground beneath her feet gave way and she stood on nothing but air.

Grae steered them effortlessly into the shadows. His stare held her captive. "Can I kiss you?"

Still feeling as though she were floating through the waltz, she nodded, caught so completely in this mysterious spell that she couldn't bear to say no. Grae ran his thumb along her jaw, softly stroking closer and closer to her lips. When he brushed a finger along her bottom lip, she closed her eyes. She was tense, yet her legs felt like jelly. Grae's finger moved away, and when she opened her eyes, he was watching her, his finger hovering over her mouth.

Arista needed to get closer to him—as close as she could. She dug her fingers into his jacket and held on as if her life depended on it. The desire was foreign and unnerving, but not unwanted, and she couldn't bring herself to pull away.

Having only been kissed once before, she felt unsure and awkward as she leaned up and pressed her lips against his. He responded immediately. His lips took hers and this time he didn't hold back. The masks helped Arista maintain a degree of anonymity, which led her to be much bolder than she would have in any other circumstance. For once, she did what she wanted—gave in to the desire to touch someone, to let him touch her in return. Deprived of this luxury for so long, Arista soaked up the feeling like a sponge. She kissed Grae back with every ounce of longing in her body. It was him, the promise in his eyes when he looked at her, that was causing this reckless abandonment. This stranger's touch was igniting something wild inside her, something she could neither deny nor control. She wanted the kiss to go on and on forever.

He could be her way out.

Arista jerked away from the man and backed up, never taking her eyes off his face. His closeness made it hard to breathe. She pressed her hand against her chest to slow her frantic heartbeat. He looked bewildered and slightly off-kilter.

Her lips still burned from his touch and she scrubbed a gloved fist over them. She had again been on the verge of asking him to take her away with him. And maybe he *would* take her with him.

But would he if he knew who she was?

He did not know Lady A or her nefarious reputation yet. He did not fear or loathe her on sight. This was cruel. As if some bigger power was dangling a beautiful silver key just over her head, promising freedom from her tarnished cage, if she only dared to reach for it. But Arista knew what would happen if she did: retribution, swift and deadly. Bones would find out, and he would do worse than kill her.

"Please, tell me your name." His voice sounded hoarse and it cracked with emotion. He already knew she would run from him again.

Arista choked on the reply. She wanted to tell him, but how could she? She was nobody. She had no past, no future. Nothing to offer anyone. She had no right to ask him to risk anything to help her escape.

"I'm sorry," she said.

He moved as if to reach for her. Arista turned and ran blindly into an opening between the tall hedges. He shouted behind her, and her street instincts kicked in. She ran down a short path to where the maze broke off into two directions. She didn't think, just chose one and then another as the path split again and again.

The maze grew darker as she made her way deeper into it. There were only a few lanterns placed sparingly, with just enough light to illuminate a specific pathway. Probably the one leading the way out. Arista chose the opposite way and the trail soon opened into a round garden. A single lantern sat atop a stone column. Most likely, she was at the center of the maze. She listened behind her, searched for signs of pursuit, but heard nothing louder than the whisper of her own skirt.

Only then, when she was finally alone, did she exhale. She stood, gasping for air. All the carefully constructed walls that allowed her to live, to exist in this godforsaken life, started to crumble. Twice now, she'd run from her very own glimpse of freedom.

It had been years since she'd really believed her life could change. Hope had given way to despair. No one would save her. No one cared about her at all.

Damn that highwayman to hell. Damn his touch that lit a spark of hope inside her again. She didn't want to feel anything. Numbness was safe. It was the only thing that got her through the horror of each day. Arista sank onto a stone bench and clenched her hands together in her lap.

Forget him. Forget tonight.

"A nice evening for a stroll, is it not?" Arista bolted upright. She had not heard anyone approach. The shadowy figure of a man stood next to an ivory-colored statue. The red tip of a cheroot cigar glowed in the low light. Not the highwayman. There had been no smell of tobacco on him either time they'd met.

Arista was entirely too rattled and exposed to have any further conversations tonight. Bones be damned. Lady A could not properly do her job in this state.

"Pardon me for interrupting. I'll leave you to yourself," Arista said. She started to back away, when the man stepped into a small pool of light. He wore a simple lion's mask over his eyes.

"Please, stay—if you don't mind, Lady A." She could not move, even as he stepped closer. Arista sensed nothing hostile or dangerous in his movements. No telltale signs that he meant to hurt her. Still, she could feel the authority surrounding him, even when he stood at a distance. A man clearly used to getting his way. And he knew who she was. He held all the advantage.

"I don't care much for social niceties when getting to the point works so much better, don't you agree?" He waved his cheroot in the air as he spoke. "Now, why don't you have a seat and we can talk business?" Arista looked around, but realized that the hedge maze had been designed for a single purpose: to hide anyone inside. She lowered her hand to her side, where she could feel the knife's handle. If he thought to harm her in *any* way, she would fight to the end.

"I'm afraid you have me at a disadvantage, sir. You seem to know me, but I don't know you." He was not a former client, because Arista would have remembered dealing with someone like him before. He must be the person she'd been sent to meet tonight. It was the only logical explanation, but still it was little comfort.

"We have a mutual friend," he said, as if that explained everything. So he *was* the client. Usually, the people she met with were nervous or angry, but this man seemed overconfident. He looked quite relaxed, in fact, for someone about to barter away a secret. The sweet fragrance of roses and gardenias filled her lungs.

Arista had no patience for games tonight. "Payment is required first. Along with the information you wish to trade." She held out her hand and waited. "And I'll take your contact information, to set up the second meeting, should your secret be of value."

He studied her intently for several long seconds before straightening to his full height. When he stepped closer, Arista saw how he towered over her. He was taller than Nic, even. His shoulders were broad, as if he were accustomed to hard work, yet his perfectly tailored clothing spoke of money. She fought the urge to take a step back. That would only show weakness. There were no sounds from the party this deep into the garden.

"I've not come to make a deal with your boss. I'm much more interested in dealing directly with you, Lady A." He was crazy. Or Bones had set her up, was testing her.

She started to move past him, but he grabbed her arm. Arista stiffened and fought the urge to reach for her knife. Nic would have had the man backed up against the wall for even touching her. Where the hell *was* he tonight?

"Get your bloody hands off me or I'll stab you in the gut." Her words came out short and harsh between her clenched teeth. Her breathing grew ragged and she took a quick breath in through her nose to try and quiet the unease.

"I don't doubt you would." The man chuckled, but his grip relaxed enough that she slipped free. "Pardon me for forgetting my manners, but I've been watching you, Lady A, and I think we can help each other."

"That is what I do. You give me your darkest secret and in return, I provide you with what you need." Having set up this meeting with Bones, he must surely know how it worked.

"Yet you are burdened with all the risk and reap none of the reward. Your services should be valued at a higher price." His face remained calm and he tilted his head to the side, studying her. "It must be a horrible life, *ma petite*. Always doing the bidding of others. You yourself are in danger, and for what? Are you being compensated, or does he take it all and force you to live in squalor?"

Arista's breath caught in her throat. How did this man know so much about her, about her life under Bones's control? She stared at him, her chest rising and falling with her quick breaths.

His hand moved suddenly, and she spun away from him in a flash. She had her knife in hand by the time she faced him again. The man only laughed, obviously happy with something. Slowly this time, he pulled his hand out of his jacket and held it palm up. Empty. She frowned. He had meant to reach for something, she'd been positive about that. She'd seen the intention in his eyes.

"Fascinating. You're as good as he said you were. There is, indeed, a pistol in my jacket, but I assure you, I had no real desire to use it on one so pretty." His smile turned almost charming and it softened his face. His gaze moved down over her bodice appreciatively, until the sharp tip of the blade under his chin forced his head back up. Amusement danced in his eyes again. He smiled at her as if they were friends. As if he were not afraid of her at all.

"I would like to offer you what that wretched excuse for a human being cannot. Lady A," he said, bowing in front of her, "I would like to offer you your freedom."

The familiar fear started again, and despite how hard she tried to push it back down, it would not budge. This had to be a test. Why would anyone, especially this stranger, want to save her?

"I'm afraid that you're not in a position to extend such an offer, sir. I don't have the time for false promises or games." Arista needed to get away. From this man, from this party—from all of it. Her ruse as Lady A had a certain structure to it. It was familiar. A part she could play with no real effort.

But tonight, Grae had thrown her off balance, and before she could recover, this man was now offering her freedom.

"How about a promise from someone that holds a much dearer place in your life? One whom you trust? One who, perhaps, has mentioned a way out recently?" he said quietly. "I assure you that I am not playing games at all. I am simply giving you the chance to live the life you dream of."

Time stopped. The space around them shrank to the very spot where they stood. Arista could find no hint of treachery in his intentions, and that fanned the flames of fear dancing inside her. He'd echoed the words Nic had whispered in the darkness last night, and she couldn't ignore him any longer. There was a connection. She needed to know what it was. "Who are you?"

"I am but a *humble* thief taker." Though he bowed his head, the square set of his shoulders told her differently. Nothing about him spoke of humility. His pride came through loud and clear. He could only be one man. Her blood ran cold.

Even in the Hells, London's darkest places where people existed almost as animals, this man's reputation was notorious. He lived with the power of the law on his side. The Thief Taker General protected the interests of the richest in society, tasked by the Crown with tracking down their stolen property.

Yet those in the Hells whispered rumors that he was also the one perpetrating the crimes against the rich themselves. Stealing. Embezzling. Smuggling. For a price, a high price, he would "find" those responsible and claim the reward. Among thieves it was well known that if you did not work for the Thief Taker, you were against him. And his enemies were dealt with in the harshest manner possible. They became the accused, and paid for the crimes they did not commit.

This man before her could make someone disappear behind the walls of Newgate Prison, never to be seen or heard from again. He could exact deadly judgment on any who might betray him, under the guise of justice.

Nic said Bones was worried about the Thief Taker. It appeared that his paranoia held merit. Jonathan Wild, the Thief Taker General, *did* know who Bones was. And he also knew what his most lucrative possession was. Lady A.

"I see by your expression you've figured it all out now?" Wild smiled at her. It almost looked . . . pleasant. Pride shone from his eyes. "We are very similar, you know. You and me. We both take from those who have too much—but while you pass along the spoils of your labor to someone undeserving, I keep mine. I am a very wealthy man, and you, my dear, could become a very wealthy woman. We are both notorious in our own way, and if we combine our . . . talents . . . the sky could be the limit. I am willing to split the profits of our joint venture fifty-fifty. You could have anything. Everything."

An uneasy feeling crossed over her skin. This could still be a setup. "Did Bones send you here?"

His lip curled in contempt. His reaction to her boss's name showed no love lost between them. She and he had one thing in common, at least.

The only man in London who terrified Bones stood before her with an offer of freedom. It seemed too good to be true. Wild dared to go against Bones and he could win—but did *she* have the courage to take what he offered?

"I know what happens to people who don't agree with you," Arista said, keeping her voice low and even. "If I say no to you now, you'll simply set me up—I'll be accused of a crime I didn't commit, and then I will disappear. Isn't that how it works?" Arista crossed her arms over her chest to hide the way her hands were shaking. She did want out. But badly enough to actually contemplate Wild's offer?

"Normally, you'd be right." His honesty surprised her. She thought he would have denied it to try and convince her to join him. "But I have too much respect for you to extort your services. If you join me, it must be as a willing associate. You could remain where you are, but we both know that when your usefulness is over, Bones won't hesitate to sell a pretty thing like you to the brothels. Is that where you want to end up? Because if it is, I can offer you a position right this moment in one of mine." Arista glared at him. "I didn't think so," Wild said.

"Why should I believe you? How do I know you won't just lock me in a different prison to use me as you see fit and keep all the money to yourself? You could dispose of me better than Bones ever could."

"You *don't* know, I suppose. But I am a man of my word, and I have made my offer. It is up to you, now, to decide the direction of your future. To choose your own fate: servitude or freedom. I am only offering you the means to obtain it if you wish." Wild bowed elegantly, then reached out and took her hand. He pressed his lips against her glove, like any well-bred gentleman would. "It has been a pleasure and an honor to talk with you this evening, my dear. I do hope that we will have the chance to work together soon. As equals. Remember that. I assure you that you can trust me in this."

Arista took a step back and cradled her hand against her chest. Too many emotions battled inside her head. How many nights had she wished for someone to appear and give her a way out? But did she dare to trust someone like Wild? It would be like trusting the devil himself.

"You of all people should know, sir, that there is no such thing as trust among thieves."

Wild laughed once more. "I like your honesty, Lady A. I dare-say I like it a lot."

CHAPTER 4

"Has Nic come back yet?" Arista burst through the door as soon as Becky opened it. A whoosh of musty air swept over Arista, so different from the exotic, clean smells of the ball. Blood still buzzed through her veins. She had to ask Nic about Wild. She had to know if what he said was true.

"No, miss. Though there's been a racket fit to wake the devil on the other side of the wall since about the time you left. I've had to tear out three rows of stitches on a new costume because of the commotion." The lamplight illuminated the frown on Becky's face before the maid turned and hurried down the hall. She had not lied about the ruckus. Voices boomed through the thin walls and something heavy thudded against the boards. Arista cringed when the distinct tone of Bones's voice could be heard over all the rest.

"You find him and bring him back here. That sorry bastard will regret the day he double-crossed me. I've got someone else to question, but you three go, now."

Doors slammed and the din quieted, which made the footsteps

coming toward the second door that much louder. Only Nic used that door to gain access to the main part of the house. No one else ever came through from that side. From the inside.

The person stopped just on the other side of the door. The rattling of keys was followed by the unmistakable sound of a lock being turned. Even through the wood, Arista could sense the murderous intentions of Bones, and the urge to flee flooded her body. "Go." Arista nudged Becky toward their room. The girl fumbled with the doorknob, and kept looking over her shoulder. Arista groaned with frustration. Her hand fell to her side and rested on the hard knife handle under her skirt.

The inside door swung open and Arista made out the shadowy outline of Bones standing there. An involuntary shudder raced over her. Her dealings with Bones were infrequent in nature, with Nic the usual liaison between them. That suited Arista fine. This, though, wasn't just his terrifying temper; it was something more, something darker. He approached, and her skin crawled.

"Miss?" Becky held the lamp up to her face and gestured hurriedly for Arista to come inside the room. She could run, but it would do no good. Others had tried to run away. They'd been made examples of.

Though she doubted Bones would harm her physically, there were other ways he could get to her, and he knew them well. Arista straightened her shoulders and shook her head. "No. You go. Close the door quickly, and lock it. Do not come out until I tell you to. Here he comes."

Becky didn't move. Her gaze flicked to the door, and the color left her face.

"Becky! Leave me." Arista hated being short with her friend, but it was imperative that she was safely behind the door before Bones got to them. Becky made a terrified sound deep in her throat, and the light disappeared. Arista heard the click of the door latch falling into place, and exhaled.

When she was young, Arista would close her eyes and pretend that in the darkness, she could become invisible. A useless trick; Bones always found her. Tonight, Arista kept her eyes open and stared directly at Bones. His pupils were dilated and his lips were a tight, thin line.

"Girl, did you have anything to do with this?" Bones's raspy voice grated across her skin, leaving goose bumps in its wake. He waved a leather pouch in her face, but she'd never seen it before. She had no idea what it held.

"I don't . . ." Arista steeled herself. It was always the same when faced with her guardian, if he could even be called that. Slave master, maybe? He owned her as if she were a piece of paste jewelry, and could reduce her to a small, scared child with a single glare.

Who could she be tonight, right now? Not that scared child. Someone else.

Arista called on her alter ego, and Lady A straightened her back. "I don't know what you mean." Her voice regained its cultivated tone, with no evident trace of street dialect.

She saw his fist too late. Pain exploded along the side of her jaw and she crumpled back against the wall. He never hit her in the face because of her value as Lady A. Something had happened to change her worth.

"Don't you dare use that uppity voice on me, girl. I made you, and I can unmake you just as quickly."

Arista held her jaw and pushed herself up to stand. She would not lie at his feet like a dog. He could beat her senseless, but she would not cower. Not anymore.

"That boy o' yours. Where is he?" Cold, steely fingers wrapped around her wrist. Bones was much stronger than he looked.

"Nic?"

"*Ni-ic,*" he mimicked. His lips turned up in a snarl. "You got more than one boy, then? Whorin' yourself behind my back, girl?"

"No!" Heat flooded her face.

Bones dug his fingers into her wrist until she thought she would hear a snap. His snarling face was inches from hers. His breath reeked of garlic and tooth rot. "Where is he?"

"I thought he was out on an errand for you," she gasped. Prickles of light danced in her vision. Bones had always been cruel, but tonight something had changed. Tonight, Arista feared he might finally kill her. "I went out alone tonight."

"You were out tonight?" Bones lifted the light over his head and peered down over her, finally noticing her costume. "What game are you up to? I didn't send you out." Spittle flecked his lips and he shoved her back against the wall. As he held her there with an arm across her throat, the flames from the lantern burned in his eyes. He looked like the devil himself. "Are you double-crossing me, girl?"

"You sent me." She tugged desperately against his iron grip.

She realized the truth in a rush. The card that granted her entrance to the masquerade hadn't been from him. Of course not— why would he send her to meet Wild? Unless Wild had arranged the meeting under the pretense of needing Bones's services. But judging by the murderous glint in Bones's eyes, he knew nothing about tonight.

Bones released the pressure on her neck, but then tangled his gnarled fingers in her wig. The pins pulled painfully at her scalp, and Arista grabbed his wrist with both hands. "I'll not be double-crossed, girl. Not by the likes o' you. Who gave you the order to go out? Do not lie to me."

Arista glared at Bones. "You did."

He yanked upward until she stood on her toes, pinned against the wall. She dug her nails frantically into his flesh, but he didn't relent. He twisted his hand, tightening his grip on her hair, then drove his free fist into her gut over and over again.

He did plan to kill her.

Bile rose up in her throat as the blows kept coming. Her entire body burned with fiery pain. She couldn't hold it in any longer. She screamed. The door to her room flew open.

"It was me," Becky cried. The girl half fell out of the door, then sank to her knees at Bones's feet. "A note was slipped under the outside door. I thought it was from you." Bones released Arista. She doubled over, gasping for breath. Each inhale sent a new, agonizing shot throughout her body. Wild had known her at the party, had even expected her to be there. Had he slipped the note under the door? No one except Becky, Arista, Nic, and Bones knew of Lady A's whereabouts—knew that the nondescript outside door led right to her.

"Please." Arista jerked her head toward the plea in time to see Becky cowering on the floor. Bones drove his boot into the girl's middle, and her abrupt scream was cut off when the next blow landed on her head. Becky lay still on the floor.

The invisible vise on Arista's limbs released, and she staggered a few steps before the pain doubled her over. "No, stop!"

Bones barked an order over his shoulder and two huge men stepped from the shadows. One, a hulking beast with a disfigured face, advanced on her with a feral gleam in his eye. "Put them inside," Bones said.

The brute grabbed her arm and pulled her against his chest. He smelled of sweat and onions and Arista gagged as he pushed her nose against his shirt. He slid his arm around her back and drove his hand into her stomach, in the same spot Bones had beaten. She cried out in pain and the man laughed, a low sadistic sound she had heard on the streets too often. He lifted her off her feet and all she could do was concentrate on breathing in through her mouth and out through her nose.

She would not faint. She would not let this monster do *anything* to her without one hell of a fight.

Arista didn't have time to contemplate it, because she suddenly flew through the air. She landed hard on her shoulder and the impact sent fresh jolts of pain through her body. The knife handle dug into her hip, and she slid her hand under her skirts until she curled her fingers around the cool, smooth wood.

Becky lay motionless on the floor. Bones took the single lantern from the room and handed it to one of the men. He stood over her, a sneer on his face. "Maybe a little reminder of how it *could be* will help you remember. There'll be no food or drink or light until I find him."

His guards left the room, then Bones followed, taking the light with him. Arista heard the outside lock click into place. She scrambled to her hands and knees and crawled to the door. Splinters dug into her fingertips as she clawed at the wood.

They were trapped in the dark.

The corset shrank with each breath until it became impossible to get any air. The room grew warmer with each exhale and Arista fought the panic welling up inside her. There were no windows— another safeguard to prevent anyone from discovering they were there. White dots danced at the edges of her vision. She could not stop her limbs from shaking as she turned and put the door at her back. She drew her knees to her chest and rocked back and forth.

What if I told you I know where Bones hides his money? That I can get to it? Where would you want to go then?

Oh God, Nic, what have you done?

She must have said it out loud. "Miss?" Becky's faint voice pulled Arista from her thoughts.

"Becky!" It hurt to talk, but she called out again despite the pain. Arista turned back onto her hands and knees and crawled toward her friend's soft cries. Each small movement sent fresh waves of agony shooting through her stomach, but she pushed on. She had to be strong for both of them now. "Where are you?"

"Here, miss."

Arista made her way over the last few feet and found Becky. As she carefully ran her fingers over the girl, something warm and sticky coated her fingers. Without any light, Arista had no idea how badly her friend had been injured.

"Becky," she whispered. Her voice sounded as though her mouth were full of muslin. "I'm going to get us out of here, and I'll get you some help, okay?" Emotion welled up in her throat, making it difficult to swallow.

Arista fought through the growing panic and pushed to her feet. Sharp pain radiated from her middle but she made her way blindly across the room, one arm cradling her aching stomach and the other held out in front of her. When she finally felt solid wood under her hand, she leaned her forehead against the wall and took in several shallow breaths. It didn't hurt as much that way.

She felt so small, so helpless. Being trapped again, in the dark room, brought back memories of before, when she was too young and helpless to fight back. Then, she would just curl up and wait.

Maybe there was nothing to do now—nothing to be done. What could *she* do, anyway? She was just a girl. An orphan. Nobody.

But she was also Lady A. She'd brought grown men to their knees. What would Lady A do? She'd fight.

And she'd win.

Arista made a fist and pounded on the door. The force rattled the locks like bells but the door held, surprisingly firm despite the rotten wood.

"Bones!" she shouted as best as she could. He thought she would admit defeat—beg to be taken out of the dark. He thought she was weak.

She was counting on it.

In only a minute, she heard his footsteps in the hall outside. Between the folds in her skirt, she found the hidden slit and pulled her knife free. He would not get the chance to lock her inside again.

A key scraped across metal and the click sounded like a gunshot. Sweat beaded on Arista's forehead and trickled down into her eyes. There would only be one chance. If she failed, he would kill her this time.

When the door swung open and light filled the room, Arista drew back and kicked out at Bones's legs. He fell into the room and the lantern he'd been carrying smashed onto the floor. The oil spread out and flames licked at it greedily.

He had not expected her to fight back, after being held in the dark. He'd expected a scared, cooperative child. But she wasn't that little girl anymore.

Bones growled like an animal and pushed to his feet. He faced her, blackened teeth bared. A small stream of blood ran down his face from a cut on his cheek. She smiled in satisfaction. But then a *whoosh* swept through the room, and the flames leapt to the bed—and the wall behind.

Fire ate at the flimsy wooden structure, spreading so fast that within seconds, thick black smoke rolled across the ceiling.

Becky moaned from the floor. Arista crouched down, the knife still pointed at Bones. "Becky, we have to get out. I need you to stand up." Arista's jaw throbbed and flashes of pain wrenched her stomach each time she moved, but if they didn't get out soon, they would burn to death.

"Die, like the scum you are!" Bones shouted over the escalating sound of the fire. He started to move past her, but he would not get away. If she was going to die, he'd go with her. Arista swung her arm in a high arc and sank her knife into his soft stomach.

He screeched and fell to his knees next to her. A deep red stain quickly spread over the bottom half of his shirt. He clutched at the knife handle but could not get a grip on it, because of all the slick blood pouring from the wound.

Bones fell forward with a hard thump. He didn't move again. Through the walls, Arista heard his men shouting. She rolled Bones over and used the material of her shirt to grip the knife, to pull it free from his unmoving body. If his men found them, she'd need it again.

The fire had eaten away half the room already and spread out into other parts of the house. The heat became unbearable. The dry wood was quickly consumed by the hungry fire.

"Becky?" Each breath took more effort than the last as smoke filled Arista's lungs. The searing temperature of the fire singed her wig, and sparks rained down around them. The old, dry wood crackled so loudly that she couldn't hear her own voice.

Becky did not respond when Arista grabbed her arm and dragged her across the floor to the doorway. Smoke was pouring out of the room and filling the hall. Heavy thumps sounded at the second door, followed by a burst of splintering wood. New voices shouted into the space. Bones's men had broken through.

Arista stood, then bent over to drag Becky toward the door that led out to the street. The pain grew so bad that she almost vomited, but she knew if she didn't keep going, they were dead. The men were battling the fire and didn't notice them in the darkness.

When Arista finally felt the wood of the door against her back, she sank down to the floor, exhausted. They'd made it. The sweet taste of relief overpowered the acrid taste of smoke. She reached to where Becky always kept the key—on a string around her neck— and found nothing. Icy panic raced up her back while the heat of the fire pressed down against them. She couldn't go back to look for it. Fire crawled across the ceiling of the hall, getting closer with each swirling orange finger.

Arista pushed to her feet and jammed her shoulder against the door. Stars danced in her vision. Pain radiated down her arm, but she tried again. And again. The street door could only be unlocked from the inside. It needed a key.

While the townhouse may have been in deplorable shape, the door had been reinforced to prevent anyone from stumbling in on them. Frustration turned to terror as the roar of the fire grew closer, all around them now. She dug at the lock with her knife, but the blade felt heavy and awkward in her grip and took too much effort to hold steady. The weight of it dragged her hand down until it rested on the rough floor. When she tried to lift it again, she had nothing left. Her strength was gone. They were trapped.

Arista turned and leaned her back against the door, gasping for air. The smoke billowed down the hallway, almost beautiful in its white, writhing dance. She watched with a sort of detached fascination. Each breath filled her lungs with more and more smoke.

Would death hurt? Could it hurt any more than being alive? Some days, she had ached almost too much to bear. And just when a chance of escape had presented itself, and given her hope for a future she'd never dared dream of, it too had been snatched away. Bones's final act of treachery.

As her head grew hazy, Arista thought of the highwayman, of the kiss they'd shared earlier, and she had a moment of regret. She would never know that feeling again. She would never find the love she craved. Never see the shores of distant lands, or feel the wind of an open sea brush over her face. Never taste true freedom.

The fire seemed to retreat behind them, holding its breath expectantly, but only for a second. It gathered itself, then reared back and roared. The thick smoke made it impossible to breathe, and the oblivion that had been threatening to overtake her finally won out.

Arista threaded her fingers through Becky's and closed her eyes as the darkness rose up to claim her.

CHAPTER 5

Somewhere in the hazy glow inside her head, Arista heard voices; wood splintered; arms lifted her. The brush of cool night air over her skin made her shiver, and each breath caused excruciating spasms in her lungs. If this was death, she must be in hell. Faces floated in and out of her clouded vision.

Then the dark was a blissfully quiet and pain-free place.

When she opened her eyes, bright sunlight streamed in through a lace-covered window. Softness cocooned her body, enveloped her in the most exquisite warmth. Hell was a strange place indeed.

There was a movement to her right, and she distantly watched an unfamiliar girl set a tray down on the small table next to the bed. Arista blinked several times, trying to chase the sleep from her eyes. The girl had on a filmy dressing robe and kohl smeared under one eye, making her seem less exotic and more like a nightmarish creature. In fact, it looked like the woman had just stumbled out of bed herself.

"Where am I?" The words scraped across her raw throat and came out barely audible. The girl glanced at her, then at someone just out of Arista's view. A new figure stood in the doorway: a man. Her vision cleared. Not just any man; Wild.

Panic sizzled under her skin. She'd heard stories of girls being drugged and sold into the cruelest brothels. Had he lied about not forcing her to work with him?

"What am I doing here?" Arista tried to push herself up, but a slice of pain cut through her middle. With a gasp, she lay back down. What had he done to her?

"Relax, my dear," Wild said. "You're quite safe here. If I may come in, I'll try and explain everything."

Arista glanced at the girl, who now stood off to the side with her hands clasped over her stomach.

"Justine will stay if it makes you more comfortable," Wild said. He waited patiently at the threshold of the room for her to grant him access: a consideration she would not have expected from one such as him. She motioned for him to enter and he made his way to the bed, standing close but not so close that it made her uncomfortable. Justine stood still, though she seemed more like a half-asleep girl than a guard.

"How did I get here?" Arista asked, and winced at the pain in her throat.

Wild picked up a glass and filled it with water from a matching pitcher. "May I?" he asked, indicating that he would help her to sit up. When she nodded, he carefully lifted the glass to her lips and tilted it just enough so a few precious drops of water fell into her mouth.

It felt as if she were drinking liquid fire. Water dribbled down her chin when she turned her head away from the pain. "Thank you," she whispered. The pain receded and her throat did feel a little better. "Where am I?"

"I brought you somewhere safe to recover," Wild said, setting the glass on a small table next to the bed. "No one saw you arrive, and aside from a few of my girls, no one knows you're here." Was that a warning? No, though her mind was muddled, she saw no ill intent in his eyes. Only concern—the way his lips turned down at the corners.

"What happened?" For the life of her, she could not remember at all. Images were jumbled together in her head. Everything remained fuzzy, as if she might still be dreaming. She had a vague recollection of shouting, and then . . . nothing. A dull throb radiated from the side of her jaw. When she raised her hand to feel along the bone, Wild scowled, though he didn't seem angry at her.

"I imagine it feels about as bad as it looks. I had my physician check on you the first night, and he said nothing appeared broken. Your ribs are quite bruised, though, and will be uncomfortable for some time."

Arista blinked. Her eyelids were suddenly so heavy. It wouldn't hurt to close them, just for a minute, would it? Wild pulled the quilt up around her neck and patted her head as if she were a child.

"Rest now, my dear. There will be plenty of time to discuss other matters when you've recovered." Wild followed Justine out of the room, and the door closed. The unmistakable click of a lock registered somewhere in the fog inside her head, but Arista barely had time to acknowledge it before the darkness swept her under again.

When she awoke once more her head had finally cleared. Night sat heavy outside the window now, and from somewhere below her, the sounds of music and laughter drifted through the floor. A lantern flickered from across the room, casting the room in soft light. The warm glow of a fire in the hearth made the room's temperature quite comfortable. As one used to waking up in a cold, dark room, it took Arista a moment to get her bearings and remember the conversation with Wild.

Gingerly she sat up, cradling her bruised ribs. The pain was at least manageable now. Her legs wobbled when she stood, but they held her upright. A demure white nightgown hung to her ankles, buttoned just under her neck. Who had put this on her? Heat burned her cheeks. Hopefully the girl she saw earlier.

The room was small but well furnished. A wardrobe sat in one corner, and next to it a dressing table. The floor was wood, but a colorful rug filled most of the room, keeping her bare feet warm. It was by far the nicest place she'd ever slept, but she still didn't understand how she'd gotten there. She could not separate dream from reality.

Arista moved to the window and pulled the curtain back. Her window looked out onto a small garden three stories below. It was too dark to make out anything that might tell her where she was. Reluctantly, she let the lace fall back into place. There were no answers in the dark.

A soft click sounded behind her. Arista swung around and reached for her knife instinctively. It wasn't there. She had just enough time to reach the side of the bed before the door swung open. She grabbed the quilt and threw it around her shoulders, just as a maid entered. She was not the same girl as before. This one looked much younger, and had on a simple blue gown with an apron over the front. Wild came in right behind her.

"So glad to see you awake, my dear." He met Arista's stare openly, then directed the girl to set her tray on the table next to the bed. The girl curtsied, not meeting their eyes, then stood silently against the wall.

Arista tugged the quilt tighter around her body. "Where are my clothes?" Her voice came out low and raspy. She swallowed against the rawness still in her throat. Wild poured water from a new crystal pitcher and handed it to her. With shaking fingers, she took it and downed the contents in two mouthfuls.

"Your dress was quite ruined from the smoke, so I took the liberty of having one of the girls—about your size—find something appropriate for you to wear. It's in the wardrobe when you're ready." The glass wobbled as she handed it back to Wild, and he gestured for her to sit. She sank to the edge of the bed gratefully. She hated appearing weak, but Wild made no mention of her state. For that she gave silent thanks.

"I've brought you some things to eat. I didn't know your preferences, so I had the cook include a few choices. Your weapon is there, next to the tray." Arista glanced to where he pointed. Her knife handle poked out from behind the tray, cleaned of Bones's blood. Some of the tension eased from her shoulders. If she were a prisoner, he would have hidden it away.

"What happened? How did I get here?" she asked again.

"What do you remember?" he asked, instead of answering her question.

An image popped into her head. "A fire?" Wild nodded. At his confirmation, more images rushed to fill her head, as if the first had opened a door for the rest. The room swam. Bones. His fists. The dark room. And, oh God, the fire.

Becky.

"Where is Becky? Is she . . ." Arista couldn't say the word. She now remembered the cold, limp feel of Becky's hand as she'd held it in the final moments before everything disappeared.

"Your friend is quite safe, though we weren't sure for a few days whether she would regain consciousness or not. She didn't have the fever you did. The physician did what he could, tended to her wounds, but left the rest up to the girl. She woke yesterday."

Fever? Days? In her own mind, only a day at most had passed. "How long have we been here?"

"Four days."

No matter how hard she tried, Arista could not reconcile that over half a week had passed. "How did you find me? You *were* the one who saved me?" Vague dreamlike recollections filtered in and out of her mind. Wild had been there at one point. Only it had not been a dream at all.

"I was," he said.

When he didn't elaborate, she filled in the blanks on her own. "You were following me?"

"It wasn't so much following, as going in the same direction. I had business to tend to in that particular area of London. When you left the party and I noticed your usual companion absent, I did what any gentleman would do. I saw you home safely."

"You followed me," she said again. How could he have followed her all that way without her sensing him there?

As if he knew what she thought, he smiled. "I can be quite invisible when I want to. And I know those alleyways as well as you."

One did not earn a reputation like Wild's without the ability to disappear, of course.

"I had concluded my business, and that's when I saw smoke coming from the building into which you had vanished. The door was locked, but I heard pounding. With my associate's help, we broke the door in. I brought you here, to one of my establishments, to recover. The rest . . . well, you know." He waved his hand around the room.

"Is Bones . . . ?" She could still hear the echoes of his furious howling; still feel his heavy hand slamming into her over and over again. Wild's eyes narrowed.

"No one else got out. The fire had consumed almost everything by the time my men broke through the door. We were almost too late to save you and your friend. The entire block is gone now."

Bones. Could he really be dead?

That meant she and Becky were free from him. And Nic . . . had he been searching for her? What if he thought she perished in the fire? "I need to let someone know I'm okay." Then she remembered that Wild knew Nic. He had alluded as much at Lady Carstair's party. "Can you bring him here?"

Wild looked at her curiously, a small smile on his lips, as if he were testing her memory. "Who would that be?"

"Nic. But you knew that already, didn't you? You two have talked before. Nic mentioned it the night before the fire. Where is he? Is he working for you now? You better not have hurt him." She started to push upright, but the room swam in her vision. Her own body's betrayal forced her to lie back down, breathless and weak. "I need to see him."

"I last spoke with your friend a day before the fire. I waited for him to accept my generous offer, and had also hoped he would convince you to join us as well. Things . . . took an unexpected turn, though, and I assure you that I've not been in contact with him since." Arista watched Wild carefully. Was that a tic at the corner of his eye? It happened so fast she couldn't be sure. Perhaps the fog in her head was clouding her judgment.

"I will have a few men ask around, discreetly of course, and if they hear any word, you will be the first to know. For now, you must concentrate on your recovery. You are alive and free, my dear. The world is at your feet. All you have to do now is take it." Wild smiled again. His eyes sparkled and Arista found herself caught up in the vibrancy she saw in them. Her own lips lifted in response.

"I have not made my decision yet." Her reply was a test. To see if his charm would be replaced by anger.

But his smile did not falter. "Perhaps after you've eaten we can discuss the terms more clearly in the garden?"

Arista glanced at the window, and saw it was dark outside. Time remained tangled in her head.

"Thank you." He was giving her a choice, something no one else had ever done. Her entire life had been dictated by other people, for their own gain. It slowly started to sink in that with Bones gone, Arista *was* free. Free to do as she wanted.

She could *choose* to work with Wild, and it would benefit her in ways she had only ever dreamed. Nic had wanted the power that went along with the money, and though she denied it, there was always a measure of satisfaction when Lady A brought a member of the aristocracy to their knees.

If Wild were telling the truth. That remained to be seen. So far, he had done nothing to make her think otherwise.

A knock came at the door. The maid hastened to open it at Wild's nod. "I have business to attend to, but I've asked the staff to draw a bath for you to enjoy at your leisure. The door locks from the inside for your protection. When you're ready, just ask Cecily to show you to the garden."

A line of servants marched into the room. Each carried two steaming buckets of water. They disappeared behind a painted screen in the corner, and poured the water into something back there. After the last person left, the maid from before moved beside Arista. "Would you be needing help, miss?"

"Help?" Arista's gaze darted between Wild, the maid, and the screen.

"With your bath, miss?" The maid crossed the room and folded the screen back. A waist-high copper tub sat in the corner, steam rising from within. They expected her to bathe in that . . . monstrosity?

She'd never had an actual bath before. Not a *get completely undressed and submerge yourself in a tub of hot water* bath.

"No." Arista looked between Wild and the maid, who then glanced quizzically back at Wild. Panic made her skin feel tight. She pulled the quilt to her neck. Would they force her into that thing if she refused? Her gaze slid to her knife.

"I can have your friend sent over to assist you, if that would make you more comfortable," Wild said softly. "At least she might help you wash up?"

Yes, she wanted to see Becky for herself, and could use the basin to wash her face and hands. "That is fine."

The maid hurried out of the room and Wild followed. At the door, he hesitated. His eyes were unreadable when he looked over at her. "I've just realized that I know you only by one name. The prudence of calling you Lady A outside of your disguise might make for unwanted gossip. As we've not yet reached a deal, I think it wise to remain silent regarding that information. Don't you?"

She nodded, but not because a deal had been made. If word got out she was Lady A, if they knew what she looked like under the mask, there would be nowhere to hide. The chances of getting killed would be high, whether she took Wild up on his offer or not.

Wild waited and Arista knew he wanted her name. She had no intention of giving him that information. Silence echoed in the room. "Ana," she lied. In the market, there was a girl that Nic often called out to. Flirted with. Her name was Ana.

Wild nodded in satisfaction and left the room, pausing long enough to hold the door for Becky, who hurried inside. Arista did not see Wild leave. Her focus was on her friend.

Arista stood and met Becky's hesitant gaze. Becky wore a simple blue dress similar to the maid's. She stayed frozen in the middle of the room, her hands clenched tightly together. She was still scared.

The covers fell off Arista to the floor as she got up.

Angry bruises marred Becky's arms; they looked like shadows thrown haphazardly across her body. A larger black discoloration covered the part of Becky's face that had been injured previously. A square of white linen had been taped over one eye to hide the damage done there.

"Oh, Becky, I'm so sorry." Arista's voice cracked and then broke. She wanted to throw her arms around her friend, but what if Becky hated her now? Arista would not blame her.

It wasn't the first time Becky had been marred by a man with angry fists. Arista's empty stomach flipped with guilt. She had promised her friend that no one would ever hurt her again, and yet she had stood by helplessly while Bones beat Becky into unconsciousness. Blame weighed so heavily inside her that Arista could barely lift her arms.

"Oh, miss." Becky quickly crossed the room and took one of Arista's hands in hers. "It wasn't your fault. That man is pure evil and got what he deserved. Mr. Wild told me about the fire and how he pulled us out. If it weren't for him . . ." Becky's hands trembled, and Arista settled her free hand over her friend's. The girl's shaking quieted under the contact.

"We got nowhere to go. No money or clothes or food. Everything is gone," Becky whispered. "What are we going to do now, miss? What will we do?" A quiet note of desperation had entered her voice. Women had very few choices for employment in London. Becky was a masterful seamstress, but no reputable shop would hire a disfigured girl with no references.

A tear splashed down onto her hands, and Arista looked up. This close, she could see the blue and green and black of Becky's bruises much clearer. A small cut ran from the corner of her mouth, covered with a thin line of crusted blood.

A fresh wave of rage and guilt burned Arista's skin. She should have been able to stop Bones. Nic had taught her to fight, to take care of herself. She should have protected Becky. But she had not. She had failed her friend. The only thing she could do to make sure Becky would *not* have to live on the street, or worse, was to work with Wild.

"You'll be safe and no one will ever get close enough to hurt you again. I promise I'll take care of you," Arista said. "Don't worry about anything except getting better."

Dealing with Wild, partnering with him, meant taking an enormous risk, but she had no other option. Arista had no skills, save those of a thief. An alliance was the only way to make sure that Becky stayed safe from now on.

She would agree to Wild's request. There really was no other choice. She had no money, no means of leaving London. But there were a few things he had to get for them first—things Arista needed in place before they made their deal. She let go of Becky's hand and turned around toward the wardrobe. The room kept turning after she stopped. Arista fumbled to right herself. Becky rushed to her side. "Miss, when did you eat last? You look so pale."

When had she? Before the fire? She'd had a small pastry at the ball, but that had been—how many nights ago? With so much lost time, she really had no idea.

"I don't know," she admitted. It wasn't like she hadn't gone days without food before.

"Sit." Becky guided her to the edge of the bed, where Arista sat carefully. Things weren't completely steady yet.

The covered silver tray had sat untouched, forgotten, but as soon as Becky lifted the cover, delicious aromas escaped from beneath. Arista's stomach growled loudly. "Oh, miss, look at all this food!" Becky said.

A meal fit for a queen. Or at least, what Arista thought a queen might eat. The tray held delicately cut triangles of toast, a pile of fluffy eggs, pastries, biscuits, a small crystal glass with what appeared to be juice of some sort, and a pile of fruit cut to resemble flowers.

"The kitchen was starting to prepare for breakfast already. I hope this is okay?" Becky said.

"What time is it?' Arista asked.

"Just before dawn, miss. Here—eat this first, to ease your stomach." Becky handed her a triangle of toast, and though she knew better, Arista was far too hungry to eat slowly. It disappeared in one bite. She reached for the glass of juice and swallowed down the contents in two large gulps.

The second piece of toast tasted even better, if that was possible. It didn't matter that both pieces were cold or that the butter sat in a greasy heap on top. The bread she knew had always been days old; stale, dry, and hard to even swallow. This melted in her mouth, and the sweet creamy taste of butter coated her tongue.

Despite the disapproval in Becky's eye, Arista took a pastry from the tray. They were common at the higher-class masquerades, but she rarely had the stomach to eat while waiting to deal with a client. "Becky, I need to ask you something. Did you tell Wild anything about me? About us?"

Her friend's eye grew round. "Of course not, miss. I know how important discretion is." Becky wrung her hands tightly in her apron. "He . . . he did ask if I knew your real name, though."

Arista's hand froze, the pastry halfway to her mouth. Only Nic knew her real name, and he never, ever called her by it. She was simply "gypsy" to him, but maybe Becky had heard them talking about it at one time. Maybe she had told Wild. Arista had not missed her friend's look of admiration when Wild left the room earlier. He had saved them, and therefore won approval.

"Becky, what did you tell him?"

Becky's gaze dropped to her hands. The small bit of bread sat like lead in Arista's stomach.

"I realized when he asked me that I don't know what it is. Is that bad, miss? That I don't know your real name? Mr. Nic calls you 'gypsy,' but I should remember it, right?" Becky was becoming visibly upset now. Her hands shook on her lap. "Do you suppose the fire made me forget?"

Arista hated seeing her friend distraught, but there was relief at knowing Becky did not know her real name. She reached out and took her hand. "I told Wild my name was Ana, so if he asks again, you can tell him."

"Ana, miss?"

"Yes—Ana." Now that Arista knew Becky had not told Wild, the panic receded and hunger replaced it with a fierce intensity. She popped the entire pastry into her mouth.

The flaky crust began to dissolve as soon as it hit her tongue. An explosion of tart lemon and sweet sugar filled her mouth. Arista closed her eyes and savored every exquisite second. When she opened them, Becky stood next to the table, her hands clasped in front of her stomach.

"Becky, eat." Arista licked sticky sugar crystals off her fingers.

"I've eaten plenty, miss. Mr. Wild made sure I was taken care of. I don't know how to ever thank him." She saw a look of pure adoration on Becky's face again. It was clear that the Thief Taker had made one ally, at least.

Arista decided to work with him, but she did not trust him yet. She wiped her hands on her nightgown and left the half-empty tray where it sat. "I need to clean up and meet with Wild. I have an idea, so don't worry about anything. We will be fine. More than fine, actually." She laughed. When had she last felt any real hope? Arista crossed to the stand and took the pitcher. If she dipped it into the bath water, she could wash enough to be presentable. When Arista stepped up to the tub, Becky gasped.

"Oh miss, a bath! I can help you. I used to help my young ladies, before . . ." Her voice trailed off. If Arista ever found out the name of the rich bastard who'd hurt Becky, hell would not be a safe place to hide.

"It's okay, I'm only going to wash in the basin." Arista tried to usher Becky back, but she would not move. When Arista looked up, determination shone from Becky's uninjured eye. Arista knew that look. When Becky was stubborn, nothing could sway her.

Arista glanced at the huge copper tub, the height of her waist, filled almost to the top with water. A thin vapor rested on the surface, and a neatly folded white square of cloth and a cake of soap sat on a small table.

"No, I'm not getting into that. It's indecent!" Arista held the pitcher in front of her like a shield.

"Oh miss, it's really not!" Becky said. "I had one in my room just yesterday and it was amazing. Just once, wouldn't you like to know what it feels like? Not to wash with freezing water, and only the parts that show? Imagine being clean, smelling like lavender or roses. I could wash your hair for you, too."

Arista had not seen Becky so excited, or so single-minded, since she had tried on her Lady A disguise and immediately demanded more frontal coverage. Well-bred ladies, though prudish in many areas, showed off ample amounts of skin when attending a party.

The last thing Arista wanted was to smell like lavender. It reminded her too much of the ladies she watched at the parties. The ones who wore their dresses indecently low to entice the men. No, she was more than happy to run a wet cloth rubbed with castor soap through her hair after that dreaded wig came off. Another swipe of it over her body and that was fine for her.

The idea of submerging her entire body in water just for the purpose of getting clean seemed unnecessary. The street men bathed in the Thames, and most of the children swam there when the heat got to be too much, but Arista never joined them.

Not out of modesty. Arista couldn't swim. Water, even in this contained form, terrified her.

Though the tub only came up to her hip, it might as well have held the entire river. Arista swallowed and ran her fingers tentatively through the water, tiny currents trailing behind. She stared in fascination. The water rippled outward from her fingers, its effect hypnotizing.

She leaned over the side and watched her reflection break apart, then come together, only to break apart again. Even in the unstable water, she could see the black smudges on her face. It wouldn't hurt to wash her arms *in* the tub. She took the soap and plunged her hands under the surface, lathering them until soft bubbles trickled down her forearms. The black soot washed away, revealing clean, pink skin. She pushed up the sleeves of the gauzy shift and scrubbed higher on her arms.

The soap felt decadent against her skin. The aroma wafted through the air, thick and sweet. She ducked her arms into the water, as far as she could from the odd angle where she was standing. Not entirely right, but not wrong either. Heat seeped through her skin and settled next to her bones. Amazing. Arista bit her lip. If Nic were here, he'd be taunting her, calling her a coward. "Becky, would you please check the lock?"

Becky adjusted the screen so it provided a barrier to the rest of the room, and then disappeared. Arista glanced once more at the bath and took a deep breath.

The buttons at her neck came undone easily, and the nightgown slipped off her shoulders. She held it tightly against her body and climbed onto the stool next to the tub. She let the nightgown fall and gripped the edge of the tub. First a toe, then an ankle, then a leg.

Her heart hammered against her ribs as she stepped in with the other leg. She stood still, arms crossed over her chest, as the water lapped gently at her thighs. She could wash like this and get clean enough, but what would it feel like to fully immerse herself in that warmth?

Very slowly, she sank down until she could sit. The water cocooned her body, and panic reared up. She grabbed the edge of the tub to get out before her heart exploded inside her chest.

"That's it, miss, just give it a minute," Becky said, coming around the corner. Arista sank back down so fast that water sloshed over the edge of the tub. Immediately the warmth of the water encompassed all of her at once. Heat soaked into her limbs, down to the bone, and Arista exhaled. Maybe this wasn't so bad after all.

Becky rolled her sleeves back and took the square cloth from the stand. She dipped it into the water and then scrubbed the cake of soap over it. The room filled with a thick, sweet fragrance that reminded Arista of the women at the masked balls, dancing by in their clouds of scented air.

"Lean forward, miss," Becky said.

Arista followed the order as if she was looking down at herself from a distance. Becky scrubbed the slick cloth over Arista's back and shoulders. When she tried to wash Arista's arms, Arista refused to unwind them from her knees. Tiny ripples covered the water from where her limbs still trembled. Each time she shifted, the water moved and pulled her slightly off balance. What if she slipped under?

"How about I wash your hair first?" Becky gently guided Arista's chin back and up, and then used the pitcher to slowly pour warm water over Arista's head.

It wasn't that much different than getting caught in the rain. Arista let out the breath she'd been holding. Another burst of fragrance filled her lungs, and then Becky's fingers were on her scalp. As Arista was not used to being touched, the sensation was both uncomfortable and luxurious.

The warmth of the water made her arms grow heavy. She let them fall away from her knees and they floated, suspended, next to her. She watched them with a sort of detached amusement. A sigh escaped, and she gave in and closed her eyes. Becky's fingers worked the lather into Arista's short hair with practiced ease.

The remaining tension in her body floated away as Becky massaged Arista's scalp. A languid calm settled over her. By the time Becky poured two more pitchers of water over her head, Arista could have fallen asleep. Baths might *not* be a terrible thing after all. Becky handed Arista the cloth when she was finished. It was all very different than washing one body part at a time with a damp rag.

"Ready?" Becky stood next to the bath with a larger cloth.

No, she wasn't ready, but the water grew cooler by the minute and Arista's teeth were beginning to chatter. Her legs shook as she stood and stepped over the edge. Becky immediately wrapped the cloth around Arista. Goose bumps sprang up along Arista's arms.

Becky took another cloth and vigorously rubbed it up and down Arista's arms. A bit of heat returned and Arista's teeth stopped chattering. Becky grabbed a robe from the peg on the screen. The bright red silk had exotic-looking tigers stitched in orange thread, rearing back with their mouths wide open. Exactly what she pictured a brothel girl wearing. The robe came only to her knees. She tugged at the hem, but it would go no lower.

"There are clothes in the wardrobe," Arista said. Hopefully something more tasteful than the robe. It would probably be a low-cut scarlet dress. Maybe Becky could find an errand boy and borrow some clothing for Arista to wear?

As Becky hurried to the wardrobe, Arista hung back, not comfortable enough to step out from behind the screen dressed in only a short robe. The door was locked, but she did not doubt that Wild had a master key.

When Becky returned, Arista braced herself for some monstrosity posing as a dress, but the garment Becky was holding seemed quite plain. The dark blue muslin material had been cut and sewn into a flattering and demure shape. The neckline was lined with lace, and not indecent at all. In fact, it covered more than any of the dresses she'd worn as Lady A.

A wide darker sash was wound around the waist. Not what the working girls would wear; it covered too much skin for them. A maid, maybe? Becky hung it on the peg and set down a pile of white underclothes, then left a pair of shoes on the floor. Not a single piece of the clothing screamed *whore*.

"Would you like me to help you get dressed?" Becky asked.

Arista picked through the pile of underclothes. Normally she wore only a shift under her man's shirt and jacket. Not even Lady A wore quite so many things. There had to be a half dozen different pieces here. She'd never get them all on correctly.

She could only nod.

Becky knew exactly what went where, though, and in only a few minutes Arista had on a chemise, a petticoat, silk stockings held up by lacy garters, and a corset laced not too loosely around her middle.

"All this when a simple shift would do just as well under a dress," Arista mumbled. The bones in the corset forced her back straight, which in turn forced her chest out. No one would mistake her for anything but a girl.

Becky lifted the dress over Arista's head and slid it down, shaking it as she did so that the material fell into place perfectly. After a few tugs here and there, Becky tied the sash in the back.

When Arista turned around, Becky's eyes opened wide and her

fingers pressed against her lips. "Oh, miss. You look beautiful." She dashed a stray tear away, then hurried to hang up the robe.

Heat flooded Arista's cheeks. She felt more exposed now than while standing naked at the tub. She lifted the hem of her dress to her waist and secured her knife to her thigh, and finally felt more like herself. More in control.

Now she was ready to go and make a deal with the devil.

CHAPTER 6

*A*rista only had to wait ten minutes before the maid, Cecily, returned. "If you'll come down to the garden, Mr. Wild will join you, miss." Cecily curtsied and motioned for Arista. "Follow me, please."

Arista took Becky's hand and squeezed. "I'll be back before you know it, and everything will be taken care of."

Becky's eye shone with unshed tears. She gripped Arista's hand tight. "What will you do, miss?"

"I'm going to give him what he wants, but on my terms. Now lock the door behind me." Arista let go of her friend's hand and turned away.

The long corridor outside her room was empty. Sounds filtered up from below, but no one else was in the hall. A well-worn runner spanned the length of the hall, stretching out to the left and right. After hearing the telltale click of the lock, Arista followed Cecily to the left, away from the music.

Most places like this had separate stairs for servants, so they could come and go unnoticed by the clientele. Cecily led her to a dark stairwell, and down it to another door. More steps wound further below them. When there were no more steps, Cecily swung open the last door. The hall they entered was empty; obviously the servants' area. The walls were rough and bare, and no rugs covered this floor. It didn't matter here.

"This way, miss." Cecily led Arista through the kitchen, where several hunched-over women tended to a line of pots hanging above a huge fire. None looked up as they walked past. Incredible smells filled the air, and despite the fact that she had eaten earlier, her stomach growled loudly. She grabbed a warm roll from a tray—a small show of defiance, if only in her own head. Cecily opened yet another door, and cool air immediately swept past her. A small, well-tended garden was just outside, with a stone walkway winding out of sight.

"You can wait on the bench if you like." Before Arista could answer, the door had closed behind her. She stood alone, with only the glow from a single window illuminating the fenced-in space. It appeared to be a small kitchen garden, filled with herbs and a few flowers. Someone had put a wooden bench in the corner by the tall fence, in the darkest part of the garden. Arista gravitated toward the shadows. The hem of her dress brushed against the fragrant foliage, and the air filled with a spicy mix of scents. She sat, her back to the fence, so that she could see Wild the moment he stepped outside.

In the silence, Arista cleared her head, and focused on what needed to be done. The warm bun practically melted in her mouth. After a lifetime of stale bread, there were no words to describe how delicious the food here tasted.

Mentally, she ticked off what her demands would be:

A place to live. A safe place, not like where they'd been before.

Food to eat.

A promise of safety for Becky, if anything should happen to Arista.

And Nic. He had to find Nic for her. Oh, he'd said he would send men to *inquire*, but Arista had no assurance that he actually would. By attaching the request to her list of demands, it might make Wild look for him just a little bit harder.

Arista had to know for sure that everything Wild had told her was true. If Nic had already planned an alliance with the man, he could tell her if Wild was in fact trustworthy. At least, trustworthy enough to get what she needed from him.

If Wild met her demands, then Arista would agree to give their deal a chance. She would become Lady A again to protect her friend. And in doing so, she would secure their future as well. With a fair cut of the profits, they would be able afford passage on a supply ship within a few months. Maybe even the one her mysterious highwayman captained.

The thought made her pulse jump, but she steeled herself against it. She had no time to dwell on him. Right now, she had to be sure that Becky remained safe.

"I barely recognized you dressed like that."

Arista swung around, reaching for her knife instinctively. Wild was there, half covered by the shadows. Behind him, a gate swung shut. Damn him. He'd taken her by surprise while she was lost in thought. "I'm ready to make a deal." She stood as he approached, his gait relaxed and confident. They were equal now. Partners.

Wild smiled and took a long inhale off his cheroot. "A wise business decision. One that will benefit you greatly, Ana."

Arista nodded and chose her next words carefully. A man like Wild manipulated and used people. There could be nothing left up to interpretation or chance. "There are a few things I will need from you first."

The corner of his lips turned down a fraction, giving away his displeasure. Enough of a pause for her to remember that Wild was not her friend. He might not get his own hands dirty like Bones did, but Wild and Bones were both used to getting what they wanted—no matter who suffered. Bones had used her. Wild sought to do the same—only now, she would benefit from this arrangement a lot more. She'd make damned sure of that.

"What do you need?" he asked. His shoulders were relaxed again, and he leaned casually against a statue of a cherub holding an urn upside down.

"We need a place to live."

Wild lifted one eyebrow and glanced at the building behind her.

Arista snorted. "Someplace that is *not* a brothel. Nothing fancy, but it has to be safe. And we need food. Enough for Becky and I to live on, though like I said, we require nothing fancy."

Wild puffed in a breath of smoke and exhaled slowly. "Anything else?"

She hesitated. Her next request wasn't as simple as providing food. "I need to be sure that Becky is safe. Always. That no one has the opportunity to hurt her again. If something happens to me, I need assurance that she will be taken care of. If you can't do this, I will not help you."

"She must mean a great deal to you," he said.

She thought she saw something flicker in his eyes, but in the darkness she could not know for sure. "I made her a promise. Do we have an agreement?" she asked briskly.

He dropped the cheroot and ground it under the heel of his

boot. He looked thoughtful, then smiled. "Agreed. So, now that we have your needs taken care of, let's discuss our mutual business agreement." Wild moved closer, and Arista could finally see all of his face.

Today he wore a tailored jacket and matching trousers, and looked every part the aristocrat. His casual demeanor almost made her forget that, underneath the costly clothes, he was lethal. He had the power to ruin anyone, rich or poor. Even the notorious Lady A could be taken down by him. Their arrangement was not without risk.

"Where would you like to start?" she asked.

"I don't suppose you have access to the secrets you traded in?" he asked drolly. "That would make things a lot easier." His tone may have been nonchalant, but Arista noticed the slight tightening of his lips, the way he unconsciously flexed his right hand. He wanted that information desperately. But if he thought she had that information, he'd be sorely disappointed.

"I was only the messenger." It was a half truth. The night he kissed her, Nic *had* told her where Bones hid the secrets, the money. But were they anything beyond ashes now? Maybe she could sneak away and check. It would give her additional leverage should Wild try and renege on their deal. "I'm not interested in becoming one of your lackeys, either. I want no part in your thievery operation."

"Of course not. This is an entirely separate matter. You are Lady A. We only need your reputation to continue doing business. I will simply make sure that those in need of your services have a way of contacting you. And of course, our alliance will be kept between ourselves."

There was a hint of warning in his tone. Arista nodded. "It

would not benefit Lady A's reputation if it were thought she was working with the Thief Taker General, either. So as far as *le bon ton* are concerned, nothing has changed with Lady A's services."

Wild nodded. "Then we are both in agreement that this arrangement stays quiet. Good." He took her hand and pressed his lips to the back of it. Without gloves, the touch was far too intimate for her liking. A voice interrupted them and she withdrew her hand.

"Excuse me, sir, but Lord Whitley is at it again. He refuses to leave again this morning." Light poured out from the open kitchen door, and Arista saw the silhouette of Cecily.

Wild scowled. "I've warned him for the last time. I'll be right there." He stalked toward the door and turned on the threshold. "Tomorrow morning, I'll send a carriage to take you to your new home. Be ready."

He left her there in the garden, the protest falling from her tongue unheard. Tomorrow. That seemed so . . . soon. Arista stood for several more minutes, unable to make her legs move. Exhaustion washed over her and she had to sit for a few minutes. Though she'd had days of rest already, weakness filled her limbs. She would never be able to sneak out later that night if she didn't rest first. And she had to return to her old home, just once, before it became impossible.

Reluctantly, Arista made her way back inside and to her room. She crawled under the quilt and watched the sky grow lighter outside her window. By the time sunlight filtered through the lace curtains, Arista had fallen asleep.

"Miss." Becky's soft voice broke through the haze of sleep.

Arista opened her eyes and blinked.

"Are you feeling better, miss?" Becky held up a lantern and a soft glow illuminated the room. Outside the window, the sky was dark.

Arista sat up and shoved the quilt off her body. "What time is it?" she demanded. Her heartbeat thundered against her ribs. Was it too late? How could she have slept the entire day?

"It's just past midnight, miss."

"I don't have much time." Arista slid out of bed and smoothed down her wrinkled dress. Her dress. She needed something more appropriate to go walking about at night in her old neighborhood. Her knife skills would not be enough. There had to be trousers somewhere; this *was* a brothel, after all.

Without a word to Becky, Arista flung open the door and made her way back down the servants' stairs. She stepped into the kitchen, through a rush of warm air, and cleared her throat. None of the kitchen girls even looked up from their tasks.

"Can someone tell me where the laundry is done?" Arista asked in her very best Lady A accent. When one of the girls looked up, Arista crossed her arms across her chest and glared down at them. She tapped her foot impatiently.

"Across the hall to the right, miss." The girl couldn't be any older than Arista, but fatigue was written all over her sweaty face. It made her look as old as Bones. Her hands were red and chapped from her duties.

"Thank you." Arista dropped the fake accent and left the room.

No one saw her, and she slipped into the laundry room easily. Huge tubs lined one wall, and the sharp scent of lye filled the air, burning her lungs. A rope was strung from one corner to the other, and clothes were pinned along it.

It took no time at all to find a shirt, jacket, and trousers that looked about the right size. All were rough and patched, probably belonging to the stable boy. She'd never been comfortable stealing, much less from someone in her own situation, so she made a silent pledge to put them back as soon as she returned.

The stairwell was dark and empty and Arista hurried up it. She pushed through the door and immediately stopped. In her haste to get back to her room, she'd exited on the wrong floor. These were the working rooms. Before she could duck back inside the stairwell, a door opened just three away from her.

"A pleasure as always, my dear." The man's words were slurred, and he stumbled as he backed out the door. A throaty giggle followed his retreat. The door closed and the man straightened, put his hat on his head, and tapped it into place, though it still sat very crookedly.

Arista didn't dare move. *Go the other way.*

He turned, as if he'd heard her thoughts, and walked right toward her.

"Well, what do we have here? You're a new one—I haven't seen you before." The man's eyes widened and then narrowed as he focused on her. He took several stumbling steps down the hall. Arista backed up, the stolen clothes clutched to her chest. She didn't miss the way he leered at her. Bile rose in her throat. *Run.* The command from her brain would not reach her frozen feet. She smelled the bourbon on his breath before he stopped in front of her. Without the benefit of either of her disguises, the boy or Lady A, Arista felt naked. Powerless. Her mind would not work at all.

"My, you're a pretty one. Where have you been hiding?" He ran a finger down her cheek and Arista pursed her lips tightly together. Still holding the clothes with one hand, she reached down with her other hand and inched the fabric of her dress up.

She needed her knife.

He must have sensed her movements, because a wide grin curled his mouth. "Eager, are you?" He leaned into her, pressing himself along the length of her body with only the rough cloth between them. His hot breath washed over her ear. "I like that." He reached down and covered her hand with his, easing her skirt up more. The weight of his body pressed her harder against the door, and she couldn't move. There was no room to lift her knee or drive her fist into his nose. Nothing Nic had taught her would work now.

One of the man's fingers trailed along her leg. Arista bit down on her lip so hard that she tasted blood. A vise tightened around her wrist and he held her hand firmly at her waist, her entire leg now exposed. She could not beat him with physical strength.

With a soft sigh, Arista forced her body to go limp. He wasn't expecting that, and lost his grip and balance at the same time. Drunks were unpredictable, except when it came to coordination. Arista had the tip of her blade pressed against his temple before he could blink. *Arista*, perhaps, wasn't experienced at dealing with men like him, but Lady A was. Something inside of her shifted. The debilitating fear was gone now.

"Leave now or I'll sink this blade right through your skull," she hissed. Becky would be proud of how cultured Arista sounded.

"What the hell are you doing? Do you know who I am? I practically funded this entire place. *I own you, whore.*" The man reared back, but his glance flicked to the knife and he hesitated.

This situation she could control.

"They tell me that I like to play with knives a little too much," she said softly, running the blade down his cheek until it stopped, right on the throbbing pulse in his neck. "But some men like that." The man swallowed loudly. "Do you still want to play with me, my lord?" Arista pushed the blade against the man's soft middle and he blanched. Men like him liked to pretend they owned the world, but underneath they were cowards. Especially when confronted with their own mortality.

"You're crazy," he spat. Hatred blazed from his bloodshot eyes.

"So I've been told," she answered with a cold smile. "Now get away from me."

The man stumbled back a few feet and stopped. Without the knife at his throat, a bit of bravado returned. He brushed off the front of his jacket and straightened his hat. "I'll see that you're thrown out on the street with nothing, girl," he sneered.

A door somewhere down the hall opened, and the man turned his attention toward it. Arista slipped back into the stairwell and ran up the stairs as fast as she could. Her hands were shaking so badly, it took three tries to open the door at the top.

Precious minutes had been lost because of that man, and her chances of being seen had increased. She had to get out of this place. As the hour grew late, more men would be roaming the halls. She couldn't get the feeling of the man's touch out of her head. If she'd had the time, she might have jumped back into the tub of cold, dirty water to wash it away.

Arista counted seven doors and knocked softly. The door immediately swung open, and Arista stepped inside the darkened room. She met Becky's wide-eyed stare in the flickering candlelight, and then her glance slid to the chair in the corner of the room. Her heart thumped against her ribs dully.

Wild raised an eyebrow. He looked at the bundle of clothes in her arms.

"I hope you have not changed your mind already, my dear?"

CHAPTER 7

"So I'm to be a prisoner after all, then?" Arista asked.

Wild laughed. "Of course not, but I *am* invested in your safety. If you'd like to venture out, I'd be more than willing to provide an escort. At this hour, it is most prudent." Just what she needed. Someone to keep watch over her every move. And report back to Wild, of course.

"I've been on the streets since I was five," Arista said, forcing herself to speak calmly. "I don't need anyone to go with me."

"It would make me feel better, knowing you were protected. You have only just recovered, and I hate to think of you on the streets alone."

"He's right, miss," Becky chimed in. She wrung her hands together and glanced between Wild and Arista. When Wild smiled at her, the girl visibly relaxed.

"I only wanted to get some air," Arista lied. "I can't move in this dress. But you're right, it's not safe. And I'm suddenly feeling tired. If you'd excuse me, I'd like to rest now."

Wild stood, and Arista hugged the stolen clothing tighter.

Though the conversation was nothing but civil, Wild's mouth tightened, and she knew he distrusted her.

"Truly, I am not used to being inside for such a long time. I only wanted to stretch my legs in the night air, as I've always done. It's safer as a boy."

"I understand, my dear. Really, I do. I don't like long confinements, either. After tomorrow, you can come and go as you please. I only ask that you honor my request tonight." He held out his hands for the clothing she had borrowed. Arista shrugged and placed the bundle in his outstretched arms, pretending the stolen clothes were of little importance to her. Of course he didn't trust her yet. That was something she would have to earn.

"Good evening to you, ladies," Wild said. With those last words, he closed the door and left Arista alone with Becky.

"Miss, what were you thinking?" Becky clasped her hands tightly in front of her, and she kept looking at the door as if expecting Wild to return any second.

"There is something I need to do, Becky. Tonight. Now, help me figure out a way to escape." Arista stalked to the window. They were high above the street, and had no way to climb down; it was pointless to try. With no idea where they were going in the morning, she had to get out now, while she still had the chance to find her way back to their old home.

Deep voices could be heard from outside the door. Arista pressed her ear to the wood. A guard. Damn.

"I need to go back to the house. Wild is looking for Nic, but I'm not sure I can trust him yet. I have to let Nic know that we're okay, and tell him how to find us. I'm afraid he may think *we* died in the fire, too." It was only half the truth. She and Becky would have the means to live any way they chose.

"But if Mr. Wild said he was looking . . ." Becky twisted her fingers together and glanced at the door.

"I'm sure that Nic will go back to the house, looking for a hint that we're still alive. I'm just going to leave something so that he knows for sure. I'll be back before anyone misses me, I promise."

She *hoped* to be gone and back before anyone missed her.

"There's a guard outside the door. I need a way to distract him." Arista looked around the room for anything that might be useful. The only thing she had was her knife. That wouldn't work. She wasn't a murderer. The heavy candlestick? Would anyone believe he was simply sleeping if he were sitting prone against the wall? She had to take the risk.

Arista picked up the heavy candlestick and glanced at the door. The man was big, but if she hit him just right . . .

"I have an idea, miss." Becky grabbed the covered tray from the stand by the bed and opened the door. Though Arista couldn't see anyone, she heard the deep tone of a man's voice just outside the room. Becky said something in reply, then the door closed.

It seemed like hours passed. Arista paced the room. What if Becky had been caught? What if Wild were questioning her? This might be the only chance Arista had to find Bones's stash before Wild had her firmly under his thumb. He had saved her, but not due to any kind of chivalry toward her. He had reasons of his own.

She had picked up the candlestick again when she heard voices in the hall. The door swung open.

"Thank you very much," Becky said, backing into the room with the covered silver tray in her hands. "You're a very nice gentleman."

"Anytime, miss," came a reply.

Arista watched as Becky smiled at the man in the hall. She very rarely ever met a man's gaze, and if it happened by accident, she always turned away first. When Becky closed the door, Arista saw the faint stain of a blush on her friend's cheeks.

Another reason why Arista had to figure out a way to get them out of this life; so that Becky could have one. Arista wondered if her friend wanted a family of her own. They'd never talked about it— never talked about any kind of future, really. Without a guarantee that there would even be a future, there had never been any point in talking about it. Now, however?

The thought took Arista by surprise. *Did* Becky want that? Her own family?

"Here, miss, I got these for you." Becky's voice broke through the strange direction of Arista's thoughts. Arista could not focus. Why was she so distracted? Maybe because for the first time in her life, there was a promise of something more. The future, the freedom of her thoughts, made her mind go to strange places. She needed to focus on the here and now.

Her friend lifted the silver lid, and underneath, there was a neat pile of folded clothes. They looked very similar to the ones Arista had stolen earlier. Becky had sneaked them into the room, disguised as food.

"Becky, you are a genius," Arista said with a big smile. She turned around, and Becky immediately began helping her undress. Soon Arista stood in just her shift and began pulling on the rough boys' clothing.

"I'm still not sure how you're planning on getting out, miss," Becky said. "That man that Mr. Wild put outside the door isn't moving."

"Maybe you'd like to distract him for me?" she teased.

Becky's cheeks turned red. "He was just doing his job," she said, and her glance fell to the floor.

Arista wanted to pull her friend into a hug. Despite the scars and bandage over one eye, Becky's goodness still radiated out.

"I only need a few seconds to make it down the hall," Arista said. She stepped out from behind the screen and adjusted the wool cap. The clothing hung a little loose on her frame, but it hid her gender more than her old disguise had. The only thing missing was shoes.

She hoped that somewhere near the kitchen door, an extra pair of boots could be found. Otherwise she'd be running through the alleyways barefoot. It wouldn't be her first time, but in the darkness she'd have to go slowly and walk carefully to avoid broken glass or sharp stones—and there was no time for caution.

Becky chewed her bottom lip. "Are you sure about this? If you get caught . . ." They'd both heard the veiled warning in Wild's tone, but really—what could he do to her? He needed her.

Still, there were ways to ensure Arista's cooperation without threatening her. One look at Becky proved that. And Wild, unfortunately, knew Arista would do anything to protect the girl.

"As soon as I'm gone, I want you to lock the door and wedge the chair under the latch—do you understand?" Arista said. "I'll use our usual knock to let you know it's me when I return. Do not open the door to anyone else. Is that clear?"

Her voice was sharp, but she needed Becky to listen to her—to do *exactly* as she said. "If Wild insists you open the door, blow out all the candles, tuck my dress under the blanket, and whisper that I'm sleeping. That should buy me a little more time. I'll be back before daybreak." Arista started toward the door.

"And if you're not?"

Becky's soft question stopped her. It was always possible, that she might not return—especially wandering the alleys alone in those dark hours before dawn. Even with her superb knife skills, it only took one mistake.

"Don't think about it. I'll return. I promise you." Arista took the girl's clammy hands in hers and squeezed. "Now, just imagine yourself at Haymarket Theatre—like the play I told you about— and put on a good show." Becky's lips trembled as she tried to smile.

If she could bring Becky with her, she would. If they had any- where else to go . . .

"Ready?" Arista asked. The longer she waited, the higher her chances of getting caught. Becky took a deep breath and nodded. She released Arista's hands and stepped to the door. Her hand shook as she reached for the latch, but she didn't pause.

"Hello again." Becky moved out of the room and left the door slightly ajar. "My mistress is sleeping, and I find that I am not at all tired. I hoped that I could find someone to converse with. There aren't many to talk to around here."

Arista heard the way Becky's voice wavered and held her own breath. Would the man notice her nervousness and become suspicious?

"Most aren't here for the conversation," the man said with a knowing chuckle.

"This isn't the kind of place I normally stay in," Becky said. Her voice got a little fainter and Arista decided to take a quick look out the door. Sure enough, Becky had moved a few feet away and the man now had his back to the door. Becky glanced past the man and saw Arista.

"I used to be a lady's maid," Becky continued. "Before . . ." She brushed a hand to her face and Arista watched her gaze slide down to the floor. Anyone would blame the maid. No one would ever dare point a finger at the lord.

Arista took a tentative step into the hallway and paused.

"Damned rich bastards think they can get away with anything." His voice grew hard with contempt. The man shifted toward her and Becky put her hand on his thick arm.

"It was the best thing that happened to me. I got away from him before something worse happened. He had a horrible reputation . . ."

Arista missed the rest of the conversation. She made it down the hall, her bare feet silent on the carpeting, and opened the servants' door before she dared to exhale. A quick glance back showed Becky and the man were still deep in conversation.

Confidence surged through Arista, making her muscles sing. Three flights of stairs and the kitchen door were all that stood between her and escape. Every creak from the uneven steps made her catch her breath, and it seemed to take forever to get to the bottom, but she finally made it without anyone the wiser.

When Arista opened the kitchen door, there was more movement in the house than before. A half dozen kitchen girls were mixing and kneading huge piles of dough on the large center island. These must be apprentices, not yet experienced enough to do anything but turn the dough.

One looked up, and an immediate spark of interest flashed in the young girl's eyes. She looked about twelve or thirteen. Arista thought it peculiar, until she remembered she was dressed as a boy. She ran the last few steps and threw herself out the door. The fading sound of laughter followed her abrupt departure.

So much for leaving unnoticed.

The garden was full of shadows. The glow from the kitchen illuminated only the area right in front of the door. And there, on the side of the step, she saw a pair of boots. The errand boy must have put them there so as not to track mud into the house.

With a quick, silent apology, Arista grabbed them and hurried toward the back of the garden, to where Wild had materialized earlier. Sure enough, a small gate was hidden in the dark. The alley that ran behind the brothel was so black she could barely see her hand in front of her face. Arista slipped the boots onto her feet as quickly as she could.

Once she was free of the alley, she didn't try to be quiet any-more. She simply ran. Her borrowed boots thumped against the ground, breaking the silence of the night with each step. In just three turns, Arista made it back to the familiar labyrinth of alleys that would lead her to Fleet Street—she could navigate them blind-folded if she had to. The shadows were quiet as she raced past. Even the ones who staggered home drunk from the taverns were asleep in their own beds at this hour.

Only the sneaks who picked the pockets of those same drunks were out. The occasional whisper of movement was the only indica-tion they were there. It was one job Bones had never required her to do, though he sent most of the children out to do this dirty work. It was a very dangerous practice. Sometimes the drunk would wake, and fight back. Sometimes an even more desperate sneak would rather stick a knife in a fellow thief than return empty-handed.

An acrid aroma filled the air, even before she made the last turn out of the alley. Wet, charred wood. A dull thumping filled her ears when she looked at where the house had once stood. It no longer reached for the sky. All that remained of her home was a lifeless pile of broken pieces.

Something inside her snapped, and all at once, Arista could see her freedom. Nothing was left of her nightmare, her prison.

Her tormentor had perished in the bowels of the hell he'd created. Laughter bubbled up in her throat. A fitting death for the likes of him. She inhaled deeply, letting the stench of this death fill her lungs.

Once, this place had filled her with a burning fear, but no more.

It was a terrifying and exhilarating thought. For the first time in her life, Arista had a say in her future. Her future might be clouded with uncertainty at the moment, but it was true nonetheless. The only thing missing was Nic.

Blackened wood crunched and snapped beneath her feet as she made her way over the pile of debris. Wild had been right. Not much remained at all. The fire had burned the building almost to the ground. Gritty soot coated everything. It smeared across her skin in black slashes.

The rubble would have been picked over as soon as it was cool enough to touch. Arista could hear the scratching of the creatures who were still salvaging inside the pile of burnt wood.

Her room should be just ahead, on the other side of the chimney. The fire had burned hottest there, where it had started. There wasn't much left, and there was nothing she could recognize, except the barest hint of where the walls used to be. The straw mattress had been there, in the corner, and under it she had hidden things only a child would find valuable. A cornhusk doll Nic had made for her. The sketch on her wall. Gone. Everything was gone.

Her gaze slowly moved to the spot where she had last seen Bones. The Watch must have removed the body, but Arista still couldn't resist the urge to dig the toe of her boot under a pile of boards and lift them up. As illogical as it seemed, she half expected Bones to come charging through the rubble and finish what he'd started. Her bruised ribs throbbed.

Arista kicked at the pile of burned boards. They fell apart into a mess of black dust and lumps of charcoal. What she wanted was buried deeper, where no one knew to look. Even she didn't know the exact location.

Nic said that Bones had hidden it under a floorboard near the stove. If that had been pilfered, she might as well give up, rather than tear apart the entire house. It took several long minutes to make her way to the middle of the house. The chimney, almost entirely intact, rose up like a signpost. With only the stray light from a lone, unbroken streetlamp to illuminate the ruins, Arista had to pick her way slowly toward it.

A dark shape grew distinct from the rest of the blackness as she crept closer. The old potbelly stove still stood, but something else was different. She knew what it was almost immediately. The space in front of the stove had been neatly cleared, and the floorboards were torn up. Arista stuck her hand in the hole, roughly the size of her head, and found nothing. The letters, the money—it was all gone.

She sat down with a bump, not caring about the soot that was rubbing off onto her borrowed clothes. The noose of having to work with Wild tightened around her neck. Images of the fire flashed through her head. Bones had been more furious than Arista had ever seen before. He'd shouted that something had gone missing.

The secrets. The money. It had to have been Nic.

Nic took it all—and then left Arista to deal with the aftermath?

He wouldn't do that to her. But she had the bruises on her body to prove that he had. No, something had gone wrong. Nic would never have left her to face Bones's wrath alone. Not after he'd spent years protecting her from that terrible man.

Arista stood slowly and looked toward the waterfront, where a sliver of light was making its way over the horizon. Nic was out there, waiting until it was safe to contact her. She had to believe that—because the alternative was too horrifying to consider. He had everything, and he was hiding somewhere, waiting until it was safe to look for her.

She had to let him know she was waiting—give him some sign. With the toe of her boot, she scuffed an A into the soot, then turned back toward the maze of alleyways. A thick fog was rolling in from across from the river, and a chill settled over her skin, seeping into the threadbare cloth and making it uncomfortably damp. The sun would be up very soon. Already, a soft yellow pushed its way through the hazy pall. A cold waft of air blew over her, and she shivered. It felt almost as if Bones were still searching for his letters and money from some ghostly plane. She didn't truly believe in such things— the streets had ground common sense into her—but when it came to Bones, no amount of horror was out of the question.

She picked her way back through the rubble as quickly as she could, the hairs on her neck standing up. She allowed herself one quick glance over her shoulder, but there were no ghosts. An eerie stillness filled the dawn. There were no sounds of children; no dogs barking; no sellers hawking their wares. An ominous feeling hung in the air. Arista started to run as soon as she was free from the burned-out row house.

Sprinting now, she wove her way through the narrow passages, making the automatic twists and turns that would lead her to Covent Garden.

Even blocks away, she felt like she was being watched.

CHAPTER 8

*T*he man stood with his arms crossed over his chest, a frown turning the edges of his mouth down. He did not look happy to be there. Arista could see the door to her room clearly from where she was, hunched down near the top of the stairs. She could not slip inside without him taking notice.

Entering through the front door had been easy. Disguised as a boy, she'd moved down the main hallway, unnoticed by two house-maids sweeping by with arms full of linens. After kicking off the boots and tucking them into a small alcove off the front door, she started up the massive stairway, the one with thick carpeting and a gleaming wooden banister. The one only paying guests used.

This side of the house was still. The rich men had gone home to their wives' beds, while the working girls on the second floor were sleeping. The back of the house would be a flurry of activity at this early hour, and she didn't want a confrontation. Not dressed as a boy.

She glanced up again, willing the man to move. Blast it. How could she be in her room before Wild arrived, if she couldn't get back in? Maybe if she went outside and threw a pebble against the window, it would alert Becky, and *she* could distract the man again. It wasn't much of a plan, but it was all Arista had.

Wild's "request" had been a test. She knew that. And if she wasn't there when he came for her . . . No, she *would* be in her room. That was that.

The carpet muffled her steps as she snuck back down to the second floor. Just before she reached the last step, a door far down the hall swung open. A man came out, his shirt tucked haphazardly into his trousers. He said something into the room that Arista didn't hear, but the tone in his voice said more than enough. The door slammed, then a fist pounded on it as the man's voice grew louder. "You thieving whore, let me back in. I'll get my money's worth out of you yet."

The threat in the man's tone made Arista's skin crawl. She reached for her knife out of habit. More doors were opening now, and disheveled heads popped out to watch. The man turned, and his lip curled into a snarl.

"I'll get my money's worth from one of you girls, then." He staggered down the hallway, and several of the girls shrieked and slammed their doors. The man bellowed in drunken rage and yanked on each of the door handles.

Arista backed up and her foot caught the edge of the step. She fell, quickly turning to catch herself on her hands and knees. A large black pair of boots filled her vision.

"Out of the way, boy," a deep voice growled. A hand on her shoulder roughly pushed her aside and Arista sprawled awkwardly across the stairs. The man pounded past and stormed toward the drunk man. It took her a moment to realize that *her* guard had shoved her out of the way. He yelled at the aristocrat to step back, but he only sneered.

Her guard outweighed him by at least four stone. Only the spirits the aristocrat had drunk made him think it would be a fair fight. But that wasn't her problem. An opportunity presented itself, and she took it. Arista sprang up the stairs as fast as she could and ran toward her room. The loud sounds of the fight below filled the air, and her heartbeat sounded equally loud in her ears.

When she got to her door, she rapped out the signal, and gulped in several deep breaths. What if Becky was asleep? Or not in the room? An icy edge of panic began to creep along her skin, and Arista knocked again. She tried the door, but it was locked, exactly as she'd asked Becky to do.

Just as she started to knock again, the door swung open. Becky stood back, blinking sleep from her eyes, and quickly let Arista slip inside.

"Thank goodness, miss. I knew as soon as you left, there would be trouble getting back inside. I waited, kept checking to see if you were back, but the guard finally told me to stay inside. How'd you get past him?"

Arista squeezed her friend's hand. "There was a commotion downstairs. Quickly, help me clean this soot off my skin. I mustn't arouse Wild's suspicion when he comes for us."

Arista stripped, and Becky made short work of the soot with a soapy rag, which was then dropped in the copper tub to conceal the evidence. Arista raised her arms and the soft fabric of her nightgown fell around her.

Becky tucked everything inside the silver domed tray as Arista crawled into the bed. "I'll take them back right now, miss." She lifted the tray and opened the door. "He's still gone—should I go now?"

"Yes," Arista whispered. The last thing she wanted was for Wild to find evidence that she'd blatantly disobeyed him. The door clicked shut, and Arista finally let her breath out. The throbbing that had started as she stood in the ashes of her burned-out home grew more painful. She pressed her fingers against her temples.

Nic would find them. He was probably waiting until Arista was alone. Even if he knew that she was at Wild's brothel, it didn't mean he could get to her. Maybe he had already tried. Yes, once they were away from this place, Nic would have the opportunity to contact her. That had to be what he was waiting for. She just needed to be patient a bit longer.

By the time Becky returned, Arista had regained her composure completely.

"Mr. Wild is coming, miss," Becky said breathlessly. "He wasn't too happy that David left his post to tend to the commotion below stairs, but I assured him that you'd been sleeping."

"David?" Arista quirked her eyebrow, but then smiled as color covered Becky's cheeks. It was nice to see something other than pain or fear on her friend's face. But her expression quickly turned more serious.

"Miss . . . what you've agreed to, with Wild I mean, it's . . . not because of me, is it?" Becky clasped her hands together tightly. Her glance slid to the door and back to Arista. "I know you can take care of yourself, and I don't want you to feel . . ."

Arista swallowed against the lump in her throat. "Becky, I'm doing this for us. For both of us. And I don't feel obligated," Arista lied. "I need you more than you need me. Who will keep me from making foolish choices?"

Becky snorted, then covered her mouth. "Sorry miss, it's just . . ." The red spots on her cheeks grew brighter.

"I know—I 'never listen,' Becky."

"No, miss, you don't. The only person who could keep you in line was Nic."

An uncomfortable silence stretched between them.

"Do you think he's okay, miss?" Becky asked softly.

"I really don't know. But I have to believe that he is." Any more talking was preempted by a quick knock at the door. It swung inward before either of them answered. Wild stepped into the room, his gaze darting swiftly between them before settling on Arista.

"Be ready to go in one hour. Everything has been arranged, as you requested." He gave her a quick half bow, then turned on his heel and left the room.

"Miss? Are we really leaving?" Becky asked.

Wild had agreed to her terms, which meant that Arista had entered into a new partnership. The wisdom of her decision would remain to be seen. "Yes, Becky, I guess we really are." Reluctantly, she pushed the covers aside and sat up. "Everything will be fine, just like I promised."

Becky didn't believe her. Arista saw it in her face, but her friend said nothing. She only helped Arista get dressed once more in the blue frock. Wild told them nothing about where they were going, but if this person was a business associate of Wild's, anything was possible.

An hour later, the carriage pulled up to the front of a neat townhouse in Talbot Court. Honest middle-class merchants lived in this part of London. The footman climbed down and opened the door, then offered his arm to Arista. Bright mid-morning sun shone down, a rarity in fog-shrouded London.

This was a home, and behind the door, there were people inside. She had not expected this.

Families lived here; real families.

"Are you Ana?" A fresh-faced girl in a beautiful pink morning dress smiled down at them from a small balcony above the front door. Her curly hair had been pinned back, but some had fallen free, and it bobbed around her face as she bounced on her toes. She appeared to be around the same age as Arista.

Arista's feet hit the ground, and she froze. This wasn't going to work.

"Oh, you *are*, I just knew it! I could hardly wait for you to arrive." The openness of the girl's expression took Arista by surprise. Scorn, contempt, fear—those were familiar emotions in faces around her. Friendliness? Rarely. But the girl was not pretending. Her smile was artless, not forced, and her body was relaxed as she leaned out over the wrought-iron rail. As she spoke her hands moved wildly in the air. Everything about the girl spoke of sincerity.

"Do come inside! I asked Mama to put you in the room next to mine, but Papa insisted you should be in the guest room downstairs. We seldom get visitors, and when we do, they're usually wrinkle-faced old men who talk business all day. I adore your short hair. Mine is an unruly mess all the time. Perhaps we can convince Mama to let me do the same with mine? We are going to be such good friends, I just know it!" Her merry laughter rang out and she disappeared back into the house.

A dull, smothering unease settled around Arista, like a coat that fit too tightly. Friends? No, this would definitely not work at all. "Becky, I think we should . . ." Her maid was already deep in conversation with a white-haired man who stood in the open doorway. They were chatting like old friends, and Becky actually giggled.

He took the valise from Becky, and then stepped back to allow her inside. "Miss?" Becky asked, looking back toward Arista. The butler and carriage driver also watched her. Her skin grew hot under all the scrutiny. The dull thump of her heartbeat sounded in her ears. Every nerve in her body urged her to flee. Becky must have sensed her distress, because she quietly moved to Arista's side.

"It'll be okay, miss. I can tell already that they are good people." Arista closed her eyes and sucked in a long breath. That was exactly what she was afraid of. Thieves, blackmailers, and whores were familiar territory. Arista knew what was expected of her, and what to expect in return. Here, she knew nothing—definitely not how to behave correctly.

Already, she had increased the awkwardness by just standing there in the small courtyard.

"Ana!" The girl waved from beside the butler. "Come!" At Becky's urging, Arista took a step forward.

"Don't let old Wilson here intimidate you," the girl said with a bright grin. She reached up and tweaked the man's cheek. Arista could see the sparkle of affection in his eyes. Even the servants weren't afraid to show how they felt.

Arista was the intruder here, surrounded by her lies.

"I'm Sophia, and it is *so* very nice to meet you. You have the most beautiful eyes, but I bet you hear that all the time. And your dress! I—"

"Sophia," a stern but equally cheerful voice said behind her.

"Mama! Come and meet Ana."

"You will scare our guest away, child."

Had there been a slight emphasis on *guest*? Did the woman know why she was really there? When her gaze met the woman's, Arista wasn't sure.

Her eyes were not cold or filled with disdain, but they were not as welcoming as her daughter's had been. "Ana, my husband said to expect you. I am so very sorry to hear of your loss. So young to already be a widow."

Becky's hands squeezed Arista's arm. In the carriage, Arista had explained to Becky what Wild had told her. They were to stay with a merchant who owed him a favor; the story was that she was a young widow, in London to settle her late husband's affairs.

"Thank you, ma'am," Arista said, careful to keep her voice low and neutral. "Truth be told, I did not know Sir Reginald very well, and had only met him on one occasion before we wed. His death was most sudden and unfortunate."

The grip on her arm turned viselike and Arista squeezed back, a gentle but firm reminder that Becky should remain silent. Thankfully, aside from a low murmur in her throat, Becky did not speak. With their lives so full of deceit, Becky knew well how to play along.

"Come inside, both of you—you must be weary from traveling such a long way," the woman said. "I am Marguerite Sinclair."

"Thank you, Mrs. Sinclair," Arista said, following the woman as she turned and made her way down the foyer.

Paintings hung on gleaming wood-lined walls. A modest staircase rose to the left, and there were three doors to the right, all closed but one. Marguerite stopped in front of the second door, which was open. "Wilson will show your maid to your rooms. My husband, Robert, would like a word with you before you rest, please. Thank you, Ana."

Each time someone said the name Ana, it wedged the lie a little deeper under her skin, like a thorn. Arista wiped her sweaty palms on her skirt. Her throat went dry and she tried uselessly to swallow.

The man inside that room knew she was not who she claimed to be. No more pretending. She glanced at Becky, but her maid could not help.

Sophia led Becky away, and Marguerite waved her hand to indicate Arista should enter. "Thank you," Arista said faintly. She stepped into the room—a study, judging by the wall of books and dark wood paneling. In the middle of the room sat a huge desk, and behind the desk a man watched her with a steady gaze.

The door clicked shut behind her, and Arista fought the urge to run and fling it open. Instead, she clasped her hands together and faced the man. Men, she could deal with.

"Have a seat," he said. His voice had a low but not unpleasant timbre. She studied him as she sat, looking for the typical signs of anger. He simply observed her with a guarded curiosity.

"You have met my wife and daughter." It wasn't a question, but Arista nodded. "If not for the *favor* owed to Mr. Wild, you would not be sitting across from me in my house." His tone held no animosity, only simple truth. And perhaps a small bit of warning.

"And if not for circumstances outside my control, I would not be here either, sir. This was not my idea. I have . . ." She hesitated, but only for a second. She admired his honesty and wanted to return it. "I have nowhere else to go, and given the choices, this arrangement was the most practical. In truth, I expected much worse. And I did not know your family existed at all, until your daughter called out from the balcony."

"Ah yes, Sophia. She is impetuous and spoiled, and unaware of our agreement. As is my wife. My son is readying one of our ships so we won't see much of him. I trust you will conduct yourself properly inside these walls. I also trust that nothing will go missing while you reside here."

Anger surged to the surface. "I am not a thief," she replied, a little too hastily.

He lifted an eyebrow, and heat splashed over her cheeks. She looked away, unable to deny the accusation in his eyes. How could he know that she had stolen all her life, but only to appease a cruel man? How it had been a matter of survival? She wasn't like the others. But in his eyes, she was the same.

"I won't take a thing that isn't necessary for my stay here," she said, finally meeting his stare. After a moment of contemplation, he nodded.

"I was told you would have odd hours and a need for privacy, so despite my daughter's pleading, I have decided to give you the rooms at the rear of the house. There is a door that leads to a small, private garden, as well. My wife has seen to the rooms, and I assure you they are presentable."

Arista blinked. He took her at her word, just like that? No questions, no demands? No threats? Again she nodded. "Thank you." He seemed surprised to hear her say that.

"I'm not without manners, sir," she said, slipping into her Lady A voice.

The man sat back and steepled his fingers under his chin. Heat crept into her cheeks when he said nothing—just watched her. Out of habit, she fingered the handle of the knife strapped to her thigh. Not because she feared for her own safety, but because she needed something familiar. Something to ground her.

"You're not what I expected," he finally said. "How old are you? Fifteen? Sixteen, maybe? So young to have such a debt on your shoulders. To owe someone like the Thief Taker General, who walks on both sides of the law."

If he only knew how long her list of transgressions was. She refused to answer, but something in her face must have given it away. It unnerved her to have her thoughts read as easily as she read other people's.

"How did you come to know Wild? I assumed since he used blackmail to place you in my home, you were one of his cohorts. But you don't seem the type. . . ."

"Neither do you," she shot back.

A flash of admiration crossed his face before he carefully schooled his emotions. "I think we can agree that often, decisions are made in less than favorable conditions, with future consequences unimaginable."

Arista swallowed loudly. Perhaps they had more in common than she had first thought. "We won't overstay our welcome, sir." She almost blurted out that she would be gone as soon as she had enough money to leave London, but she stopped herself. He didn't need to know how truly destitute she was. "When my business is concluded, we will leave promptly."

He studied her for a few more seconds, then stood and walked to the door. Wilson appeared as soon as it opened.

"Please show our guest to her rooms," the man said.

"Very good, sir." Wilson inclined his head toward her. "This way, miss. Your maid is waiting."

As she moved toward the door, Mr. Sinclair stepped aside to let her pass. She glanced up and what she saw in his eyes almost stopped her cold. Understanding. Compassion. No one had ever shown either to her. She stumbled and he reached out to steady her.

He released her almost immediately and took a step back. "Thank you," she said again.

This dynamic confused her. This man should hate her. He would be right to demand that she leave his home and never return, despite Wild's threat. This family was real. It didn't need someone like her, a liar and a fake, defiling their honest lives.

Yet they had welcomed her without question. Even Mr. Sinclair, who knew she was connected with Wild, was still kind. She followed Wilson, and glanced over her shoulder to see that the door to the office was now closed.

Wilson led her to the right, down a short hallway that led to another hall, and finally to a door illuminated by soft candlelight. The aroma of fresh bread permeated the entire space, and Arista inhaled hungrily. Though she had eaten well at Wild's, the edge of hunger never truly left her. Years of starving made sure of that.

"Here you are, miss. The kitchen is there, and Sara, Miss Sophia's maid, has a room off the kitchen if you need anything." When Arista made no move to enter, Wilson opened the door for her.

"Dinner is at six, miss. If there is anything you need, please ring for one of the staff." With a formal bow, Wilson stepped back, turned around, and disappeared down the hall.

Suddenly, in spite of her good, homey surroundings, the house seemed stifling.

Wild wanted her to live among a family? He knew where she came from, yet he'd thrust her in with people who thought her a lady. Why? He could have put them in any room in any seedy boarding house and it would have been better than where they had been.

Was this part of his game? To show her what she had missed all her life? If so, it was a cruel move.

Before, survival had taken up almost every second. There was no time to dwell on the possibility of anything different. Here, in this quiet neighborhood, with genuine people just steps away, people who welcomed a stranger into their home, she saw what she had missed.

She had time to think about it.

Time to wish, in that secret part of her mind, that she really belonged there.

Arista entered the room blindly.

"Oh, miss, isn't this wonderful?" Becky said from behind her. Her bright smile said it all, and Arista forced the unease aside. Already Becky looked better, more relaxed and happy. How could Arista relocate them to someplace else, a place that could be much worse?

Everything about the room spoke of home. The yearning was back, so swift that it took her breath away. The pale floral tapestry reminded Arista of a garden. A colorful rug covered most of the gleaming wood floors. The porcelain pitcher and bowl on a small stand were not chipped at all, and the towel hanging next to them was a beautiful crisp white. Curtains were pulled back from two windows, through which she could see the gardens. Sunlight streamed inside, casting the room in a golden, almost dreamlike glow.

What would it have been like, to grow up in a room like this? With security and comfort? Love?

And the bed. So far removed from the straw tick that made up her own mattress. Arista had never seen anything like it. White wood with tall posts at each corner, it took up almost half the room. There was even a small stepladder so you could climb in.

Becky smoothed her hand over the thick quilt. "This will be a good place for us, miss. I can feel it already."

The longing in Becky's eyes dug under Arista's skin like a burr. She had never seen hope on her friend's face before. Becky had accepted her duties under Bones without one complaint, but there had never been this light in her eyes.

Resolve straightened her spine. That was why she was doing all this. To give Becky the life she deserved. To get her away from the hopelessness and fear. Arista wasn't sure if happiness was something she could ever find, but making sure that the light in Becky's eyes never dimmed again was within her control.

"I'm going to get some air. I won't be long." Arista stepped outside and shut the door behind her. The household noises faded, and were replaced by the distant sound of children's laughter. It sliced through her like a knife. She stumbled and dug her nails into her palms.

The pain helped to dull the ache, but it didn't go away completely.

Her shoes crunched in the loose stone walkway. *One. Two. Three. Four.* She counted the steps under her breath so she would remember them in the dark. Exactly twelve steps to the fence. Tall shrubs lined the intricate wrought iron, creating an intimate garden space. Brightly colored flowers bloomed despite the lateness of the season, and their delicate aroma hung in the air. Two benches were placed facing each other in the center—to encourage conversation, she thought.

She could imagine the family out here, with the soft glow of candlelight illuminating animated discussions. What did they talk about? Parties? Politics? She'd known shouting and fear all her life. Try as she might, she could not imagine these people arguing with hate in their voices. She could not envision them fighting over a scrap of food or a straw bed.

Arista glanced up at the townhouse, which loomed over the garden.

It's only a house. They're strangers. They don't matter.

She repeated it over and over until some of the distance returned. *You are nobody. You are nothing.*

The voice in her head dripped with ugly undertones. It was eerily similar to Bones's, reciting a mantra she'd heard all her life. One which she had desperately fought against, but which time had proven true.

"I am nobody," she whispered, turning her back on the house.

A throat cleared from somewhere behind her. "Am I interrupting you?"

Arista froze. Every muscle in her body tightened—first from fright and then from something else. She closed her eyes, willing away her body's second reaction. It did no good. Heat coursed through her veins, reigniting a familiar fire.

She heard him take a step closer. Gravel crunched under his feet. She wrapped her arms around herself, a useless barrier against the surge of emotion. She could run out the gate, away from this place and him, but her legs barely held her upright.

"Father said we had a guest. I'm Graeden, but everyone calls me Grae. And you are?"

Grae is here. The thundering beat of her heart drowned out all outside noise. Arista swallowed against the lump of dread and excitement lodged in her throat. He was right there behind her.

"And you are?" he prompted again, so close she could almost feel his breath on her neck.

With no other choice, Arista turned, and looked up into the eyes of her highwayman.

CHAPTER 9

"You." The word came out in a long exhale and Arista could not help but look at his lips and remember.

She hugged herself tighter. What cruel fate had brought her to this house, of all the houses in London?

Emotions played across his face. Surprise. Relief. Rage. His eyes narrowed and he grabbed her upper arm. "What the hell are you doing in my father's house?"

Arista stepped back, shocked by his reaction. Before, he had been all soft words and warm eyes. There was nothing of that in his face now. The emotions that she saw there were all too familiar. The urge to flee made her muscles spasm painfully.

They're all alike.

She should have known he had no real concern for her.

"Let go of me." She tugged at her arm, but he would not release her. She reached for her knife, but Grae spun her around so fast that she lost her balance. Before she could exhale, he had her back pressed up against his chest and his free arm around her waist, holding her immobile against him.

"What are you doing here?" he growled in her ear.

"Let go of me! I'm a guest. The daughter of a business partner." She gasped out the lie. His hold tightened and she clawed at his arm, kicking back uselessly in a tangle of skirts. He released her suddenly, and fear seized her body. Next his fists would rain down on her. Instinctively she cringed, pulling her arms to her chest. His expression faltered, but the anger never left his eyes.

"I know who you really are, *Lady A*." He practically spat the name at her.

The fight left her body, and she glanced around to see if anyone had heard his accusation. They were still alone in the garden, which was both good and bad. Had he known all along? Her stomach rolled and her entire body shook. Her own anger swiftly replaced the fear. He'd used her.

"You knew? When we met, you knew who I was?" she said accusingly. Unwanted tears burned the back of her eyes. What did it matter? Everyone wanted something from her. Except she'd wanted him to be different. She'd believed the lies he'd whispered in her ear.

Grae shook his head, and Arista thought she saw a flash of hurt in his eyes.

"I didn't know who you were when I met you. I just knew I had to see you again. I asked a few discreet questions. They kept leading me back to the same thing: a woman who traded secrets for money. A cunning blackmailer who wore a mask of raven feathers." His gaze darted over her face as if he were trying to reconcile the woman in the mask with the girl who stood before him.

Arista tried to still the shaking in her body. No one knew her identity outside the mask, aside from Nic and Becky. He could out her to everyone, and her value to Wild would be gone. Any chance at safety for Becky would be lost with it. Once again, someone else held the power of her future in his hands.

She straightened her shoulders and forced her face into a mask of indifference. He had no proof against her. "You're mistaken."

He laughed; a dark, hollow sound. "I've never been more sure of anything in my life." His stare burned into hers and she couldn't look away. He lifted his hand and traced a finger along her jaw. His voice was deceptively calm now. "I know it's you. Your eyes. I won't forget them until I take my last breath."

The urge to lean into his touch gripped her. He had haunted *her* dreams, as well. She could keep denying who she was, but they both knew the truth. "So now what?" she asked, raising her quivering chin at him.

"Now that we have established your identity, I want the bloody truth. What the hell are you doing in my father's house? Are you blackmailing him? My family?" The hand on her face slipped lower and he gripped her bare shoulder. His touch burned her skin.

"I . . ." What was she supposed to say? No answer would satisfy him. She started to shake her head.

"Graeden?" Mrs. Sinclair's voice floated over the garden. "Is that you?" Grae tensed behind her; then his arm slowly fell away. Arista took a quick step away from him.

"I'm here, Mother."

"Your father said you were home." Marguerite came to the gate that separated the kitchen garden from Arista's private one.

Arista pressed her hand against her stomach and turned away, sucking in a quick breath. She kept her gaze on the ground, not wanting to see the hatred in Grae's eyes. Not that she blamed him one bit. She was an imposter. A fake.

"There you are. . . . Oh, I see you've met our guest, Ana."

"Yes, we've met." His tone dripped anger. "Actually, Mother, I think you should know . . ."

Arista gasped. She met his stare and saw his determination. He would tell the family. That could not happen. Not only would it put her in danger, but then they would know Grae's father had done something very unscrupulous. Secrets like that destroyed families. She would not allow that to happen.

"It's not what you think," she whispered quickly.

Marguerite moved closer to them now. Arista looked up at Grae, silently begging him for a chance to explain. Grae's penetrating gaze stripped Arista of all her defenses. She hoped that he could see that there was no deception in her eyes.

"Should know what?" Marguerite asked, looking between Arista and Grae.

Please. She sent one last silent request to the man who held her future in his hands.

After several tense seconds, his jaw relaxed.

"That I'll be joining you for dinner tonight." He seemed to tear his stare from Arista's face with difficulty.

"Oh, how wonderful. I'll let Jane know. Will you be staying overnight, too?"

Arista heard the joy in his mother's voice, but could not look away from Grae. Behind the anger, something else was burning, far more dangerous than any threat he could make. She swallowed against a dry throat.

"Yes, Mother. I think I will."

"Excellent. I'll have Wilson open up your room." She started to turn away, but seemed to change her mind. She said nothing, but Arista saw the question in her eyes—whether or not it was wise to leave them alone in the garden together.

No, Arista screamed in her head.

"Tell Father I'll be there in just a minute," Grae said. "I've a new shipping route to discuss with him."

Mrs. Sinclair smiled. The simple gesture was so full of love that it took Arista's breath away. In that moment she knew that Grae would do anything to protect his family. The only defense of this charade that would be acceptable to him was the truth. But if she told him why she was really there, he would know that his father had made some kind of deal with Wild already.

Never in her life had she wanted to keep a secret that was not her own this badly.

Arista sat down hard on the nearest bench. She glanced up in time to see the look of warning Marguerite directed at her son as she left the garden. She might not know the truth about why Arista was there, but something made her wary nonetheless.

Grae sat on the bench opposite her. This would not be a pleasant exchange. He leaned back and crossed his legs at the ankles. His shoulders were squared and rigid, a sign that his irritation had not yet dispersed. Everything about his body spoke of anger, and yet Arista wasn't afraid for her safety. Before, blind fear had taken over, but she knew now that Grae would not harm her physically. She knew that as surely as she knew he would accept nothing less than the truth. Which she could never give him.

"Talk, *Lady A*."

Arista looked around before narrowing her eyes at him. "Stop calling me that."

"Ana, then? Is that really your name?" His eyes narrowed. When she could not look at him, he sighed. "Of course not." He unfolded his arms and leaned closer. "I've gone to every damned party and ball since Lady Carstair's, you know. Looking for you."

Her pulse quickened, despite the precarious position she was in. There was a tone of vulnerability under the steely rage in his voice. It made her stomach twist in unexpected ways. It made her remember their brief time together. She, too, had wished they might meet again under the safety of a disguise. Heat surged to her cheeks. She had to be glowing like a lantern. Did he remember the kiss as well as she did?

His voice lowered, took on a dangerous undertone. "It was an acquaintance of mine, Lord Kalman, who finally informed me that the lady I sought was a *notorious* blackmailer."

Lord Kalman. Arista wracked her brain but could not put the name to a face. There were so many faces she wished to forget. She closed her eyes to ward off the accusation in his stare.

"Were you marketing your skills for new clients that night, *Ana*?" he asked roughly. "Did you think I might be of some use to you?"

Her gaze dropped. She had been excited about the fact that he'd sailed to India. She'd only wished to know everything he'd seen and done. It had nothing to do with Lady A. He mistook her silence for guilt. "Do you provide such a hands-on service to all who employ you?" Hurt radiated from his eyes, and she knew that some of the anger wasn't because she was there in his home; it was because he thought his feelings were one-sided. His entire body was tense. "Did you lose interest once you figured out that I didn't need what you were offering?"

His cruel words dug under her skin. Arista shook her head. She wanted to tell him that he'd made her feel things she'd never felt in her life. That she had planned to seek him out again, but the fire changed everything. No one had ever affected her as he had. She knew from the first time they'd touched that he could be trusted—a feeling so rare that Arista was sure she'd been mistaken. Their second meeting proved she had not been wrong.

She could tell him that despite the pretense on both of those nights, what she'd said—how she'd acted—it had been real.

His accusation—that she'd faked everything between them, simply to gain a new client—hurt more than anything he could physically do to her.

"You have no idea who I am. You know nothing about me or my past, or what I've had to do just to stay alive." Arista covered her mouth and stood. She hadn't meant to say that much. The tears in her eyes were treacherously close to spilling over. "Just leave me alone." She whirled around, running blindly for the door.

"Ana! Wait—" Grae's words followed her through the door.

She stood with her back against the hard wood, taking deep, shuddering breaths. Why did she have the urge to tell him everything? To make him understand that none of this was her doing? She hated the look in his eyes when he'd called her by her name— Lady A—like it was an accusation. That look was familiar, and it made her feel ashamed of who she had to be. How many people had looked at her with the same disgust on their faces, every day of her life? How nice had it been that Grae only knew her as a girl at a party, and not a notorious extortionist?

A quick knock at her inner door sent her pulse racing. Had Grae come back? Would he demand the truth from her? The knock came again. She could not ignore it. He knew she was in her room. Steeling herself, she walked to the door and opened it.

It was not Grae. A strange disappointment settled inside her.

"This just came for you, miss," Wilson said, handing her a card. "The messenger said to bring it to you straightaway."

The address was written on the outside, along with her made-up name: *Ana*. The writing looked unfamiliar, but it could only be from one person—the only other person who knew she was here.

"A trunk was also delivered. It's in the front hall. Should I bring it to you?"

"A trunk for me?"

"Yes, miss."

It couldn't be hers—she had nothing now, after the fire. Not that she'd had much before that. Certainly not enough to fill a trunk. Wilson stood there waiting. She could argue, but she had a feeling it would do no good.

"Yes, please—bring it in."

Arista quickly closed the door and swung around to press her back against it. She clutched the card tightly in her fist. She had not expected Wild to call so soon. She slipped her finger under the seal and opened the card.

An invitation. Tonight?

Another soft knock came from the door and when she opened it, Wilson stood there with a rather large trunk behind him. "Your things, miss."

Things? She owned nothing. "Are you sure that's for me?"

"It came with the card, miss. And this tag has your name on it." Wilson looked at her as if she'd lost her mind.

"Of course." It had to be from Wild, but what on earth was in it?

Wilson pulled it inside the room and set it down. "Your maid is with Sara in the kitchen, if you need her." He waited expectantly.

"No, that's fine. Thank you." She could not keep from staring at the trunk. It was about the size of a crate of vegetables at the market.

As soon as the door clicked shut behind Wilson, Arista pulled the straps free. She lifted the lid and gasped. Inside the chest were clothes. Clothes that were most definitely not hers—she had never owned that many nice things in her life.

She pulled the first dress free and shook it out. The fabric was simple cotton, a rich brown color that looked almost like chocolate. It had a modest neckline lined with delicate lace. Arista held it up to herself. Of course the length was perfect.

She carefully laid it on the bed and dove back in, pulling out several more dresses and undergarments. They were all dark colors, appropriate for a girl in mourning. Wild had thought of everything. At the bottom were shoes and stockings and a pile of dark clothes tied together with string. A note had been pinned to them.

For the esteemed Lady A.

Her fingers shook as she lifted the bundle; it was a reminder that there was a price to the luxuries bestowed upon her.

She set the package on the bed and untied the string, then folded back the paper, revealing more clothing. But this was different. There was a blouse, stark white with a low neckline, lined with ruffles. Next she found a brightly colored skirt, seemingly made from hundreds of different pieces of cloth, sewn together in patchwork fashion. A black corset lay under the skirt. A plain black mask sat on a pair of tall black boots at the very bottom of the pile.

This was all for Lady A? She'd expected a black dress. A raven-feather mask. Instead she'd gotten . . . the mismatched clothes of a beggar? Arista took the shirt and skirt and walked to the oval mirror in the corner, holding them up.

As soon as she saw her reflection, she knew. A cold dread seeped through her and sank down into her bones. She could almost hear Nic's teasing whisper in her ear. Wild had not meant for her to go as a beggar at all. Somehow he'd known.

Arista stared wild-eyed at the gypsy looking back at her.

CHAPTER 10

An unfamiliar thrill washed over Arista as she stood at the edge of the ballroom and watched the costumed dancers fly by. She was there as Lady A, but no one would recognize her this time. Behind the plain black mask, she was simply a guest. They were expecting a black dress and a raven-feather mask. Lady A's signature costume.

But dressed as a gypsy tonight, no once glanced at her with disdain. No one whispered as she walked by. And without the threat of Bones over her head, she could not stop the smile that curled her lips. Freedom. This must be what it tasted like.

Dancers whirled around her as she stood watching. Laughter floated through the air, and more than one touch grazed her arm, both male and female. They were subtle invitations. Unspoken offers. How many times had she wished for this very thing?

Lady A's identity was still anonymous behind the raven feathers, of course—no one knew the girl in the mask—but it was different this time. Not only did they not know the girl under the disguise, but they did not even know she was Lady A.

Spiked punch gave the confident guests reason to talk more. To boast and flirt and disclose secrets meant to be kept silent. Mouths shut tight when the black-cloaked Lady A approached, but a gypsy girl attracted no notice.

It gave Arista the chance to eavesdrop, and make note of bits of gossip that might come in handy at some other time. It also allowed her to move about the room freely, searching for the person she was to meet tonight. Wild had sent another note later that day. She must look for a red kerchief in the left breast pocket of a man dressed all in black.

Wild had supplied no name. Perhaps that was how he intended to conduct business, which was fine by her. She didn't need a name. Usually she could pick out the guilty party simply by observing the telltale signs of stress. Fidgeting with a neck cloth. Trembling hands. Furtive glances around the room, followed by mopping the brow. All signs that the person was most uncomfortable in their current surroundings.

Given the anonymous nature of a masked ball, discomfort should be the last emotion in a guest. In fact, most times it was the opposite. Complete abandon and indiscretion led to gaiety and false comfort.

Each stride she took exposed a long length of leg, which did not go unnoticed. There were looks of interest in several gazes she met. They reminded her of Grae, and in a moment of self-indulgence, Arista allowed herself to think of him. To wish that he was here with her like before—just two guests, with nothing but time to explore the unfamiliar longing between them.

It was not an uncomfortable thought at all. On the contrary, she'd liked the quickening of her pulse when he had stepped too close. At

Lady Carstair's party, his kiss had rendered her senseless. It was something she wished to experience again—there was no doubt.

With a secret smile on her lips, she made her way around the room, leisurely taking in each person that she passed. Though in disguise, Arista knew there were several of Lady A's clients in the room tonight. What would they do if they knew she stood so close, brushing against their arms as she walked by?

It was a heady feeling, this power of complete anonymity.

It took her two turns around the perimeter of the room, and two refusals for a dance, before Arista spotted the person she was to meet with. A flash of red caught her eye. A second glance proved the man was dressed entirely in black from head to toe, except for the bright handkerchief in his pocket.

He stood to her right, and in the dim light she could not get a clear look at his face. A jewel-encrusted cane rested on the floor by his side: a grotesque overstatement of wealth, for anyone to see. She curled her lip and moved closer. Tonight there was no threat of physical retribution over her head. Bones was gone. She did this for herself and Becky alone. She walked taller, knowing that *she* would reap the benefits of this encounter.

She had relied on Nic to protect her before, but tonight she didn't need a bodyguard. She would control the meeting from this point forward.

Arista moved toward him, the swirling colors of her skirt dancing above her knee. The hem on the right side of her skirt had been fashioned in such a way that when she walked, most of her thigh was exposed. She had strapped her knife to the covered thigh, the opposite side that she was used to.

The practical white blouse had become much less demure when

Becky fastened the black corset around it. The top of her chest was pushed out, exposed by the low neckline. Knee-high black boots completed her outfit. Becky had tied the plain black mask in place and wound Arista's brightly colored silk scarf around her head, letting the loose ends trail down her back.

She stepped in front of the man and met his gaze brazenly.

He wore no mask and once he might have even been handsome, but his vices were written clearly in the lines on his face. He looked haggard and desperate. A slight, constant sniffle made her wonder if he had an opiate problem as well. His gaze roamed over her, and interest sparked in his eyes.

"Are you looking for someone special, my lord?" Arista kept her voice low and friendly. She didn't want to give herself away just yet. Meeting out in the open like this afforded a small measure of safety, since she had no idea who this man was and what he was capable of.

"Aren't we all?" His gaze slipped over her shoulder, then it came back to rest below her chin. "Maybe you could be that one tonight?" A sly grin curled his lips up.

"I am here to arrange an exchange of information only, my lord." She lifted one eyebrow above her scarf and watched the realization dawn in his eyes.

"You?"

Her smile grew bigger and she gave him a mock curtsy. "The one and only." Arista laid her hand on his chest and reveled at the way his heart pounded furiously under her fingers. If she were not mistaken, she could detect a trembling in his body as well. A sheen of sweat covered his forehead.

"How does this work?" His gaze darted around them. People

crowded the room, but none paid any mind to them. They were just another couple, standing intimately in a shadowy corner.

"You have something for me?" she asked.

The procedure before had always been to give the client the desired information first, and take their payment—the first install-ment of money and one of their own secrets—because Bones did not trust anyone. Wild had told her in the note that she would be collecting only a payment tonight.

If the man could pay what Wild demanded, then she would later deliver what he wanted in return.

Perspiration dotted his forehead, and he patted it away with a square of white cloth. He stroked the end of his cane with his thumb and shifted his weight onto his good leg. Then he squared his shoul-ders, giving the appearance of height, and let his eyes roam back to her face.

"How do I know you'll honor your part of this exchange?"

Arista smiled slowly. "You really don't, my lord. But I guess it depends on if the information you seek is worth a small bit of trust."

He snorted. "You're a glorified extortionist. Why would I trust you?"

"Then I guess we're done here. Good evening, sir." Arista turned away and counted to three under her breath. There was no way this man would let her walk away. Not after he'd gone to the trouble of setting up a meeting with her.

"Wait."

When she turned, she kept her face a mask of cool indifference. "Yes?"

"Take it." He thrust a pouch at her, and she took it from him just as quickly. The small reticule at her wrist was the perfect size, and she slipped it inside. "And if you think to double-cross me, I will make you pay," he threatened.

How many times had she heard the exact same thing? "That's the chance you take for your own greed, my lord. Provided that what you've given me is worth the information you seek, I will be in touch soon."

"You had better." With that, he turned and stormed away.

"Thank you, my lord. It was a pleasure," Arista called out at his retreating back. A few curious heads swiveled her way and she smiled. Tonight had been a success, and if Wild held his end of the bargain, she would have a nice-sized reward.

The first time she'd be compensated for the risk she took. The idea made her insides feel fizzy, like the punch at the Carstairs' party.

One bold gentleman moved in front of her.

"Would you care to dance?"

He was tall and had broad shoulders, and smelled of sweet cigars. The exhilaration of the exchange filled her with tense energy. Perhaps one dance would help to ease the pressure.

"Yes, thank you." The man swept her into his arms and onto the dance floor. They twirled around to an upbeat tune and laughter broke free from her throat.

She had not danced like this ever before; not this wild and carefree. With Grae it had been all about the contact, the slow swaying that set her body on fire. Tonight she felt as if she could fly away.

Before, at the end of each exchange, Nic had led her away from the party, more for her own safety than anything else. Tonight she had no worries. Lady A had appeared, and she did what had to be done; and now Arista was free to enjoy herself for a little while.

No one knew who she was.

The man spun her around, her feet barely touching the floor.

The tension in her body faded and a new excitement took its place. Never in her life had she embraced such freedom.

By the time the last strains of the orchestra fell silent, Arista could not catch her breath. Her face hurt from smiling so much. The man had been a gentleman, and his hands fell away as soon as the music stopped.

"I won't ask for your name, but would you care to stroll in the garden?" His low-timbred voice caused pleasant vibrations along her skin. Nothing like when she was with Grae, but she didn't feel her usual distaste at having a man so close to her. Still, leaving the party with him might be one risk too many.

"You'll have to excuse me," she said with a smile, and left before he could protest. A breath of cool night air did sound nice, so she headed toward the door herself.

A figure stepped out of the shadows. Grae? Arista blinked. He wore no disguise tonight, so it was definitely him. He didn't look happy to see her, and truth be told, she was not happy to see him. Not here, not when she was conducting business he had no right to know about.

"What are you doing here?' she demanded.

"I came here so I could watch you conduct your *business*," he said. "To try to understand why you were doing it." She saw raw pain in his eyes as he pushed past her.

Arista stood in stunned silence. Grae was halfway to the doors before she could move her feet. By the time she reached him, he had stepped outside. She grabbed his arm and tugged. "It's not what you think."

"I know what I saw," he ground out. "You asked me to trust you? I almost did."

He jerked his arm free and stormed toward the street. This

was not how it was supposed to be. "Grae, please wait." Arista ran to catch up with him. Carriages were still bringing people to the party, so she took his hand and pulled until he followed her farther down the street, away from anyone who might overhear.

"So you can tell more lies?"

"No, so I can tell you the truth." Frustration welled up inside her. She didn't want to lie to him, so she had to tell him at least part of the truth. She hated the way he was looking at her now. "I despise my job." The doubt in his eyes only made her want him to understand all that much more. "It's never been my choice, what I do. I hate controlling people's lives, but it's not something I can simply refuse to do."

"And dancing with strangers, that's how you find new business?"

Embarrassment heated her cheeks. Why had she given in to the urge to let loose tonight? Of course it was the same night Grae decided to follow her. "That's not it at all. I'm only the go-between. I make the deliveries and collect the information." She kept her voice low in case anyone was near enough to hear. Her pulse thundered in her ears. This was more than anyone outside of her circle knew.

Grae now held Lady A's fate in his hands.

"So, what was that, then? The dancing. The laughing with that man?" Grae demanded. He held her shoulders and looked right into her eyes. His gaze was hard, his lips thin with anger. "Because from where I was standing, you didn't seem to despise your work at all."

She set her jaw, and her lips thinned as well. "It's complicated."

"It didn't look too complicated to me. In fact, it all seemed quite clear."

Arista balled her fingers into fists at her side. How could he understand the small taste of freedom she'd gotten tonight? How it made her feel so alive inside that she'd *had* to dance? Grae had no right to be angry.

"Then you mistook what you saw. Someone like you would not understand."

"Then explain it to me." Grae dragged a frustrated hand through his hair. "Simple enough so that I don't feel the need to tell my mother who you really are. That our houseguest is actually a blackmailing liar!"

"I'm not," she gasped. His words stung. "I swear I'm only doing this because . . ." She almost spilled out Wild's name. There was no explanation she could give that would satisfy Grae, not without revealing everything. And she could not do that. Even now, raging at her, he was so vulnerable. She didn't want to hurt him more. It would be her burden to bear. Her secret.

She sighed, her body suddenly heavy. "I'm sorry—I wish I could make you understand, but there is so much I can't tell you." She took a step away from him and felt her body protesting. For a few glorious nights, she had felt something, had felt truly alive. Grae had given her that, and she didn't regret a second of it. "I'm not like you. I didn't have a family who loved me, who protected me, and I've only done what I had to do to survive. But I promise you that the person you met, the one who danced with you, that *is* me—the real me—behind all the pretense. I want you to see who I really am."

Arista stared at the ground, unable to look at Grae. She finally dared to meet his eyes. "I would never lie about this, Grae, because it's one of the only real things I've ever had in my life. I hope that you can at least trust that." She prayed he could see the honesty in her face, because there was nothing more she could say.

From the corner of her eye, Arista watched a black carriage make its way slowly down the street. She knew Wild would be waiting. "There isn't anything else I can say. Good-bye, Grae."

Her heart cracked as she walked away, and he didn't come after her.

That was it, then. He would tell his mother who she really was, and she would be kicked out of their home. The only place she'd ever felt welcome.

She had almost reached the parked carriage when a pair of arms wrapped around her from behind. Taken by surprise, she reacted without thinking, and had her knife out from its sheath and pressed back against her assailant's ribs in a flash.

He froze. "I see that you can take care of yourself, at least." At the sound of Grae's voice, her hand dropped. Yet her traitorous pulse sped up. He *had* come after her.

"I do want to trust you," he said in her ear. "Because whatever this is between us, it feels real to me, too. But you have to tell me everything so I can help you. We can figure this out together."

Up ahead, the carriage door opened, and blind panic gripped her limbs. Would Wild approach her with Grae right here? Wild glanced their way and nodded his head, then entered the gates of the party.

Arista exhaled. That was why she couldn't tell Grae the truth. Because someone like Wild would ruin him, for the sport of it. She wouldn't let that happen—not to Grae. For his own safety, she had to push him away.

"I'm not sure I'll ever be able to tell you the truth." She felt him tense up behind her. "This is my life. This"—she waved her hand that held the knife—"is how I stayed alive. None of this is my choice, but you have no idea what it's like. You can't understand what it's like to have nothing."

"But you always will have nothing if you refuse help," he argued. "Unless this is all really just part of the lie, too?"

The denial was right there, but it would not come out past the lump in her throat. He was right—she always would have nothing. But at least she had nothing to lose. If anything happened to Grae, she would never forgive herself.

"Is it, Ana? Is this all just a lie?" Grae demanded.

Silence stretched between them. She took a deep breath in.

"My name's not Ana."

"What?" The disbelief in his voice nearly broke her.

"My name. It's not Ana, it's Arista." His grasp loosened and it took all of her strength to walk away from him again.

CHAPTER 11

*A*rista closed the door softly and crept into her room.

Wild had left her by the back gate to the garden, after giving her half the money as he had promised. The coins sat heavy in her reticule. Tonight had not gone as she'd planned. How had Grae known where she would be? She'd told no one except for Becky, who had worried about Arista going alone to meet the client.

Arista groaned. Becky had told him. "Of course."

In the morning, she would have to have a talk with her friend—try and explain the danger that Grae would be in if he were to get caught up in their world.

It wouldn't matter now anyway, she realized with a pang. Whatever had been between her and Grae lay in pieces on the street. Admitting that even her name was a lie must have been the final straw. But it was better that Grae hate her than have him be in danger.

With a heavy heart, she sat and undid her boots, setting them carefully aside. Then she stood and began to unlace the corset—she could do it herself, as it was tied in the front for her costume. The light from the lantern on the side table cast the room in a soft glow. The colorful skirt came next, and then the white blouse and stockings. Finally she stood in nothing but her underclothes.

Arista blew out the gas lamp and the room sank into darkness. In the morning, would Grae demand answers? Or worse yet, would he continue to ignore her? Either option left a sick feeling in her stomach. She sank down on the edge of the bed. What was she going to do?

She pulled back the quilt to get into bed. A barely discernable scratching noise sounded at the door—the one that led to the garden. She listened—there it was again. The hairs on her neck stood up. She reached for her knife, tucked under her pillow, and crept to the door. When she pressed her ear against it, she heard nothing. The latch clicked, overloud in the quiet room. Very slowly she pulled the door open, inch by inch. Her eyes, already accustomed to the darkness, easily scanned the lines and shapes of the garden beyond. There were no shadows out of place. Nothing moved.

Had it been an animal? She started to close the door, and then looked down. Something lay on the stone step. A bundle of some sort.

Had Wild left it there? Another assignment, already? Why had he not told her in the carriage, only an hour ago? But it could not be her next task, because it was too thick. And it wasn't just one letter—there was a stack of them, tied with a crude piece of string. She ran her thumb over the wax seal of the letter on the top.

There was no way she could sleep without knowing what this was. She carefully relit the lantern and held the packets closer. Her eyes swept over what she held in her hands before the shaking in them caused her to drop it. The packet landed on the floor with a soft thump, but she didn't hear it. She was already out the door and in the garden. Cool night air washed over her uncovered skin, but she didn't care. Barely even noticed.

"Nic," she whispered as loud as she dared. "I know it's you."

She paused, listening to the sounds of the night. Nothing moved within the walls of the garden.

"Why did you leave those for me?"

Only silence answered her.

Coldness seeped up from the ground, chilling her bare feet. Goose bumps sprang up along her arms and she wrapped them over her stomach, rubbing her hands up and down her arms for warmth.

"Nic?" She tried one more time, but she already knew. He was gone.

With no other choice, Arista went back inside her room and latched the door. The packet lay on the floor, in the shadow cast by the side table. How did Nic know where she was? Why hadn't he stayed, so she could see him, talk to him? She picked up the letters and pulled the string loose, letting them spread out over the bed. She picked one up at random and read it. Then another. And another.

Nic had not just left her letters; he'd left the secrets she'd collected as Lady A over the years. The same secrets that the aristocracy had paid enormous sums to either procure or hide.

Did Nic expect her to use them? *The one who controls the secrets controls those rich bastards.* Nic had always thought that way. He wanted to own them all, just like Bones. So did he now expect her to use them, and continue the blackmailing?

"What am I supposed to do with these?" she asked the empty room.

After tucking the packet safely away in the back of the wardrobe, she crawled under the quilt to fight off a sudden wash of chills.

She lay awake in the darkness for hours. When sleep finally pulled her under, her dreams were filled with shadowy alleyways and voices cutting through thick fog. And faces: Nic, Grae, Bones, Wild. They changed from one to the other until they seemed to merge into one terrible image, staring at her through deep, vacant eyes.

✺

"Good morning, miss," Becky said cheerfully. Arista blinked her eyes open and was surprised to find the room bathed in morning light. "I thought you might like some help getting ready. The family will be eating in a half hour. Miss Sophia has been hovering outside your door all morning, waiting for you to wake up."

Becky pulled back the covers and urged Arista to sit. "Everyone here is so nice," she continued, chattering away. "Do you know that Wilson and the cook, Jane, are married? Mr. Sinclair had rooms added to the house just for them. And Sara, Miss Sophia's maid, is sharing her room with me, and she gave me this new bonnet."

Arista watched Becky move around the room, efficiently gathering what she needed. Her steps were light, and she kept smiling between words. A fresh bandage covered her injured eye, and a pretty blue bonnet sat atop her neat curls.

She wore a new dress, too: a plain light-grey uniform with an immaculate white apron. In this attire, her step seemed more sure, her head higher, despite her injuries. Becky caught Arista's eye and smiled.

There was one thing that needed to be said first. Arista frowned. "You told Grae where I went last night."

Becky's face fell, and she clutched Arista's underclothes to her stomach. "I was worried, miss. You've always had Nic to watch out for you, and Mr. Graeden said he just wanted to be sure you were safe. I'm sorry, miss, I shouldn't have told him."

Arista sighed. It was hard to be mad at her friend for anything. Becky had only done what she thought best. "When I'm out, no one is to know where. It's better that way, okay?"

Becky hung her head. "Of course, miss."

Arista moved across the room and gently took the bundle of clothing from Becky. "Thank you for caring, Becky. That means a lot to me. I don't mean to be harsh, I just want to keep Grae away from that part of my life."

Arista didn't tell her that it was too late. That he knew who she was—what she did. Her friend was happy in the Sinclair home, and Arista vowed to make sure she stayed that way.

This is what she wanted to give Becky for the rest of her life. Security and happiness. Things that a cut of Wild's money could buy. And maybe now, with the secrets Nic had left for her, she might find a way to earn even more. Ideas flashed through her head, but she needed to think them through before she did anything rash. There might be a way to get everything she needed.

"Are you ready to get dressed, miss? Breakfast will be starting soon. You needn't worry about Mr. Graeden," Becky chattered as she helped Arista into her day dress. "I heard him tell Wilson that he went back to his ship. That there were things he needed to attend to."

Arista's spirits sank. A part of her had hoped that he might understand in the light of day. With a heavy sigh, she sat as Becky started tending to her hair. It had gotten longer since the last time Nic cut it. Small curls hugged her neck and framed her face. Becky had pinned up a small section in the front, pulling the hair away from Arista's eyes. Had they always been so blue?

"You look beautiful, miss."

She looked . . . very much unlike herself. Arista missed the rough feel of her wool trousers and the comfort of her oversized jacket, which gave her the anonymity she craved. Things with Grae would not be in such a state of discord, had she been allowed to keep up her disguise. But she couldn't go around dressed as a lad when she was the guest of a family.

Becky led her down the short hallway and opened the door. Arista stepped into the room and everything went silent. Three pairs of eyes were staring at her. Had Grae told his family about her?

"Good morning, Ana," Marguerite said graciously. "Please come in and join us." Arista tried desperately to remain calm. It appeared he had not.

Arista sat in the chair Wilson pulled out for her. She had avoided taking meals with the family so far, unsure of how to act in such a civilized and normal setting. Becky had taught her the graces of a lady, but they did not include dining.

Heat climbed her cheeks, and she didn't dare look up from her plate. But what she saw there only caused her more unease. There were so many utensils. Why did anyone need three forks to eat, when one would suffice?

Arista curled her fingers into her palms and held her hands in her lap to hide the trembling. She could stare down grown men, yet facing a table setting put the fear of the devil in her. If she wasn't so terribly uneasy, she might have laughed at the absurdity. Nic *would* have laughed. He would have declared all of this as pompous as hell, tossed the utensils aside, and eaten with his fingers. It wasn't like they'd had the luxury of eating with anything *but* their fingers growing up.

"How are you this morning, Ana? Are you feeling better?"

Sophia asked. She sat across from Arista and looked bright as sunshine in a pale yellow dress. "Maybe after breakfast we can sit in the garden and gossip? You can tell me what goes on outside of London! Father never lets Grae tell me tales of his adventures." Sophia playfully poked her father, who held up his hands in surrender.

"Those tales are not for the ears of young ladies." Mr. Sinclair smiled at Arista. "Last year, Sophia dressed herself as a boy and snuck onto one of my ships, under the guise of a new cabin boy. They were halfway down the Thames before she was discovered."

Innocent-looking Sophia had done that? Arista's mouth fell open, and Sophia giggled. "I wanted a grand escapade, like in the books I've read."

"Never should have taught the girl to read," Mr. Sinclair said, though there was nothing but love in his smile.

"That's enough," Marguerite chided with a smile. "We have a guest at our table. Ana, what are your plans? Will you stay in London after your visit?"

"I don't think so," she answered. Finally, one truth in the sea of lies. "As soon as things are . . . settled . . . I plan to leave with Becky." She knew that they would assume what would be "settled" was her late husband's estate, and not her business with Wild. Mr. Sinclair nodded and smiled at her explanation, but she could feel his assessing gaze.

"Where will you go?" Sophia asked. Her eyes were wide with excitement. "I've always wanted to travel, to see the world."

"I'm not sure," she lied. Why was she keeping her dream of going to India a secret? Would it matter if they knew?

"Perhaps we can discuss all of the places, and I can help you decide," Sophia said.

"That would be fun." Except she already knew where she

wanted to go, and had hoped that it would be with Grae, on one of his ships. That might be difficult if he continued to avoid her.

Wilson set a covered dish in front of her and Arista seized upon the interruption. She dug her fork into a steaming meat-filled pastry and concentrated on taking a bite. It still made her uneasy, talking about getting away from London—even in the relative safety of the Sinclairs' home.

"Well, there are many ships that sail all over the world, my dear. When you're ready to go, I'm sure we can assist with proper arrangements." Mr. Sinclair nodded his approval at his wife's words and picked up his fork.

"Oh, and I *must* take you to the bonnet shop, Ana," Sophia said from across the table. Her eyes glinted with excitement, and something very close to mischief. Arista smiled and nodded, not at all excited about bonnet shopping.

The family finished their meal with more conversation between Mr. and Mrs. Sinclair about trade routes and finding new crew members. Mrs. Sinclair had as many opinions as her husband, and Arista watched in fascination. Mr. Sinclair took her suggestions to heart. Even when they disagreed at one point, a spirited debate ensued instead of a fight. Arista waited with bated breath.

"Your idea is ridiculous," Mrs. Sinclair said at last, throwing her napkin down.

Every muscle in Arista's body tensed. Now the anger would come. The destruction. Something must have shown on her face, because Mr. Sinclair looked at her with concern.

"Are you okay, Ana? I apologize for the business talk, it must all be very boring for you."

And just like that, the tension in the room disappeared. No one had used fists. There was nothing thrown; nothing broken.

"Usually father and Grae talk for hours after breakfast," Sophia said, rolling her eyes. "But my brother had to get back to the ship for something early this morning."

"That boy works too hard," Marguerite said, though Arista could hear the pride in her voice. "Just like someone else I know." Her pointed gaze wandered to her husband, but it turned soft when their eyes met.

"Well, he must have had something important to see to, as we had plans to go over a new route I've been studying." Disappointment shone in his eyes, and the pastry Arista had eaten sat like a lump of coal in her guilty stomach.

"If you will excuse me, I'd like to get some air in the garden," Arista said, rising to her feet.

"I'll come with you," Sophia said, pushing back her chair. "And maybe later we can go look at the bonnets I told you about."

Not once had Arista mentioned that she needed a bonnet, yet Sophia seemed almost fixated on the errand. When they got to the garden, Arista thought, she would plead a headache and go back to her room. Once they were out of earshot, however, Sophia wound her arm through Arista's and pulled her out into the garden through a pair of open patio doors. "You must think I am frivolous to go on about a bonnet, but . . ." Sophia looked over her shoulder, then leaned in conspiratorially. "There *is* no bonnet. Well, I suppose there is, technically, but in this case, 'bonnet' refers to a place I want you to see."

As Arista had never before had a real young lady for a friend, she had no idea if this was normal behavior. Sophia looked positively giddy with excitement, while Arista only felt shivers of apprehension. "I'm not sure I understand."

"I can read people pretty well, and I think that you and I are very similar." Arista flashed back briefly to a different Sinclair sibling who'd said the exact same thing to her. Sophia guided her to the same bench she and Grae had sat on the night before. "What are your thoughts on arranged marriages? About women not holding positions of power? About the poor being treated as garbage, while the rich walk over them on the way to the opera?" Arista's head swam as Sophia fired off the questions one after another.

As Sophia waited expectedly for her answers, Arista realized that the girl actually wanted to know her thoughts. "I think unless you are a rich, overly pompous man, you get no choices in life," she finally said.

"Exactly!" Sophia clapped her hands together and Arista jumped. "See, I knew we were similar in our views. If you promise not to tell Mother, I have something to show you." Sophia had leaned in close and dropped her voice to a whisper. "This afternoon. We'll take a carriage ride together, and I'll introduce you to several like-minded friends. I think you will fit right in." Sophia grinned and her eyes sparkled.

Arista had no idea what she had agreed to with her silence, but it made Sophia happy—and that, strangely, made Arista happy. Sophia reached out and took Arista's hand. "I'm so very glad that you're here, Ana."

Ana.

And just like that, Arista was reminded how much of her life was a lie.

CHAPTER 12

Sophia tucked Arista's arm into hers and they walked around to the street entrance of the garden. "I asked Tomas to bring the carriage around earlier, so we're all ready to go." Outside, in the bright light of day, Arista felt too exposed. People walked by as they waited for Tomas, and they made eye contact and smiled at her. They saw her. No disguise hid her features. She was neither Lady A nor an urchin boy. She was Arista.

"Maybe we can do this another day?" she asked Sophia. Unease prickled over her skin.

Sophia looked so disappointed that Arista forced a smile and nodded. They would go. No one would ever know her like this. What harm could it do to act like a normal person just for one day?

The carriage pulled up to the curb and Tomas helped them in, and then she decided. Today she would simply be a girl, who wasn't really shopping for a bonnet. Such a normal thing; it made her smile. Soon they were rocketing down Tulane Street, and the panic began to recede.

Sophia appeared to be enjoying herself immensely—waving to a woman walking along the sidewalk, joking with the driver that he had gotten much better at avoiding pedestrians.

Arista watched her new friend with a mixture of awe and envy. It was clear that she had never suffered by anyone's hand. She had never been so hungry that moldy bread was a feast. Her eyes were full of an innocent light Arista's had never had. But her openness made it hard to dislike her for her privileges. Sophia had a family, and was a highly valued member of it.

Arista, on the other hand, had been tossed aside. Unwanted. And maybe that's what drew her to Sophia and the girl's delight with the world.

"Tomas, a left here please," Sophia said. They'd stopped at an intersection, and were waiting for a storage cart piled high with barrels to lumber through.

"Miss?" Tomas couldn't be much older than Sophia, but he wore the same look of warning that her father had had at the breakfast table.

"I've changed my mind. I wish to shop on Cheapside instead." Arista saw the gleam in the girl's eyes; this detour had been the plan all along.

The cart passed through the intersection, and Tomas turned their carriage left onto Cheapside. The street was filled with carriages, and crowds of people made it impossible to see into the shop windows from the street. Buildings loomed four or five stories high, and Arista could see the steeple of St. Paul's Cathedral farther down the street. This area was familiar to her, as she and Nic had often ventured here to pick pockets on days like this.

"Here is fine," Sophia said after only a few more minutes. They both stepped down, while Tomas glared at Sophia.

"Isn't that laundry shop where your sweet friend works near here?" Sophia asked. Arista looked over her shoulder and saw that Tomas's cheeks were red. Still, his gaze darted down the street to where Sophia pointed.

"Go. I promise to be right in this very spot, at two o'clock on the dot," Sophia said.

Arista turned to the window of the closest shop and saw a display of bonnets and gloves. One bonnet in plain blue caught her eye. The lack of frills and decoration appealed to her. She gave herself a mental shake when Sophia grabbed her hand. A bonnet? Since when did she care about such trivial things? She turned, expecting Sophia to start down the long street of shops, but instead she pulled Arista to the edge of the sidewalk. When Arista glanced at her, Sophia's eyes widened with excitement. Clearly she had not brought Arista to Cheapside just for bonnet shopping.

"Thank you," Sophia said. She linked their arms together, then looked for an opening in the heavy traffic. "You don't know what this means to me."

Before she could argue or ask what Sophia had planned, the girl jumped off the sidewalk and dragged Arista with her. A hackney swerved around them and the driver swore loudly. Sophia paused, then pulled Arista in front of a supply wagon horse, which looked half dead and moved as if it were, too. When they finally reached the relative safety of the opposite sidewalk, Arista let out a pent-up breath. "Where are we going?"

This side of the street was just as crowded, and they were swept along for several feet before Sophia yanked Arista between two women and into an alley.

There was an immediate change in the air. Out of the sun, the air was cooler against her skin, but a dank odor wafted through the narrow space. Arista reached for her knife, remembering too late that she had not put it on that morning before lunch. Every shadow seemed to move. She stopped and tugged on Sophia's hand.

"I don't think this is a good idea." Arista's gaze slid left, then right. This place would be where criminals hid in waiting. It's where *she* would hide. The sound of horse hooves on the cobblestones filtered through the maze of buildings, but there were no other people taking this shortcut.

"Don't be frightened," Sophia said, mistaking Arista's hesitation for fear. "We're nearly there. Trust me."

Just as Arista was starting to dig in her heels and insist they return to the street, the alley opened up onto another street, quieter than the last.

"We're here," Sophia said. Her smile grew wider.

Here appeared to be a small coffeehouse tucked between a shoemaker and a bookbinder. The sign on the plaque read LLOYD'S COFFEEHOUSE. People lounged inside, gathered around the square tables that were crowded into the space. Lively discussions were going on in every corner. Suddenly, a hush fell over the crowd. Sophia grabbed her hand and squeezed, then pulled them inside to stand along the wall.

"There he is," Sophia whispered. Excited murmuring spread throughout the people gathered there.

"Who?" Arista asked. She had never been to a coffeehouse, though she knew what often took place inside them: discussion, mostly political, mostly among men. There were no class distinctions in many of them, and Lloyd's appeared to be the same. Arista saw fine tailored suits and threadbare cotton, silk and muslin. She and Sophia were, however, the only women in the establishment.

"Voltaire." Reverence filled Sophia's voice.

Even Arista had heard of the man in conversations at the parties she attended. He was part of the Enlightenment movement, and the aristocracy hated his message. They fought to have him silenced, because he spoke of equality and the dissolution of the classes. She had often wondered how one man could cause such resentment and fear in others.

Until he began to speak. His soft, French-accented voice carried over the hushed crowd. He spoke of privilege and wealth and how each person, regardless of the circumstances of their birth, deserved to be treated as an equal to everyone else.

Shouts of agreements rose above them.

Sophia gripped her hand tighter, nodding her head. Her eyes shone with the fervor that filled the room. And Arista? Her skin prickled with excitement as she got caught up in Voltaire's words. Never had she heard such conviction. Such belief in one's own words. She found herself nodding, too.

"Sophia, love, I hoped to see you here."

A new voice came from behind them. Sophia released Arista's hand and swung around with a happy cry. "Louis!"

He took her hand and bowed low, brushing his lips over her fingers. A blush rose in Sophia's cheeks. A cocky grin split the handsome young man's face and he stepped closer, resting a hand on her hip in a familiar way.

"Louis, this is my house guest, Ana."

Louis's gaze turned assessing as he looked over Arista. When his eyes finally stopped at her face, he stared at her unapologetically. "You have the look of a gypsy about ya. Do you read fortunes, too?" Arista froze. Nic had only ever called her "gypsy" in jest.

"Louis!" Sophia gasped. She looked between Arista and Louis, clearly embarrassed.

"What? We could use a fortune teller, love." He laughed, but the emotion didn't quite make it to his eyes. There was nothing threatening about him; he appeared relaxed enough, and made no indication that he would reach for a weapon. But instinct—a familiar feeling in her gut—told her that he wasn't all that he appeared. The way he dressed, the threadbare wool trousers that were a little too short, the scuffed boots that looked too big, all spoke of poverty. The kind that Arista had grown up in. What was Sophia doing with someone like him?

The crowd shifted, moving closer as one to hear what the dynamic speaker was saying. Sophia took Arista's hand so that they would not be separated.

"So, you're another one for the cause, aye?" Louis leaned around Sophia and addressed Arista. At her questioning stare, Louis tugged Sophia closer. "This one believes that we are all the same, regardless of social standing. I tell her it's a lost cause, but she refuses to listen. Them with the money won't ever let people like me into their circles. Not that I want to rub elbows with that stuffy lot." Sophia elbowed him, and he grunted. "Well, there are a few lovely exceptions, I admit."

Arista saw the way they looked at each other, and turned away. It was too intimate to watch. Voltaire continued to talk. Arista tuned out the couple and let his words wash over her.

If enough people would rise up and denounce the way things were, he said, if they no longer accepted the boundaries of the classes, it could all begin to change. He made it sound so simple. It could have been five minutes or fifty, she was so caught up in the spell Voltaire had cast.

"Love, I'll be back in a few minutes," Louis said to Sophia. It wasn't his sudden disappearance, but his tone, that piqued Arista's interest. Resigned—to whatever it was he had to do. He didn't want to go, that much was clear. She followed his progress as he made his way outside the crowd. Even in the thick mass spilling out of the doors, Arista knew the man that Louis had stopped to talk to.

Wild.

Louis pulled a thick packet from inside his jacket and handed it to the Thief Taker. Wild, in turn, gave Louis a small drawstring bag that he immediately tucked away. Arista wanted to get closer, to hear what they were saying, but she didn't want Wild to see her. To let him know that he'd been seen.

But now she needed to know what business Louis was conducting with the Thief Taker. It seemed too big of a coincidence that he and Sophia were on such friendly terms, while Sophia's father owed Wild an unpaid debt. Was Louis toying with Sophia to gain some kind of information?

He would find himself less one vital organ if Arista found out it was all a ruse. It was obvious by the way Sophia looked at him that she was in love. For the second time, Arista reached for the familiar shape of her knife handle, but it wasn't there. The crowd suddenly became suffocating around her. Too close. Too little room to move. Stars began to dance at the edge of her vision. Ripples of tension raced up her spine.

Louis came back and grinned as if nothing were amiss. When he caught Arista's stare, his smile faltered. She was not one to back down. Louis swallowed visibly and took a step away from her.

"Sophia, could we go, please? I'm feeling suddenly unwell," Arista said. She had to get her friend away from Louis, at least until she could figure out what was going on. "It must be the crowd and the heat. I'm not used to so many people."

"Of course," Sophia said right away. Her gaze moved to Louis and a wistful look crossed her face. He glanced at Arista, then lifted Sophia's hand to his lips once more.

"We can meet here in another two days, love. Every second will feel like forever. Nice to meet you, Ana." With a sideways glance at Arista, he disappeared into the crowd.

A dreamy smile drifted over Sophia's lips as she stared at the place where Louis had been. When Sophia saw Arista watching, her cheeks turned red. "I know it's unconventional, but I really think I love him." Her face immediately fell. "Papa will never allow it. He's a poet."

"How did you meet him?" Arista asked Sophia.

She guided Sophia along the sidewalk, toward the intersection. There was no way she'd go back through the alley, not with the possibility that Wild was still nearby. She didn't want him to know that she'd seen him meeting with Louis. Not yet.

"Papa had business with a blacksmith a few months ago, and I talked him into letting me ride along if I promised to stay in the carriage. This very bold boy, the blacksmith's apprentice, kept walking past, sneaking glances at me and smiling. I thought he was quite forward, and told him so. He laughed and said someone as beautiful as me must be used to stares." Sophia looked up becomingly from under her lashes.

He was probably trying to figure out the best way to pick your pocket.

Arista kept the thought to herself.

"A week later, I saw him again at the market. And then I found a poem he left—it was in a corner of the garden where I like to sit and read. A few days later, I found a note. It asked me to meet him on Lombard Street, at the coffeehouse." She grinned at Arista. "I'm all for a grand romantic adventure, you know. That was three months ago."

They were at the intersection and Arista scanned the streets. There were more carriages and people on this one, and she stepped closer to Sophia. Nic used to do the same for her, to keep watch of everything around them. Looking for danger.

It had to be Sophia's innocence that made Arista feel this way. Sophia had no idea that there were bad people in the world, who would use her or hurt her for their own gain. Arista knew it too well. Without knowing for sure what Louis's real intentions were, she vowed to keep an eye on her new friend.

Louis had to have ulterior motives, especially if he knew someone like Wild. They should be easy enough to find out. All she had to do was follow him, eavesdrop, and she'd know the truth. Better that Sophia feel the sting of betrayal rather than the pain of something much worse.

As they neared the carriage, Tomas turned in surprise. "Done already? And no packages?"

His eyebrows rose in suspicion, but Sophia only grinned. "Can you believe there was absolutely nothing that caught my eye after all?"

"No, I cannot," Tomas mumbled as he helped them into the carriage. He climbed in and picked up the reins.

A very pretty but disappointed-looking young washerwoman stood in the doorway of the laundry shop and watched them pull away. Tomas gave her a quick wave, and the girl blushed before ducking back into the doorway. The streets were even more crowded now, and it took almost an hour to make their way back to the townhouse.

"Tell me more about Louis," Arista prompted, and Sophia eagerly told her everything about him.

By that time they arrived home, Arista knew what she had to

do. Grae might not want to talk to her, but she had to tell him about Louis. It all seemed too contrived, especially given that the young man clearly had ties to Wild.

Though she couldn't tell Grae everything, she had to tell him enough so that he would intercede and protect his sister.

Arista would not let Sophia get mixed up with a thief.

CHAPTER 13

Tomas had no idea that Grae did not want to see Arista, so he was more than willing to take her to the docks. She'd never been there dressed as a girl before, and more than one admiring glance was thrown her way as Tomas maneuvered the carriage through the tight spaces created by the crates of goods in the process of being loaded and unloaded. Shouts and loud thumps and the sharp smell of unwashed bodies filled the air. How had she never noticed it before? Dozens of men from various ships moved about as if they were following the steps to an intricate dance. How they didn't crash into each other, especially while pushing carts piled high with cargo, she'd never know.

When Tomas finally stopped in front of a massive three-masted ship, Arista could not stop the warm rush of admiration. It was beautiful. Moored next to the wharf, bobbing on the river, the ship's elegant design was on display. Intricate carvings covered the hull, and a figurehead of a woman stretched proudly out in front. Small windows lined the front of the hull in a neat row, and the mahogany wood gleamed in the sunlight. Hundreds of lines of ropes stretched in all different directions, creating a weblike effect that she could make neither head nor tail of.

On board, men rushed all over, checking ropes and scrubbing down the decks. Arista and Nic had sat watching enough times to know that the rituals of sailors rarely deviated. They were preparing the ship for another departure. Grae would sail away from her in the near future.

Small panels in the side of the ship brought Arista back to the reality of how dangerous Grae's job was. If attacked, cannons would be pushed through them to fire on pirate ships. Had he fought another ship on the open ocean? Faced pirates?

There was so much she didn't know about him. That she wanted to know. She rubbed her arms to push away the chill at the thought of Grae in danger.

"I'll go get Mister Graeden, miss. You stay in the carriage. The docks ain't no place for a lady." Tomas jumped down and tethered the horse to a post, then jogged to the gangplank that led to the deck.

She almost protested that she'd spent plenty of time in the area, and had never suffered more than a swipe to the ear, when she remembered that it was different now. Then, she had been dressed as a boy, and had garnered nary a glance; but now, men eyed her as they passed. They grinned with interest, and a few were brazen enough to say hello. Arista ignored them all. Instead she sat quietly, clenching her hands tightly in her lap. She had her knife strapped to her thigh if she needed to use it, so that provided a small measure of comfort.

It was only a few minutes before Grae appeared. The top buttons on his crisp white shirt were undone and he had rolled his sleeves up, revealing tanned forearms. He had on black pants tucked into tall black boots, and he stood with his feet wide apart. In this light he looked less a highwayman and more a pirate.

She saw Tomas point to the carriage, and Grae's gaze caught hers. He stood, hands on hips. From this distance she wasn't sure if he was happy to see her or not. Tomas jogged back to the carriage.

"I'll just grab a pint at the tavern there. Send for me when you're ready, miss." Tomas nodded politely and walked away down the dock.

Arista braced for more anger. Given their last conversation, she didn't doubt Grae would dismiss her altogether. When he started down the gangplank toward her, she couldn't stop her pulse from quickening.

The wind blew his dark hair across his eyes and he pushed it back absently. He looked as wild and strong as his ship. Possessiveness washed over her, though she had no claim to him. He stopped next to the carriage and cocked his head at her. "I didn't expect to see you here."

God, he was beautiful to look at. Every time he was close, she found it hard to breathe. To even remember what excuse she had invented to see him again. "I needed to talk to you. About Sophia."

"Is she okay?" Worry immediately replaced everything else. His knuckles turned white where they gripped the side of the carriage.

"She's fine. She took me . . ." Would Grae tell his parents what Sophia did when they thought she was shopping? Coffeehouses were not exactly the place where proper young ladies went. "There's a boy. Louis. I'm worried that he may not have her best intentions at heart and she seems . . . very fond of him."

She couldn't tell Grae that he was working with Wild without revealing her own connection.

"You're worried about Sophia?" His expression bordered on disbelief.

"Of course I am. She is young and beautiful and trusting and I don't want her to get hurt. Maybe you should look into this boy, make sure . . ." She stopped talking. Grae had started to smile at her and it was very distracting.

This close, she could see flecks of dark blue mixed in with the grey of his eyes.

"Why are you smiling? I'm being serious. He's . . ." she tried again.

"Do you know why I was angry the other night?" he interrupted.

Her head spun at the sudden turn in topic. "No."

"I was worried your actions would cause harm to my family. That you had no regard for their safety and were simply using them to obtain your goal. That you were using me as well."

"I told you . . ." she started to say, but his finger against her lips stopped her cold. Or, red-hot, judging by the heat coming from where he touched her.

"I believe you now. You came here despite every hateful thing I said to you, in order to protect my sister. I wouldn't have been surprised if you had never wanted to speak to me again, given my behavior. I will look into this Louis person, and thank you, for looking after Sophia."

Her eyes darted away from his, landing on the ship behind him. "I wanted . . ." She sighed, finally pulling her eyes from his ship. "She's my friend. I care about what happens to her."

She looked everywhere but at Grae. Things between them had shifted again and she wasn't sure what to say. Maybe she should find Tomas and go home?

"Arista?"

Warmth flooded her entire body when she heard her name from his lips. It had been so long since she'd heard it spoken and the fact that it came from Grae only made it that much more special. She sought out his gaze and found him staring at her, but she couldn't say anything. Not when so many unfamiliar feelings were making themselves known at once.

It was as if all sounds on the wharf had fallen silent and it was only the two of them.

He leaned closer and took her hand, pulling it to rest on his chest. "Knowing what you're doing only makes it worse. People don't hide their distaste for your Lady A persona. Every time you go out, you put yourself in danger, and it makes me sort of crazy to think about it now. I'm sorry I overreacted last night. I just want to be there at your side to keep you safe, even if it puts me in danger as well."

"That's the problem," she said. "I would never do that to you. This is my life, and I have to deal with the consequences of it. You don't. I can't drag you into it."

Grae lifted her hand to his lips, and heat bloomed under her skin. "What you don't understand is that I'm already one hundred percent in it. There's something about you I can't stop thinking about. You have an air of mystery that is intriguing." He grinned at her, and she knew his anger from the previous evening had evaporated. "But there is more. There's a look you get in your eyes—as if you're on a great journey, but have gotten lost along the way. All I want is for you to let me guide you back."

She choked on her own breath. He'd seen that? She tried so hard to hide any emotion. Bones loved to find any weakness and exploit it. Arista had learned to become numb very early on. Yet Grae had managed to find her beneath the shell she'd erected.

The fact that he saw her, really saw her and not someone Arista had created for protection, meant more than she could ever say. Around Grae, she didn't even want to hide. The thought was terrifying and exhilarating.

"Would you like a tour?" he asked. "You said you've never been on a ship before. I'd love to show you."

A small gasp escaped from her lips, and she smiled. "Very much."

He reached for her hand and helped her out of the carriage. Excitement bubbled in her veins. Grae steered her toward the gangplank, keeping his body between her and the men moving about on the deck. His hands settled on her waist to steady her as she started across the wooden bridge between the dock and ship, which was much narrower than it looked. The water lapped at the wharf as they climbed, and she tried not to look down. Tried not to think that if she fell, she would drown.

The ship dipped suddenly, and the wood beneath her feet shifted. She scrambled to hold on to something, but there was nothing except for a rope strung as a makeshift rail. "It's okay, I've got you." Grae's soothing voice in her ear stopped the frantic movements of her arms. His arms tightened around her waist and he drew her back against his front. "Relax. The more you move, the more the bridge moves. One step. Now another. That's it." Grae guided her and she clung to his voice, careful not to look down. When she finally set foot on the solid wood of the deck, her legs were almost too wobbly to stand.

All thoughts of Louis and Sophia were gone, replaced with the awareness that she could have fallen into the Thames.

"Are you afraid of the water?" Grae asked softly.

"I can't swim," she whispered. "Someone tried to teach me once, but I could just never learn."

"Well, if you fall in, I promise I'll jump in after you."

Arista swallowed the lump of fear still stuck in her throat. "That would be greatly appreciated. Should that day come."

She met his stare and saw more than just that one promise in his eyes. He seemed to offer so much more without saying anything, and she didn't want to look away.

"I'm okay now," she said. "Thank you."

Grae nodded and took her elbow. "We'll start above deck with the basics. I don't want to bore you." He steered her away from the railing, away from the crew working steadily on what seemed like every part of the ship. How they knew where every rope went baffled her. There were so many, strung up and down and across.

"I want to know everything," she said breathlessly. "How do they know which rope does what?"

"When you spend all your life on a ship, it becomes second nature. I could shimmy up that main mast when I was six." He pointed to the tallest mast, which stretched proudly toward the sky.

Her pulse thundered in her ears. Why would anyone willingly climb that thin pole? "That's crazy."

"It's a necessity. The crow's nest—that platform you see there— it's a lookout. Land, pirates, storms—they're all easier to spot with a spyglass from up there." The rocking of the ship seemed to make the crow's nest sway dangerously back and forth. She could hardly keep her footing on the deck. Up there, she would probably tumble right out.

"I can safely cross 'lookout' off my list of possible future positions," she said with all seriousness, which made Grae laugh again.

"You'd make a better cabin boy, anyway," he teased. Heat climbed into her cheeks. He had no idea how close he was to the truth.

"What do all the ropes do?" she asked as Grae led her farther up the deck. He spent the next half hour explaining the intricacies of how the sails were raised and lowered, and how the ropes wound around pulleys were used to change direction at a moment's notice. There were even more ropes connected to cables that could raise and lower the cargo below deck. Arista tried to follow the lines to see how they worked, but there were just too many to make sense of them all.

"There are one hundred men on board when we sail, and every one of them knows how to work the ropes. Even the cabin boy," he teased.

"I'm slowly losing any usefulness I thought I might have had on board." She meant to jest with him, but his eyes darkened and he grew serious.

"If you sailed with me, you would never have to lift a finger. I wouldn't let you," he said into her ear.

She pulled away and walked several steps toward the front of the ship, then looked over her shoulder with a smile. "I'm not used to being idle. There must be something I could do."

Grae took three long strides and he was there, right behind her. She felt the heat from his body and waited for the touch she knew would come. Whenever they were together, it seemed like he could not keep from initiating some kind of connection.

But this time, he did not. She didn't dare move, and it became a test of wills. The muscles in her neck tensed as she fought the urge to take a step back, enough so that their bodies would be touching.

"The front of the ship, where you are currently standing, is called the bow. Below this deck are the crew's quarters and the cannons, and then on the lowest level, the cargo hold." His hot breath washed over the edge of her ear as he spoke, and she really didn't hear much of what he said. Something about cargo, maybe? A shiver of anticipation raced down her spine when she felt the faintest brush of a touch on her neck.

"This is my favorite place to be when we are at full mast, slicing across the open ocean. It feels almost like flying." The ship bobbed and dipped suddenly, and Grae wound his arm around her waist and pulled her securely against his front. It was second nature to rest her hands on his forearm.

They stood like that, staring out over the Thames together, until someone cleared their throat behind them. They turned and Arista almost lost her balance.

"What can I do for you, Joseph?" Grae asked, not taking his arm from around Arista.

The huge bald man nodded to Arista, and she tried to smile. He seemed to be as wide as he was tall, and without a shirt, she could clearly see the thick cords of muscle that covered his torso. But that wasn't what caused her apprehension. A long, jagged scar ran from just above one eye, down across his face, and ended under his jaw on the opposite side. Men with scars like that were usually fighters. Bones employed men like him because they had no morals.

"'Scuse me, sir. There's a problem with part of the rigging. It won't take but a minute."

Grae clapped him on the shoulder. "I'll take a look with you. Oh, Joseph, this is Arista. Arista, this is Joseph, my right-hand man. He'll be the second in command on this next trip—isn't that right, Joe?"

Joe grinned and shook his head. "It's nice to meet you, miss.

And no, I'll not be his second in command. I'll feed this bunch, but I won't be telling 'em what to do unless they set foot in my galley."

"You're the cook?" she asked.

"Not just a cook. Joe is a genius. The meals he manages when we're down to the last crate of dried parsnips and some dried fish would make you weep. I wouldn't sail without this man." Grae beamed at Joe, who actually looked like he was blushing now.

The banter between the two men belied their friendship. It was clear that there was a deep bond there.

"Will you be okay here for a few minutes?" Grae asked her.

"Of course. I could stand here all day and never grow bored with it."

Joe grinned at her, then raised an eyebrow at Grae. "Found a like-minded soul, I see." Grae smiled right at her and it warmed her heart. That look made her feel like the only person in the world. Now a blush was filling *her* face.

"I'll return him posthaste," Joe said, practically dragging Grae back down the deck behind him.

Arista walked to the very front of the ship and stood at the rail. A light breeze ruffled her skirts and brought the thick odor of the river to her nose. What did the ocean smell like, so far out at sea? The river was a muddy brown color, but she imagined that out at sea, it was so blue that the sky and water blended together. The ship swayed and bowed again, but this time Arista kept her balance. Already she was getting used to being on a ship. She could do it. Go all the way to India.

Lost in her daydreams, she didn't hear Grae return several moments later.

"It's a much better view when you're at sea," Grae said.

She turned and found him holding a tray with some bread,

cheese, and exotic-looking fruit that was yellow with bumps all over it. "Joseph insisted I bring you something to eat. Said a good wind would blow you away." Grae set the tray on a barrel next to the rail and motioned her over. "So what do you think of the ship?" He watched her expectantly, as if her answer really mattered to him.

"It's amazing. I've sat and watched the ships from the wharf for years, but never imagined what they looked like from this side. It really is beautiful." She smiled at Grae and he stared back at her. The moment was perfect.

For once, the grey fog that sat heavy on London had parted and the sun shone down on them. Birds chirped and the sounds of the men getting the ship ready were almost comforting. She felt like she belonged for the first time ever. Nothing had ever felt so right.

"Are you really a widow?" His question took her by surprise. She'd all but forgotten the ruse that had brought her to his parents' home.

She shook her head. "That was just a story made up to explain why I was there." She wanted to trust him, more than she'd wanted anything in her life. "Tell me more about your travels," she said, walking to the front of the ship. She needed a moment to collect herself. "What's it like, being at sea?" She closed her eyes and tilted her face into the breeze. She wanted to imagine every detail he told her. Grae moved next to her and the fresh scent of cedar joined all the other aromas filling her lungs.

"Indescribable. Sometimes, when I see the coast coming into view, I don't want to come home yet. Once the ocean gets into your blood, it stays there forever. My father took me out on his ship when I was only four that first time. Ever since then, I couldn't stay away. There is no freedom like water as far as you can see."

Inside her chest, Arista felt her heartbeat thumping wildly. That was what she'd always envisioned. What she wanted to feel. "Tell me about something you've seen."

Grae thought for a moment, then turned to her with a grin. "There are ports along the Indian coast that make you think you've gone to another world. There are the most beautiful animals roaming free. Women carry great baskets of fruits on their heads. You've never seen such colors. And the smells. Spices and tea and smoke."

"That's what I want. A place with color. London is so grey. It feels . . . hopeless most days."

"Is that why you've decided to travel to India, then?"

"When I was very young, an Indian woman at my orphanage was kind to me. No one else cared whether I lived or died." She risked a glance at Grae, and he looked pained. "Nalia was good to me. She was the laundress. I'd sneak to the room where she stayed, washing clothes for days on end. She told me stories about India as I sat under her folding table. It became this . . ." Arista stared out over the river, watching it wind through London and disappear into the horizon. She'd never said any of this out loud before, but it felt right and she didn't stop. "It became this magical place across the ocean that I wanted to escape to. Whenever things got bad, which was most of the time, I clung to the idea that if I could one day get there, everything would be okay."

A self-deprecating laugh escaped from her. She couldn't look at Grae again, afraid of what she'd see in his eyes.

"The man who took me from the orphanage—he came often, taking the smallest ones to steal for him in the markets. The night he chose me, I was five. I remember being scared, so I ran to Nalia. She gave me her scarf and told me to never forget that there was a big world out there. I only ever dreamed about it. I never really expected that I might see it one day."

She turned to look at him. His hair danced in the wind and he stood firm despite the rocking of the ship. She never wanted to stop looking at him; would never grow tired of listening to him tell stories about his adventures. Only, she wanted to be part of them now.

"So, what changed?" he finally asked.

"Everything," she whispered.

CHAPTER 14

The same man stood on the edge of the crowd, as he had done before. Arista had been watching him for the past ten minutes as he grew increasingly agitated.

Arista had gone to the harbor almost every day for the past three weeks to visit Grae's ship, learning everything she could from him. She now knew the difference between a mizzenmast and a foremast. She could tie a serviceable knot, and it no longer made her ill to watch the men shimmy up the masts to tug on the ropes. The best part was watching Grae work. His interactions with his men, who clearly respected him, and the way Grae never hesitated to jump in and help with any job that needed to be done, made her heart swell. He was hard-working and kind and when he would catch her staring, his grin lit up her insides.

And now, she could walk across the deck while the ship rolled beneath her feet without stumbling. Joe even tried to show her how to clean the fish they were to put on salt for the voyage, but that hadn't worked out so well. Arista now knew that fish guts caused retching. At least for her. Even then, Grae had been tender and insisted she rest in his cabin until she felt better.

In the evenings, Grae joined his family for dinner. Afterward in the parlor there was always lively conversation, about anything from politics to shipping routes. The Sinclairs always included Arista in their discussions, even though she had very little to add. Mostly she would sit and listen, especially when Grae talked. His eyes would light up and he would gesture wildly with his hands, and she couldn't look away. The way the family interacted with each other intrigued her. They were always respectful, even when they argued, and the love they shared was very clear.

She looked forward to those after-dinner moments, but what she really enjoyed were the few precious minutes when Grae would sneak out into the garden and then knock on her door. They'd stand on the threshold of her room, hands occasionally brushing together as they whispered to each other.

Those moments made her ache for so much more than she deserved. They almost made her forget that she still had a job to do. When a messenger finally arrived one morning with a note, reality came crashing back down. Wild specified that she was to meet the same man as before at midnight the following night. There was a packet included that she was to give him.

Now it was quarter past, and she found herself hesitating. She should have concluded their business already, but tonight—the disguise, the lies, everything about what she was going to do—it all made her stomach hurt.

It wasn't nerves. It was something else. Something even more terrifying. The blackmail felt wrong. She was aware of a sense of guilt that had never before been present in her life. The time spent with the Sinclairs, especially with Grae, had shown her what normal was like. He treated her like a lady, and she found she liked it immensely. For the first time in her life, she'd found a place where she fit in, something she'd only ever dared to hope for in the quietest hour of the night. And putting on Lady A's disguise was like wearing a dress three sizes too small. It was confining and uncomfortable.

It scared her, this sudden burst of conscience. If she wasn't Lady A, then who was she? Where did she really belong? Arista shook her head. This, right here, was where she had to be. It didn't matter who she wanted to be—only who she was right now. To get out of this life she had to play the game.

Her client was waiting. It was time to do her job.

"Would you care to dance?" a low voice from behind her asked. Arista turned, a shiver of excitement running over her skin, but it wasn't Grae.

"No thank you. I'm waiting for someone."

"A shame," he said. A small smile passed over his lips and he nodded his head. "If you change your mind, you have only to ask."

As he walked away, she couldn't stop herself from the obvious comparison. His shoulders were narrower than Grae's, and he wasn't quite as tall. From what she saw of the lower part of his face, he wasn't hideous to look at, nor did his breath reek of brandy. His behavior was polite enough. All things considered, he appeared to be a decent enough gentleman. And yet she felt nothing for him. There was only person she wanted at her side. And for that reason alone, she had made sure he did not know where she was.

Grae would not be there tonight, as she had given Becky explicit instructions not to tell him anything. Part of her wished that she had said nothing to Becky. Watching couples dance and flirt behind the safety of their disguises made her want Grae there. She missed being in his arms more than she wanted to admit. No one would be an adequate substitute.

"I grow tired of waiting for you to come to me."

Arista swung around and came face-to-face with the man she'd met before. His eyes glinted dangerously in the candlelight. He was gripping the head of his cane tightly, and she had the distinct feeling that he would just as soon beat her with it as lean on it. Keeping him waiting had not gone over well at all.

Which pleased her greatly.

"I'm on no one's schedule but my own, sir. But since you are standing here, we may as well conclude this business." He took her arm none too gently, pulling her closer to the darkened side of the room. Once they were away from curious eyes, Arista pulled out the packet Wild had given her and held it out to him, but yanked it away when he reached for it. "You have something for me?"

He glared at her, but took out another purse of coins. Once the purse was in her hand, she dropped the packet into his outstretched palm. He quickly tucked it into an inner pocket, then patted his jacket. A self-satisfied smile curled his lips up.

His greed was the ticket to her freedom, but someone else would ultimately lose when he used this information to blackmail them. "Good evening to you, sir," she said, starting to turn away.

He grabbed her arm again, and this time squeezed it until she winced. Arista tried to pull away, but his fingers dug into her flesh painfully. "If I don't get what I want from this deal, I will personally come after you, my dear."

Fear clawed its way over her skin, and she took a deep breath to push it back down. Lady A resurfaced. Deftly, her hand fell to her thigh, and her knife was free before he could move. The tip pressed against his groin. "If you ever threaten me again, sir, I will make sure that your line ends with you. Is that clear?" This was a dangerous game she played. The people around her were too engrossed in each other to care if she was hurt. Nic had been the one who kept her safe before, but now there was no one. She needed to appear strong and unafraid.

His eyes narrowed, but he released her arm and stepped away from her. "A wise move," she said pleasantly. "Again, good evening to you, sir." Arista slid the blade back into its sheath and turned her back on him. Without glancing back, she knew her casual dismissal of him would fuel his anger. Men like him did not like disrespect, especially from a woman who held power.

It wasn't until she'd made it to the patio doors that Arista allowed her hand to drop from the knife's handle under her skirt. Tonight she felt like a fraud. No matter what Wild promised her, no matter how much money she extorted from the aristocracy for him, she knew it would never be enough. Men like him, led by greedy hearts, took and took until there was nothing left. She might be better paid now, but she was still as much his pawn as Bones's. She had to get out before it was too late.

The idea that had been dancing in her mind since Nic left her the letters grew stronger.

If she contacted the people in the packet and offered them their secrets back in exchange for a reasonable sum, she could get the money she needed for passage to India—while also freeing them from further blackmail. She could make some amends for her part in Bones's blackmail scheme.

She knew that Grae planned to sail in about a week. The cargo was due soon and once it was on board, the ship would be ready. And she would be on it.

With her mind made up, Arista made her way to the street. She had only gone a few steps when a carriage pulled up alongside her. "A lovely evening for a stroll," Wild said from the window. "Did everything go well with Lord Raffer?" Raffer. So that was the despicable man's name. She tried to keep her face as neutral as possible. If Wild had any inkling that she intended to deceive him, this night would not end well for her.

"Yes, he gave me his payment." She stepped closer and handed Wild the small bag through the opening. She heard the unmistakable jingling of coins, and then Wild handed her half of tonight's money. Tucking it safely in her reticule, she started to move past the carriage.

"I have arranged a meeting for one week from now—a new client who is very interested in meeting Lady A. He has indicated that masks won't be necessary." A thin line of white smoke drifted from the window of the carriage.

Arista's feet froze to the ground. No mask? "That's not how it works."

"The meeting will be held in a discreet place, I assure you, so you don't have to worry that anyone else will see you."

"Why?" Something didn't feel right. Anyone dealing with Lady A had no need to see her face to conduct business. Not unless they had ulterior motives.

"He simply wishes to see the face of the woman he does business with. As I said, your safety is my utmost concern." His bored tone told her more than his words did. Her safety did not interest him at all.

"No. If what you said is true, if this is a real partnership, then I have a say in how things work, correct? Or is this where you reveal your true colors, and I find you are no better than Bones?" It was a bold move, calling him out on the promise that he'd made her at Lady Carstair's party. He would either prove to be a liar and demand she do as he bid her, or he would relent.

Wild leaned out the window. She did not miss the steely glint in his eyes. "This is a very *lucrative* offer. You could have the money you need to go to India after only a few meetings. Isn't that your goal?"

The ground beneath her feet shifted, and Arista stumbled. How did he know about that? She had only ever talked about it with Becky and Nic. And Grae. *In public—several times now.* The air left her lungs in a soft whoosh.

He chuckled, a dark sound that made her cringe. "I have ears everywhere, Lady A. London belongs to me, and I know everything that goes on in it. It really would be foolish to pass up this opportunity. If we both get what we want, we can conclude our partnership."

The tiny tic in the corner of his mouth gave away his lie. He had no intention of letting her go. But she had no intention of staying. It was only a matter of time before one of them would betray the other.

Play along. Let him think he has you.

She gave an exaggerated sigh. "How much is he offering?"

"More than the rest put together." His smile told her everything. He thought he'd won already. She would need to fit in as many meetings as she could before Grae's ship left, in order to collect enough money to put this life behind her.

She was to meet Wild's new client in a week. It was scarcely enough time to enact her plan, but it had to work. "It's not as though I have any other choice, do I?" she said.

"Oh, there are always choices, my dear," he answered pleasantly. "But I trust you will make the wise one. I will send instructions for the meeting's place and time." Arista jumped back as the carriage sprang forward and disappeared into the night.

She would begin sending notes tomorrow, and by the time Wild sent for her to meet with this mystery person, she would be on a ship heading far away from London.

CHAPTER 15

The very next morning, Arista sent out a dozen notes, the addressees carefully chosen based on their ability to pay quickly—only familiar names, those she knew were well off. Time could not be wasted with those who did not have the means to meet her offer quickly.

Those others would receive their letters after she set sail. There would be no demand for money, only their secrets returned, free and clear. Yes, she could make demands of all of them—threaten to expose their secrets—but then she would be no better than Bones or Wild.

She was not like them. She would not cause fear and pain for profit. Not anymore.

They may have set their own blackmail in motion by contacting Bones in the first place, but desperation caused a good many people to make bad choices. People like Grae's father, who years later was still being manipulated. No, she would end everything before she left. And if they chose to move back into that world, well, she couldn't be the one to help them.

Grae had meetings with suppliers most of the day, preparing for his upcoming trip, so she didn't have to worry about him showing up unexpectedly as she snuck out. She didn't want to have to lie to him anymore.

By midday she had already heard back from six people who wanted to meet immediately; all promised her the sum she requested. Three hundred pounds each. The amount would be a pittance to those who could afford to pay so much more than she demanded for their secrets.

Four others wanted to meet her tomorrow morning. That left only two she had not yet heard back from. They were to meet her on Fleet Street at staggered times. An hour was all she needed. She had no desire to dally, and neither would these people.

At noon, she tucked the six chosen packets into her pocket and told Becky only that she had a job to do. Her friend knew better than to ask questions. Arista snuck out through the garden exit. The midday sun sat high in the sky, and she was sweating in her black mourning dress within minutes. Every so often she stopped to make sure that no one was following.

The veil over her face held in the heat, and sweat beaded on her skin as she walked to the next street over. From there she hailed a hackney cab. It was even hotter inside the carriage, yet she didn't dare open the shade covering the window, or even lift the veil farther than her nose. In the light of day, even with her disguise, discretion was of the utmost importance. No one could know what she was doing. Especially not Wild.

When they reached their destination, a busy but discreet inter-section, Arista held her breath until she heard the impatient knock. The door opened, and a man climbed in and sat across from her. The space inside the carriage seemed to shrink.

"Do you have it?" he asked.

Arista nodded and pulled out the packet of secrets that belonged to him. It was one of the thicker ones, as Lord Sommersville had used Bones's services more than once.

He reached into his jacket and removed a bag of coins. "Three hundred pounds, as agreed." They made the exchange and Sommersville did not bother with niceties. He exited the carriage before she had even tucked the money away.

The other five transactions were almost exactly the same. No one wanted to spend a second longer in her company than necessary, and in less than an hour, she was on her way back to Talbot Street. When she returned, Sophia insisted they spend the day together, and Arista didn't mind the shopping at all. Spending time with Sophia, learning how a normal girl spent her days, was quite nice. In fact, Arista had a rather good time when she was with Sophia. And if Grae had found out anything about Louis, he had not mentioned it to her; by the way Sophia's disposition never wavered, Arista doubted Grae had said anything to her either.

Days like today gave Arista hope that a better future was within reach.

The next day, the remaining four exchanges went as smoothly as the first half dozen. By the time she returned to the Sinclairs' and tucked the collected money into the small chest she had bought, a weight was gone from her shoulders. She only had to arrange passage on Grae's ship, and everything would be ready.

Except she had not seen Grae to ask him.

Sophia said he and her father were trying to woo a new client and that they were terribly busy, but there was a mischievous sparkle in Sophia's eyes that didn't quite fit with her explanation.

When they returned home from their second afternoon of shopping, Sophia followed Arista to her room. The girl was practically bouncing off of the walls, and Arista knew that something was going on. She didn't have to wait long to find out.

There on her bed lay a beautiful light blue gown. It was much fancier than any day dress Arista owned now, and she could only stare at it in wonder.

Sophia clapped her hands together. "Do you like it? It was one of mine, but you are smaller than me, so Becky spent two days altering it to fit you. I do so hope it fits, because the color will be exquisite with the shade of your skin." Sophia lifted the dress off the bed and held it up in front of Arista. "I knew it," she beamed.

"It's very beautiful, but I don't understand. I have no need of a dress this fine." Still, she could not resist reaching out to run her fingers along the silky material. Tiny beads had been sewn along the neckline in the pattern of flowers. The dress was truly fit for a queen.

Sophia giggled. "You can't go to the opera in a day dress, silly."

"Opera? We're going to the opera?" She had been to the theater once, when Nic paid one pence apiece so they could stand in the back and watch *Romeo and Juliet*. It had been crowded and sweaty, and she had barely glimpsed the actors who spoke such beautiful words with all the other people standing in front of her.

And still, it had been one of the best nights of her life.

But the opera?

Those productions only happened at King's Theatre, where the wealthy liked to go. She never dreamed she might see the inside of such place, let alone watch an actual performance there.

"Grae will go mad when he sees you in this dress," Sophia gushed. "And I have just the combs to wear with it."

"Grae is going, too?" Would Sophia and Robert and Marguerite also join them?

"Grae is taking *you* to the opera, dear Ana. He enlisted my help in getting everything that you would need ready. He'll be here at seven to pick you up."

"You're not coming?" Arista asked, still in shock. The opera. With Grae. Just the two of them together?

"I don't think my brother would appreciate my presence tonight." Sophia grinned. "Come. We'll have tea, and then I'll send for a bath and Becky will help you get ready." Sophia carefully set the dress back on the bed and Arista followed her blindly to the parlor. It was as though she were walking through a dream.

They would be alone tonight in a crowd of hundreds. She would be exposed and vulnerable, at Grae's side, dressed only as herself. Well, herself in an exquisite gown.

She wanted to take Grae's breath away tonight, and she had a feeling that Sophia would not let her down. Arista smiled, feeling giddy.

"For what it's worth," Sophia said, taking her hand, "I think that you and Grae are perfect together. I've never seen him happier on land."

CHAPTER 16

Arista sat in the parlor, nervously twisting her gloved fingers together. The dress flared out from her hips, accentuating her small waist, which both Becky and Sophia had exclaimed over. Lace lined her décolletage, but the dress still showed off more flesh than any of her other dresses. Sophia assured her that it was the current style, and that it was actually modest compared to most others.

Her new friend had given her stockings with garters, and beautiful shoes in the same delicate blue color. Becky had fashioned a wrap from a darker blue material that Sophia said Grae had given her after his last trip. There were intricate designs embroidered into the silk, creating a stunning pattern of birds and flowers. Her hair had been pulled away from her face and held in place with a jeweled comb, again borrowed from Sophia at her insistence. Everything had come together, and Arista felt like a princess.

Sophia sat across from her, eyes shining with excitement. Becky kept darting forward to fiddle with a flyaway strand of hair, or smooth out a wrinkle on the silk that didn't exist.

"You're both making me very nervous," Arista said, toying with the fan that was tied around one wrist.

Preparing for an evening of Lady A was nothing like this.

"Grae!" Sophia shouted.

Arista turned slowly and her gaze met Grae's. He wore black trousers with black stockings. His shoes gleamed in the candle-light. The charcoal-grey vest fit him perfectly, and over it he wore a jacket of the same color with buttons running down each side of the lapel. Snow-white cuffs peeked out from each sleeve.

He had not powdered his hair, nor worn a wig as fashionable men did. His black hair fell over one eye, giving him that rakish highwayman look she had first fallen for. He took her breath away.

Though Sophia had gone over to him, Grae had not taken his eyes off Arista. She stood slowly, suddenly feeling unsure. Was it too much? Not enough?

"Isn't she beautiful, Grae?" Sophia asked slyly.

"Indeed." His voice seemed lower, hoarser than she remembered, and it sent thrills of excitement over her skin. He was practically glowing with happiness and unabashed appreciation. He moved into the room and took her hand, raising it to his lips to kiss the back of her glove.

"Truly a vision. I will be the envy of every man there." Arista felt a blush climb up to her cheeks. "Are you ready to go?" He offered her his arm and she slid hers through it. Her heart thumped against her chest. This somehow felt different than the past month they'd spent together. More intimate, even though they were not alone.

"Good night, you two," Sophia sang. Grae chuckled and led Arista out to where Tomas waited.

Tonight they were using the Sinclairs' closed carriage. She and Grae would be inside together. Alone. Again, her pulse leapt.

Arista glanced over at Grae and found him still watching her. "What?" she finally asked.

"I thought you were breathtaking before, but tonight, I have no words. . . . You are exquisite, Arista." Heat burned in his eyes.

"You look quite handsome yourself. I'm sure there will be more than one lady vying for your attention."

"I've only got eyes for the one that happens to be with me." They climbed into the carriage and Tomas closed the door. As soon as he did, Grae leaned across and kissed her. He cupped her face with both hands and she gripped both his wrists.

If they stayed right there for the entire evening, she'd be perfectly happy. But the carriage jerked forward and Grae sat back, a satisfied smile on his face.

"I can't believe you arranged all of this. It's kind of overwhelming. No one has ever done anything like this for me before."

"Someone should do something like this every day of your life," he said. Arista ducked her head. "My compliments embarrass you?"

"I'm just not used to it," she admitted.

"I plan on changing that." He took her hand and held it all the way to King's Theatre. When Tomas opened the door and assisted Arista out, it was as if she'd stepped into another world. She had been to the Haymarket Theatre before with Nic, but it was nothing compared to the grandeur of King's Theatre. Arista walked in on Grae's arm amongst the grandest ladies of London. She held her head up high and swallowed the nerves that made her stomach tumble. No one knew who she was. They only saw a girl on the arm of a very handsome gentleman—if they even noticed her at all. There were so many breathtaking people there, both men and women, that Arista felt plain next to them.

"You're still the most beautiful," Grae whispered in her ear, as if he knew her thoughts.

As they stepped inside, a man in white gloves handed Grae a program. *Alessandro.* "What's it about?" she asked Grae.

He only smiled. "You'll see."

As they made their way closer, Arista couldn't help but be impressed—not only with the people and their attire, but with the opera house itself.

She ran her fingers over the intricate carvings that ran along the walls. As the two of them moved with the crowd, Arista felt at ease. This was so unlike the masquerades where people knew who she was—knew her reputation, and hated her for it. Tonight she was anonymous. It felt wonderful. Free.

She smiled shyly at Grae, who had not taken his eyes off her. How would she ever thank him for this?

They made their way slowly through a sea of brightly colored silk and satin, of wigs so high Arista feared they would topple off. She tightened her hold on Grae to keep herself grounded when they finally entered the main room. On either side of the stage, the boxes rose four stories high. People moved about in them, peering down at the crowd on the ground floor through glinting opera glasses.

The boxes held the most distinguished Londoners. Only the wealthiest had box seats: the dukes and duchesses, barons, earls, and of course, the King. Grae led them to two seats just five rows away from the orchestra pit. Around them people talked and laughed while Arista tilted her head back and stared at the painted horses and chariot flying through the clouds above.

Her chest tightened. This was the most perfect moment of her life, and she had Grae to thank for it. Her vision grew watery. Never in her life had she ever expected to meet someone like him.

He gave her hope and he didn't even realize it.

A hush fell over the crowd, and everyone rose to their feet. Arista stood up with them. Grae leaned close. "The King has arrived." He pointed to the very top row of boxes, the one in the center. King George stood at the rail, nodding his head at the crowd below.

Arista struggled to take a breath. She was in the same room as the King of England. A woman moved to his side and waved down at the crowd.

"That's Ehnrengard Melusine von der Schulenburg, Duchess of Kendal—the King's longtime mistress," he whispered. Her eyes widened. The King brought his mistress to the opera? Of course Arista knew the rumors, that the Queen had been exiled to a far-away land years ago. And yet here they were at the opera, as if nothing was unusual about any of it. A short laugh broke free from her throat.

Grae turned, his eyes shining with happiness. "You like this?" he asked.

"I have no words." She leaned in close so that she could whisper in his ear. "I'm in the same room as the King." Then she laughed again.

"Indeed you are. And this is only the start. Look, it's about to begin." He motioned toward the stage, where the giant red curtains were starting to move.

The King sat, then everyone else followed suit. Murmurs died down to whispers. The curtain lifted.

Immediately they were thrown into battle on stage, and Arista's heartbeat did not slow for the next three hours. She sat transfixed as she watched the story of Alexander the Great. Arista traveled with him to India; suffered the betrayal and treachery of his closest allies; cheered on the two women who vied for his love, until finally he chose Roxana; and fought alongside him in a final battle, emerging victorious.

Though she didn't understand the words they sang, the story came alive on the stage. Every note sank into her very bones and stirred a storm of emotion in her that grew wilder with each passing minute. By the time the actors took their elaborate bows, her face was shining with tears. She was exhausted, not from the time spent sitting, but from the passionate longing that gripped her body as she watched the story play out.

She had held Grae's hand the whole time and when she glanced over, she saw he was watching her, too. "That was . . ." Her breath caught on a soft sob. "That was amazing," she whispered.

He lifted her hand to his lips. "I thought you would like to see a glimpse of India, even if it's only on a stage."

"I can't believe you did this for me." Fresh tears ran down her face, but instead of being embarrassed at this show of raw emotion, she felt even freer. Grae had given her so much in the past week, but the most important thing had been hope. And she loved him for it.

She felt as if she were walking on air as they made their way back to the carriage.

Once inside, she pulled their entwined hands to her cheek, then turned and pressed her lips to the palm of his hand. She heard his sharp intake of breath; saw the way his eyes burned with passion.

She was caught in his gaze and could not look away. There were so many promises in his eyes, begging her to open up and trust him. And she wanted to, more than anything. Because she did trust him—with her entire heart.

"Arista," he murmured, tugging her closer. He brushed his lips over her cheek, and she felt the kiss down to her toes. "Come with me to India so that I can show you what it really looks like. So we can see it together. Please say you will." His whispered plea washed across the sensitive part of her ear and she shivered. "I can't bear the thought of being away from you for months and months."

She could not say no now, even if she had not planned on leaving London.

"I had planned to buy passage on your ship. To go with you if you would let me."

"You can have my cabin." His eyes glowed with excitement.

"Your mother would faint away at the idea, Grae." Even though Arista had no need for the constraints or propriety of the wealthy, there were rules that people like Grae had to follow. "I can buy separate passage . . ."

"Then marry me," he said.

Her startled gaze flew to his face to see if this was a cruel joke. The sudden acceleration of her pulse threatened to send her heart straight out of her chest.

"What?" she whispered.

"Marry me, beautiful girl. I can't imagine anyone else I'd rather spend my life with. We can sail the world, have all the adventures you want, together. I'm in love with you, if you didn't know that by now."

So many emotions crowded in her throat that it became impossible to take a full breath. Tears filled her eyes and she blinked rapidly to keep them from spilling over. This was so much more than she'd ever allowed herself to dream of that it completely overwhelmed her.

Unable to make her voice work, and almost afraid of what she'd say if she could, she nodded her acceptance.

CHAPTER 17

*L*ord Ellington stood in a shadowy alcove near the string quartet. He had not arrived in costume, didn't even have a mask on. He didn't appear uncomfortable at all as he watched the disguised partygoers.

Arista stood near the patio, where the doors were opened to let in the fresh evening air. He had arrived five minutes earlier, with a few other guests who were trickling in. She had requested the meeting at ten, to allow her to return home unnoticed.

This was it, her last exchange. After tonight, she would have time to fully realize what Grae had offered her in the carriage. Thinking about it sent a fissure of pleasure and fear through her body. Marriage? An absurd and foreign idea for someone like her.

And yet she could not stop the smile each time she thought about it.

Ellington scanned the sparse room and his gaze came to rest on her. He had picked her out, even in her widow's garb. Impressive. She stared back, then inclined her head once to let him know she was, in fact, Lady A.

Ellington made his way across the room, his strides long and purposeful. Of all the clients that she'd dealt with when working for Bones, Ellington had been the most unusual—as if he didn't care much that he had to give up one of his secrets to get a secret. The overall exchange had been quite pleasant as well, with Ellington kissing her hand and thanking her before she left. As if he were a suitor, and not being blackmailed.

Even now, as he got closer, Arista could see that the lines of tension or anger, so normal in her line of work, were not there on his face. He looked a little bored, but not angry.

"Good evening, my lady." He came to a stop in front of her and lifted her hand to his lips. "I must say, your invitation took me quite by surprise. I had expected to remain indebted to you for this lifetime, at least. Not that it would be a hardship." He grinned when he said it, and his gaze dropped to her décolletage.

"Thank you for meeting me on such short notice, Lord Ellington," she said, directing his stare back up to her face. "My note said it all. I'm willing to give back your secret, and you will be free from any further obligation."

"For three hundred pounds." He quirked one eyebrow and this time she smiled.

"Yes, for three hundred pounds. A bargain, you'll have to agree."

"I'm curious as to this sudden change in strategy. It seems . . . short-sighted, in the grand scheme of trading secrets for secrets. Even you must see the folly in this plan?"

"It was never my plan, Lord Ellington. I was merely a player. And I now have the ability to set things as right as I can."

He raised an eyebrow. "Interesting."

She reached into her reticule and pulled out his letter.

"I admit I had thought this all a ruse to get me here and demand something more." He reached inside his jacket and pulled out a bag of coins. "Would you like to count it first?"

"There is no need." She took the bag and at the same time put the letter into his hand. It would not matter if he shorted her several pounds. She had money. With what she had collected already and what she had from Wild, she had enough now. "Thank you, Lord Ellington."

He stared at her, a bemused smile on his lips. "I would ask you to dance, and perhaps offer to escort you home after a whirlwind evening, but I am averse to rejection, and can see on your face that you do not harbor a similar curiosity about me."

Lord Ellington was still flirting with her? After everything that had happened?

"Thank you for the flattering offer." And she *was* very flattered. But she only ever wanted to dance with Grae. Only ever wanted his hands on her.

Ellington smiled and bowed. "I find I am almost saddened to be freed from your web, Madame Spider. If you find yourself in need of . . . anything . . . in the future, you have but to ask." He lifted her hand and she didn't miss the way his lips lingered a few seconds longer than was proper. "Good evening to you, my lady. I wish you luck."

With a slight bow and a genuine smile, he left her there on the patio.

Arista watched him until he was out of sight. Elation slowly filled her body. She couldn't stop the smile that spread over her face. She had done it. She had actually done it. In two days' time, she would be on board Grae's ship, sailing away from London for good. If Grae were here with her, she would dance until her feet were too sore to move another step.

Grae. Arista wrapped her arms around her middle and hugged herself. Grae was waiting for her; they would leave together. It was almost too good to be true. She pinched herself, and laughed.

Several curious glances were thrown her way, and she didn't even care. Tonight marked the end of Lady A. The end of her life as a thief. Of being controlled by those who only thought to use her.

A hush fell over the crowd, and Arista looked up. A woman dressed in glittering turquoise silk stood midway up the grand staircase, watching the guests. People called out and she waved, making the bouquet of peacock feathers bounce and dip. It had to be Lady Amanda, Lord Luckette's daughter. Arista had seen her only once before, at a different masquerade ball. She had a reputation for promiscuity.

The lady's eyes momentarily settled on someone, and Arista followed her gaze. A darkly clad man stood in a plain black mask along the perimeter of the room. Looking around, Arista could see at least three more dressed exactly the same, spaced evenly throughout the room. Alarm shot through her body.

The Watch? The ones in charge of upholding the law and finding criminals. They were known to be ruthless in dispensing justice, and only their word was needed to send someone to Newgate for life. Arista shivered. There had been many close calls with the Watch when she was younger. Several of the children she had lived with had been hauled away by them, never to be seen again.

The threat of the Watch was only one hazard of their jobs as pickpockets, though. And Bones's wrath was a worse fate; so each day, they took the chance of getting caught.

Had Wild sent them for her? Though the Watch and the Thief Taker General were separate posts, she knew many of the Watch were also on Wild's payroll. According to the rumors, at least.

Sweat trickled down the back of her neck. It was time to leave anyway.

Arista skirted the darkened edges of the room, toward the door where she had entered earlier. One of the Watch stood between her and the doors. Had he stared at her a little too long? She forced her steps to slow. The man looked away and Arista moved past, exhaling in relief.

Until a hand shot out of the dark and pulled her into a secluded alcove.

She whirled around, and her knife was out and pressed against the offender's throat in one fluid movement.

"I see some things never change," Nic said with an easy grin.

The room suddenly dipped again and she grabbed his arm. Was he really there? *"Nic?"* She sheathed her knife and threw her arms around him. "Where have you been?"

He took a step back, looking around them. His eyes became guarded. "You got what I left for you, I see?"

"Yes."

"Not exactly the way I hoped you would use them, gypsy. Those secrets were to be a negotiating tool with Wild. To ensure he didn't try and double-cross you."

"How do you know about Wild?" She glanced around to see if anyone had noticed them talking. She pulled the veil up over her face so she could see him better. "What's going on, Nic?" She could read him as easily as she read everyone else. Guilt made the lines around his eyes and mouth heavier.

His voice lowered and he leaned in close. "Wild knows what you're doing, gypsy. He's had his eyes on you the whole time."

Thoughts slammed together in her head. Nic knew about Wild? About their deal? And Wild knew what she'd been up to?

She gasped. "You've been watching me?" Her heart slammed against her ribs, threatening to break free from her chest. No. No, it wasn't true. Nic would never betray her like that.

But his eyes, hooded with pain, refused to meet hers. Oh God . . . she was going to be sick. She covered her mouth and pushed outside into the fresh night air.

Her stomach tightened and her throat burned as she leaned over a hedge. When the convulsions stopped, her body ached. She glanced over her shoulder to where Nic stood just behind her.

"Nic?" she said desperately. "Please tell me that it wasn't you feeding him the information."

"I'm sorry, gypsy." His voice sounded strained and tight. "You don't understand."

The floor could have opened up and swallowed her, and it would have been less of a surprise.

"You're working for him? How long?" The words caught in her constricted throat, and she desperately swallowed the sob building there. This was Nic. Her best friend. She had trusted him.

He dragged his fingers through his hair, inhaling through his teeth with a sharp hiss. "You know it's always been about the money for me. I'm not good, like you. Wild came to me months ago, offered me a position in his operation. We'd break into a few houses, take some valuables, and then those rich bastards would pay Wild to 'find' their stolen belongings. Wild knew about you— knew that I escorted Lady A to her meetings. He wanted to meet you, so I set up the meeting with Wild at Lady Carstair's. Left the note for Becky to find."

Rage burned through her veins. She took a step closer and pressed her fingertips against his chest. "You set me up. I almost died that night. *Becky* almost died."

He met her agonized stare. "That wasn't supposed to happen. I was coming back for you, I swear. Wild was going to meet us in the alley, but I got tied up with something else and ran late that night. When I finally got there, the building was on fire, and had been burning for hours. I was sure nobody was alive in there. I didn't know Wild saved you until almost a week later. I wanted to see you, but he said you'd agreed to work with him, and he wanted me to stay low."

It all fell into place with sickening clarity. The heat inside her vanished, replaced with a heavy coldness that seeped into her bones. Wild had known where Nic was the whole time. He had never looked for him—didn't need to—because Nic was working for Wild. Long before the fire.

Nic knew how much she valued the little freedom she had, and how much she wanted to get out of this life. He'd basically indentured her to Wild without her even knowing.

"I didn't give you all those secrets so that you could just give them all back. Damn it, gypsy, you were supposed to use them to negotiate with Wild. To solidify your partnership with him. To make sure he didn't set you up."

He ran agitated fingers through his hair again and glared at the space behind her.

"Secrets destroy people," she said. "I'm tired of being a part of that."

Nic scrubbed a hand over his face. "They deserve it. You always thought so, too. Those rich bastards who think they own the world—they deserve everything they get for being greedy."

"I'm done, Nic. I'm getting out. I don't want this life anymore. It's killing me from the inside."

"It will kill you from the outside, too, gypsy. Wild won't let you double-cross him. Did you think you'd just disappear after you agreed to work with him? You think *Bones* was vengeful? I promise that anything he did to us would pale in comparison to what Wild is capable of." His voice turned low and urgent. "He already knows what you're doing, gypsy, but you have one small advantage. He doesn't know that I've told you. He won't expect you to try and run yet. That's why you need to get out of here."

A sob caught in her throat and she stiffened when he pulled her close. The arms that had once been so familiar were like a stranger's. His drawn-out sigh brushed across her ear. There were no spikes of excitement, no goose bumps now.

"I'm sorry. I thought I was finding you a way out." He sounded so lost that for a minute, she believed him.

"Come with me," she said desperately. "There's still a chance for you, too."

Nic shook his head and chuckled, a dark sound that sent shivers down her spine. "You should know by now that I'm a thief, through and through. I love this life, gypsy, just as much as you hate it."

"I've got passage on a ship in two days," she admitted.

Nic shook his head. "That's not soon enough. I mean it—you have to get out of London tonight."

"I'll hide. He won't find me. I know how to go unnoticed."

A sad smile crooked his lips. "*Everyone* notices you, gypsy, you just don't see it. Go to the ship's captain. See if you can board early, and then don't leave your quarters. I'll see if I can distract Wild long enough for you to sail."

"Are you sure you won't come with me?" He shook his head. "Be safe then, Nic. And thank you for keeping me safe all this time. Without you, I would never have made it."

Nic leaned close and gently kissed her lips. It was a goodbye. The kind that said, *I'll never see you again.* Tears danced in her eyes.

"Goodbye, Nic," she whispered. Unable to be near him anymore, knowing that this was the end, Arista spun around and started for the doors. Her vision was watery and she almost didn't see the member of the Watch that stood just to the side of her exit.

She expected him to reach out and stop her as she passed, but he barely glanced her way.

It took her an hour to navigate the dark streets and return to the townhouse. Several times, she had the feeling she was being followed, but doubling back and waiting revealed no one. It had to be her own paranoid mind working against her.

She would pack tonight—sneak out before anyone knew she was gone.

Maybe leave a note for the Sinclairs, thanking them for their hospitality and mentioning she had left London by coach. It might buy her enough time to keep Wild from looking for her at the docks, at least until they sailed. Exhilaration and dread and sadness all mixed in her chest. She hated to lie to Marguerite and Robert, but there was no other way.

The garden was dark as she snuck through it. In her room, she pulled off her black wool dress and slipped into a dark blue day dress that did not need to be laced tightly. Over it she wore a dark grey traveling cloak.

She pulled out two dresses from the wardrobe. Neither was remarkable. She laid them on the bed and folded them, then carefully rolled them up to take advantage of the limited space. Becky

would not be pleased at her handling of them after her careful iron-
ing, but, with a pang, Arista realized the girl would never know.

Next, Arista pulled stockings and undergarments from the
drawer and slid them into the bag next to the dresses. She would
wear the sturdy gypsy boots under her dress; they were new enough
that she could get a lot of wear out of them.

Satisfied that she had what she needed, Arista set the bag on the
floor and crept to the door. She pressed her ear to the wood and
listened. No one moved outside the room. Becky slept in the room
with Sara, so she could not chance waking Sophia's maid.

Tomorrow first thing, she would ask Grae to send for Becky,
before Wild might find her.

She opened the door and walked into something that had been
placed on the threshold. It was a medium-sized box, with a note on
top. It didn't weigh much at all, and Arista carried it back into her
room and set it on her bed. On the front of the note, someone had
written *Ana* in flowing script. Whatever it was, it was meant for her.
She tugged the note free and unfolded it.

> *My dear Ana,*
>
> *I saw you admiring this when we were shopping and*
> *thought it would suit you beautifully. You may find it*
> *useful in the coming weeks.*
>
> *Your friend always, Sophia*

Arista set the note aside and undid the ribbon. Inside the box,
wrapped in several layers of tissue paper, sat a bonnet. It was the
same one she'd seen earlier, dark blue with a lighter blue ribbon
woven along the edge. How had Sophia known *that* was the one
she'd found most appealing? How had she even remembered one

overlong glance? It had been nothing more than a pause as she'd waited for Sophia to finish talking to Tomas.

She took it from the box and went to the mirror. Somehow it fit in a way that made the edges of her short hair curl up around it, framing her face. The color brought out the blue in her eyes, and when she tied the ribbon under her chin, it accentuated her cheek-bones. She might even pass for middle-class, a merchant's daughter like Sophia.

Could Arista's father have been a shipmaster, or maybe a watch-maker? Did he used to have a shop on Cheapside or Lombard, or any other number of streets filled with merchants? The past weeks had shown her what life might have been like had she grown up with a real family—because in truth, she did feel like she was part of the Sinclair family now.

Arista set the box aside and tucked the note into her pocket. She would wear the bonnet on her trip. A reminder of everything Sophia had done for her. And when they got to India, she would find the perfect gift to send back to her new friend.

With her bag tucked tightly against her chest, Arista opened the inside door and crept toward Mr. Sinclair's office. The note and bag of coins were heavy in her hand, but she had to be sure that if Becky chose to leave, she would be taken care of. She trusted that Grae's father would see that Becky got the money Arista left for her. A shadow moved at the end of the hallway; she couldn't see who it was. Probably just Wilson or Jane.

"Hello?" she whispered.

"Who the hell is that?" She heard the slight slur in the man's words, but she recognized Grae's father. He stumbled, then swore.

"It's Ari—Ana. It's Ana."

"Ah yes, my *guest*. Do you drink, Ana? I could damned well use another, and since you're awake, we can toast the man that made this all possible." She didn't miss the contempt in his voice. Or the anger.

There was a scratching sound, then a flare of light. The scent of sulfur made its way down the hall. In the circle of light, Arista could see him now. His hair stood up everywhere, as if he'd run his fingers through it over and over again. He'd taken off his jacket, and his shirt was half untucked.

In the light, Arista clearly saw his pained features. He looked defeated. "No thank you," she said.

He grunted as if he didn't really believe her. "Blast it, I'll drink enough for the both of us. Well, anyway . . ." He stumbled, and the candle tilted precariously to the side.

Arista hurried down the hall and took it from him. "What would your wife say if you burned the house down around her?" She only meant to lighten the mood, but he covered his face with his hands.

"She would probably wish I would perish with it."

Arista awkwardly patted his arm. She had no idea how to comfort someone. Usually she ran away from drunken men. "I'm sure that's not true."

He jerked his head up and glared at her. "Did you have anything to do with this?"

Arista took a step back from the anger simmering in his eyes. Liquor and anger were never a good combination. "I don't know what you're talking about." That only seemed to agitate him more.

He stumbled again and tried to focus on her face. Under the anger, she saw the raw agony. His eyes were full of it. "He is smuggling humans and he wants my ships to do it," he choked out. "The wickedest, most heinous—"

That made no sense. Wild wanted *what*? As repulsive as the man was, she didn't figure him a slave trader. "I don't understand."

"I made a deal with a man," he moaned. "Years ago, I agreed to use my ship to smuggle tea for him, in exchange for a choice India trading route. That's what allowed my fleet to grow so fast. I wanted to build something to leave for my son. The man had someone forge the bills of lading. For my risk in it, I was given better access routes. But now, that bastard wants me to transport slaves for some godless nobleman. I won't do it."

With a strangled groan, he pushed past her and staggered to his office door. Once inside the room, Arista heard something crash to the floor. She held the candle tightly as she hurried inside. He sat sprawled in the chair, holding a glass full of amber liquid. The sharp smell of brandy filled her lungs. On the floor at his feet lay the decanter, its fragments reflecting the candlelight. A puddle spread closer to the thick Oriental rug.

"Should I get Wilson?" she asked.

He looked at her from over the rim of the glass. "No one can help me now. I made a deal with the devil, and he's finally come to collect." With that, he tipped the glass back and downed the entire contents in one loud swallow. "I don't know what to do."

His eyes drifted closed and Arista waited. After several moments, she decided to leave him alone. Someone would find him in the morning and clean up the mess. There was very little time for her to get to the docks and get on a ship.

Arista picked up the candlestick, afraid he might knock it over and start a fire, and took it to the massive desk. Her boots were silent on the thick rug. Papers were scattered all over his desk. How did he find anything in that mess?

She held up the candle and leaned in closer when she noticed several maps laid out, with dotted lines extending from land mass to land mass. Each had a piece of parchment on top, and in tidy writing, lists of goods beneath what must be the ship's name.

Her pulse leapt when she saw Grae's name at the top of one list, under the name *The Marguerite Heart*. She traced the letters of his name with her finger. Her gaze drifted over the room, settling on the wall to the right. There were paintings hanging there, and when she moved the candle closer, she saw that they were portraits. Grae and Sophia as young children, posing with a spotted dog at their feet. Mrs. Sinclair and Grae's father, his hand on her shoulder as she sat in a red chair. Grae, older now, standing in front of a three-masted ship. She stopped at that one. It was the same ship that she'd been on. The artist had managed to capture the seriousness of his expression, but also the sparkle of happiness in his eyes. Pride.

It was a look she knew well.

Arista set the candle down on the desk, careful to move a stack of papers well out of the flame's reach, then crept back toward the door. She must have made a sound that woke Grae's father, for he opened his eyes and stared blindly at her. "No matter what he offers you, he still owns you in the end. He controls us all like marionettes."

Arista froze. "What?"

His eyes became a little bit clearer and he tried to push himself upright in the chair. "His promises mean nothing. Be careful or he will suck you down to the depths of hell alongside him."

"Who are you talking about?" She already knew.

"The man who sent you here. The man who ruined all our lives. That bastard, Wild. I won't do it—I won't be party to humans being sold like cattle. Never . . ." Before she could ask anything more, his eyes closed, and the back of his head hit the chair. Soft snores came from his half-open mouth. His hand fell to his side, and a piece of crumpled paper fell to the floor.

Arista stooped down to pick it up. Whatever had caused Grae's father to drink himself into darkness, she was sure it was written on that paper.

> *Mr. Sinclair,*
>
> *I now have within my possession proof of your smuggling activities in recent years. Don't bother to deny them—they are irrefutable. A certain mutual friend of ours has given me everything I need.*
>
> *You have turned me down before, but I now hold the future of your very livelihood in my hands. I will have access to your fastest ships at any convenience it serves me to transport my cargo. There will be no questions and there will be no denying me anymore. You will agree this time.*
>
> *Unless, of course, you are willing to give up your children's legacy and lose everything you have worked for. You will have nothing if I do not hear from you.*
>
> *Lord E. F. Raffer*

No. This could not be. But the dual R's imprinted in the red wax seal told her otherwise. She tried to take a step, but her legs would not support her. The knots in her stomach grew until it hurt to take a breath. The secret that Wild had given Raffer, the money exchanged—half of which was sitting in her traveling bag right that second—had been used to blackmail Grae's father into transporting slaves.

Innocent men, women, and children, kidnapped from Africa and sold into slavery. Nothing sickened her more than the trade that made some of England's wickedest men some of its richest. She'd played a part in this.

Tears burned her eyes and she crumpled the paper in her fist. Grae would never forgive her if he found out. No, *when* he did. Because he would. Her dreams shattered and fell around her feet. There would be no leaving London with Grae now.

How quickly could she arrange passage on another ship? Wild knew what she was doing. There was no more time. Her carefully thought-out plan was ruined.

Mr. Sinclair groaned in his sleep.

He was a good man, and she believed that he would deny Raffer what he wanted no matter the threat. If Raffer exposed Mr. Sinclair's previous smuggling activities, Grae's father would end up in Newgate with his livelihood taken away. With no ships, no trade routes, the family would have nothing. Grae would have no future.

She could not let that vile man destroy this good family. Even if she had to face the wrath of Wild, she had to save them. There were a dozen more secrets she might be able to offer to Wild in exchange for his help stopping Raffer. He was greedy. He'd see the value in that.

And she owed it to the family for treating her so well. For accepting her without question. She owed it to Grae. Because he'd showed her that she was worth something after all.

Soft snores still came from Grae's father. Maybe he couldn't fight Wild or Raffer, but someone could. She had no explanation for why determination burned so hotly in her chest, but there was one thing she knew for certain. "I promise I won't let this happen," she whispered to the unconscious man.

Arista hurried back to her room and tucked the bag into the wardrobe. She wrote a quick note for Becky, telling her where the chest of money was hidden. If she didn't return, she had to be sure that her friend was taken care of. She took the remaining letters and started to bundle them when one caught her eye. Lord Huntington. He'd blackmailed his way into a title that granted him a seat in Parliament. She could offer him a trade—give him back his secret, if he would spearhead an investigation into Raffer's business. It might be enough to stop Raffer.

She tucked Huntington's letter into a separate pocket from the rest. He'd been at the ball earlier. If she hurried, she might make it back in time to catch him.

To make him an offer he could not refuse.

CHAPTER 18

inding Lord Huntington proved easier than she
expected.

He was positioned at the buffet table, stuffing
his face with anything he could reach. The ridiculous jester vest seemed even tighter than it had been only a few
weeks ago. Arista made her way to his side, swallowing back revul-
sion at being so close to the man again.

"Lord Huntington," she said near his ear. He smelled of sweat
and sickly sweet cologne. He glanced at her, but there was no recog-
nition in his eyes. She had grabbed her gypsy mask before leaving
the Sinclair house, but still had on her traveling dress. It must have
made an odd combination.

"Who's asking?" he mumbled as crumbs fell from his lips.

"I believe I have something that used to belong to you." Arista
waved his letter in front of his face before tucking it back into her
pocket.

Huntington narrowed his eyes. "You have some nerve, girl.
There are men from the Watch all over the place, and you think

you can just show up and demand—what, more money?" Hatred glittered from his eyes. Arista moved away from the table, toward a quiet alcove. Huntington followed, scowling at her the whole time.

"I'm offering you an exchange. Your help, for the return of your information."

"What kind of help?" Clearly he did not trust her at her word.

"If you can start an investigation into Lord Raffer's activities concerning slave trading, I will give you your secret back and we will be done. You won't have to worry that I'll ask for anything else again."

Huntington licked his lips and eyed the pocket where she'd put the letter. "Never again?"

"You will never see me again—I can assure you."

A calculating look came over his face and he leaned closer. "I think I can help you get what you want. Stay here while I find a colleague of mine who might be interested in what you have to say. If I can get his cooperation, we have a deal."

"Twenty minutes. No more than that," she said.

Lord Huntington hurried away and Arista fought back the feeling of unease. Wild might be here, but he would not know her in this disguise. She had to remain vigilant. Alert. Being careful not to draw attention to herself, she started making her way around the room, keeping to the darkened edges.

When thirty minutes had passed, Arista sighed in frustration. She would have to negotiate with Wild after all. It had been a long shot at best, to hope that Huntington would be agreeable to a trade. The man hated her and made no secret of that fact. Now she would have to go to Covent Garden and confront Wild.

Just before she stepped outside to leave, a young servant tapped her shoulder. "This is for you, miss." He handed her a folded note, then faded into the crowd.

> *At the fountain. Have what you need.*
> *H*

Arista smiled in relief. She'd been wrong about Huntington. Now she could return to the Sinclairs' with assurance that the blackmail would not take place. She could finally tell Grae the truth about her part in all of it.

There were no guests outside. It was only just past midnight, and everyone was still too busy dancing. In the main circle of the garden, a huge stone fountain stood sentry. Water gurgled softly in the still night. Light spilled out from the open doors and illuminated the front of the stone basin, while deep shadows stretched out behind it.

She was close enough to the fountain to see that no one was waiting there. Huntington had lied. Then something caught her attention—a movement just past the enormous fountain, in the shadows there—and she moved toward it.

She reached for her knife, in case Huntington thought to trick her, but it wasn't there. Had she left it back at the Sinclairs' house when she'd changed? Had she become so accustomed to being normal that she'd really forgotten to wear her knife? Maybe the threat of it would be enough to keep Lord Huntington in line, if need be. The fountain was only a few steps away now.

Just as she reached the edge of the large bottom basin, she tripped and fell to the ground in a tangle of skirts and limbs. Tiny bits of gravel dug into her palms as she pushed herself onto her knees. It took a moment for her eyes to adjust to the dim light. The thing she had tripped over lay across the pathway, partially hidden in the shadows. She used her hands to feel her way to it. After the first brief touch, she froze.

A body was lying there.

Panic took hold of her. Her feet were unsteady as she stood and stumbled toward an ornate glass lantern that sat next to the patio steps. The hot glass burned her fingers, but she didn't feel it. Her entire focus was on the dark shape behind the fountain.

As soon as she set the light down, she saw the knife, *her knife*, protruding from the man's large, jewel-colored chest. Arista stared at the still form in horror.

It was Lord Huntington.

He had on the same ridiculous bright green jester costume as before, and the vest still strained the buttons in front. A bright red stain was spreading rapidly across the green material.

She had seen a figure moving by the fountain only minutes ago. Whoever attacked Huntington had been right there.

Arista leaned over the body and listened for a breath, tried to see if his chest rose or fell, but it was too hard to see in the dim light. She leaned in closer and finally realized that there was no sign of life left in the body, though it was still warm.

Her fingers came away from his chest sticky and warm. Blood. She hastily wiped her hands on her black dress. They shook uncontrollably. What should she do? Call for help? Slip away before anyone saw her? Her knife was in Huntington's body, but she didn't know why.

A twig cracked behind her.

Arista whirled around to meet the wide-eyed stare of Lady

Amanda Luckette. Her piercing scream filled the night. People poured out of the house. Four Watchmen ran to where Arista knelt. Two dragged her to her feet. Lanterns were held up, illuminating Arista and the grisly scene at her feet. Another man of the Watch knelt beside the body. "He's dead," the man said.

"It's Lord Huntington. She's killed Lord Huntington." The whispers flew through the crowd.

"It's Lady A." The voice came from the outskirts of the crowd, deep and familiar. Wild. Dread pooled in her stomach. Nic had warned her, but she'd thought she had time. "That's her. She once threatened me with a knife. That same knife in Huntington's chest!"

Mob mentality took over like wildfire.

"Lady A killed Lord Huntington."

"I knew this day would come."

"She's a bad one, deserves everything she gets."

The voices swirled around her as the men's grip tightened on her arms. The one who had knelt by the dead man came to stand in front of her. She shut her eyes against the lights and noise as he ripped the mask from her face. Gasps and more excited whispering followed.

"Who is it?"

"Who is she?"

"She's just a young girl?"

"A girl's been blackmailing *le bon ton* all along?"

Several more of the Watch pushed through the crowd. There were now half a dozen standing around her.

"Send for the coroner and get this crowd back inside," barked the one who'd unmasked her.

"I did nothing," Arista said in a strained whisper. "I found him like that."

The man sneered at her. "You were found with the body. No one else saw you. There is blood all over your hands. Your knife's been identified as the one sticking in the man's chest. That is more than enough evidence to see you hang." He leaned in closer, so close his rancid breath made her gag. "Do you know how many will be glad to see the infamous Lady A hang? And you *will* hang for this. I'll just take what's inside your pockets, too. *He* said he'd pay extra for 'em."

He pulled out the letters that she'd meant to return to their owners. The blood inside her veins turned to ice.

This man was on Wild's payroll.

Her heartbeat thumped dully in her ears. She stood exposed in front of all these people. It was over. It was all over. Frantically she scanned the crowd for help. Nic had warned her to leave, or something bad would happen. She'd never dreamed she'd be exposed for all of society to see. To be framed for murder. Her knees buckled and, if not for the guards, she would have sunk to the ground.

Nic.

No.

Again she searched the departing faces, but there were no allies to be found. Several of the men Lady A had had dealings with looked nervous, like she would spill their secrets right there in the garden, but most of the faces she saw were cold.

No one would help Lady A. Not when they had been waiting for this very moment.

"Bring round the carriage," the man in charge snapped.

Pain shot through her arms as the guards twisted them behind her back and pushed her forward. Her toe caught a rock and she stumbled, sending a fresh sharp stab of agony through her arms.

She fought back a wave of nausea at the pain radiating through her limbs.

One of the men pulled a length of rope from the carriage, and for one panicked second she thought they meant to hang her right there in the street. She fought against the hands holding her, but there were too many, and they were much stronger than her. They lashed her hands together behind her back, so tightly that the rough rope instantly chafed the skin on her wrists, creating a new kind of torture.

"I didn't do anything," she said to the men around her. They only laughed.

With her hands tied, only one of the Watch was needed to control her now, and he shoved her roughly through the open carriage door. Without the use of her hands, Arista stumbled and fell, landing hard on her shoulder.

More laughter sounded from outside the carriage before it dipped as another man from the Watch stepped inside. A single lantern hung from a hook in one corner, throwing sinister shadows onto his face as he watched her.

Arista pulled her knees as close to her body as she could and lay in a ball on the cold floor. The carriage took off with a lurch, and her head slammed into the hard wood of the seat. Stars danced in her vision. Each time the wheels hit a rut, the carriage rocked and spikes of pain drove into her body.

The guard watched her closely, as if he enjoyed the agony that was inflicted. He most likely did, as the Watch's reputation was not any better than that of the men Bones employed. It made her even more desperate not to show how much she was hurting.

By the time the carriage rolled to a stop, Arista could taste blood from biting her lip so hard. Tears were burning in her eyes, and her nose was running. She couldn't stop crying; her body seemed out of her control. The Watch man dragged her upright by her arm, and it was finally too much. Fire exploded in her shoulder.

A frantic sob escaped her lips. He held her there on her knees and grinned. Tiny lights danced in her vision, and she fought the darkness creeping in. Through her life, she had experienced pain, but nothing compared to the raw agony ripping her apart now.

The door opened and the man shoved her out. There was no way to brace herself. The cobblestones raced toward her head—

She refused to scream—

Arms caught her before she hit and dragged her to her feet. A huge stone building loomed up out of the darkness, and even from the street she could hear the shouts and screams coming from inside. Her blood ran cold. Looming above was the massive stone structure every thief in London feared. Most who went in never came out. It was a dark and desperate place.

When she refused to walk, they simply dragged her through the huge iron door at the front of Newgate Prison. A hulking figure stood just inside to meet them. He was easily six feet tall, and had arms as thick as tree trunks. He watched her without a trace of emotion.

"What do we do with this one?" the jailer asked.

"There is to be no trial. Hundred witnesses. She's to be hanged for murder at dawn."

CHAPTER 19

The Watch man yanked at the ropes. When they fell away, the blood returned to her fingers, causing prickles of pain each time she moved them. Angry red welts covered her skin where the rope had scraped.

"I'm not a murderer!" she said, but no one listened.

Instead, the jailer looked her up and down and grinned.

"I got just the room for her."

He pulled a pair of manacles off the wall and snapped them shut around her aching wrists. Thankfully he let her keep her hands in front of her body, with a small length of chain that allowed her to move, albeit in a limited manner.

"Fill out the paper there, listing her crime, and I'll be back." His keys jingled as he turned and led her through a maze of dimly-lit hallways.

The groans and screams were so much louder inside, and the stench—God, it was bad. Arista had to fight back the bile that rose to the back of her throat. Fingers reached through the holes in the iron doors they passed. The people inside hissed and growled like animals.

The jailer finally stopped and jammed his key into the lock of a door that looked like all the rest. "Here." When the door opened, he shoved her inside the dark room and she heard the door slam shut before she could even catch her balance. Arista stood in frozen terror.

She heard movement—scuffling sounds all around her—but could not see what made the noise. There were no lanterns in the room. She moved until the door was at her back, then slowly sank down until she sat, propped up, facing a room full of who-knows-what.

The walls echoed with tortured moans, and the stench inside the room overwhelmed her. The tears she had been fighting finally broke free and slipped down her cheeks unchecked. This had to be a nightmare. It could not be real.

Even as she repeated that to herself, the cold seeped up from the floor and chilled her to the bone. The one saving grace was that it made her too numb to feel any more pain, and she sat deathly still.

The room was about twice the size of the room Bones had kept her in. As her eyes grew accustomed to the dark, Arista could make out dozens of bodies sprawled across the floor.

At the far end of the room, a figure detached from the shadows and started toward her. A misshapen figure, walking with an awkward *shuffle-thump* gait. Arista pushed clumsily to her feet, trying to force the cold from her limbs, at least enough so that she could move if needed. Others were stirring awake now, and several sat up, rubbing their eyes until they saw her.

Arista pressed back against the steel door, but it would not give under the pressure. A scratching sound came from near her and Arista saw a young girl cowering in the corner. There was something so familiar about the look in her eyes. The fear. Arista took a step toward her, but the girl scrambled back until she had wedged herself in the corner. She had the look of a wild animal about her.

It was a look she remembered well.

"Are you a lady, then?" a different woman asked. She had on a dirt-stained shift and her feet were bare and black. Her hair had been nearly all chopped off, and stood out from her head in uneven peaks. "We don't get many hoity-toities in here. That dress would fetch me a nice hot meal." A gleam came into the woman's eyes as she stood.

Arista watched the woman warily. She'd had run-ins with people like her before. They weren't all there in the head, and that made them more dangerous than if they were in their right mind. Arista slowly wrapped the extra chain around her fingers.

The woman crept closer, licking her cracked lips.

The others would be no help—already they were cowering away from the crazy one. A low whimper came from the girl in the corner. Arista's stomach rolled. A sour taste coated the back of her tongue. It would not be the first time she had fought for what was hers. She could scream, but her voice would only be one among hundreds. No one would come to her aid here. She gripped the chain tight in her fist and waited. There would only be one chance to take the woman by surprise. The woman outweighed Arista by at least four stone.

"Time to pay up, your ladyship." The woman lunged at her. Arista waited until the woman's hand was almost at her neck before she swung her chain-covered fist as hard as she could at her jaw. Her fist connected with a thud, and the woman's head snapped back. She moaned low in her throat and fell to the ground in a heap. Arista stared down at her, panting for air, but the woman didn't move.

Everyone in the cell froze, looking at Arista. The girl in the corner pushed herself to her feet, and her gaze kept darting to the woman lying on the floor. Arista didn't know what to do next. She loosened her grip and the small length of chain unraveled. There was blood on her knuckles, but she wasn't sure whose it was.

A woman leaned over the body. After a moment, she looked up. "She ain't dead. Don't matter much—heard you'll be swinging from the rope at dawn. Corpses don't need clothes, so they'll be hers come morning."

A loud metallic *clink* sounded on the door right by her head, and she jumped away as it swung open. "You." The jailer pointed at Arista. "Outside."

She looked over her shoulder, then took several hesitant steps out of the cell.

"I warned you, gypsy." Nic stood in the doorway, his arms crossed over his chest.

What the hell was he doing there? Had he come to gloat? Rage filled her, fast and fierce, and she yanked free of the guard with a primal growl. Her fists hit his chest, but it was like striking a stone wall. Nic grabbed her hands and held them with just one of his. He leaned down very close to whisper in her ear.

"What the bloody hell were you thinking, going back to the party? Huntington couldn't wait to tell Wild what you wanted."

"I needed something on Wild. Raffer is blackmailing someone I care about, and I have to help them," she sobbed. "You have to help me, Nic."

"You should have listened to me, gypsy. There's only so much I can do to protect you now. The next time I say run, you *run*," he hissed low in her ear before spinning her around and shoving her back at the guard. Instead of catching her, the man stepped back and Arista sprawled onto the cold stone floor. A sharp pain shot through her knee.

"I see you've met my new right-hand man," Wild said, stepping from the shadows. "Ah, sorry, you two know each other already—don't you." Wild crossed to where she lay and reached down, wrapping his fingers around her neck. There was no sign of mercy in his eyes. He lifted her to her feet. "Did you really think you could double-cross me?" he growled. Arista dug at his fingers, but could not loosen his grip.

"Please." Her voice came out raspy and faint. She could barely breathe. When she kicked out at his leg, he only laughed.

Blackness crept into her vision, and she struggled against his hold. She could see Nic standing by the door, watching but not moving, not helping her. There was no emotion on his face at all. Tears burned her eyes. He would never have let anyone touch her before.

"You're a monster," she spat at him.

He finally looked away.

"Time's up," the jailer barked as he came back down the hallway. "You'll not rob anyone of a good hanging." He yanked Wild away. As soon as she was free, Arista gulped in a huge lungful of air, almost making herself ill.

Wild straightened, brushing imaginary dust off his shoulder. "It was a pleasure doing business with you, my dear. I'll be in the front row at your hanging come dawn. You've made me quite popular, now that I've caught such an infamous blackmailer. I should thank you." He bowed to her, an elaborate mocking gesture that made her feel even sicker. Then he turned and walked away.

Nic watched her for a few seconds longer, then turned and followed Wild out the door.

She screamed and lunged after him, reaching for her missing knife out of habit. The jailer grabbed her around the waist before she made it more than a few steps. Wild's contemptuous laughter echoed down the hall. Arista screamed again. The inhuman sound echoed off the stones.

She kicked and twisted and pounded her fists against the thick man's arms, but he only walked over and dumped her back into the cell. She lay where she fell and curled into a tight ball. Her shoulders shook as she tried to hold in the sobs that built inside. *Nic.* Nic had betrayed her for Wild. Agony clawed its way up her throat and choked off her air.

"I'm sorry," a small voice whispered.

There was a soft touch on her shoulder and Arista looked up into the eyes of the young girl from the corner. In her expression, Arista saw the truth.

She was going to die.

Hours later, the keys jingled again and Arista scooted backward until she came up sharply against the stone wall. What now? Had Wild decided to come back and torture her even more?

Two of the quieter girls in the back of the cell detached from the shadows and sauntered forward. They were both rough-looking, but one had cuts along her arm that looked like they needed a doctor's attention.

"What do we have tonight?" the older one asked the jailer.

"There's a new one with some coins wanting a little female company."

The girls nudged each other and the jailor laughed as they walked out of the cell. "Here's your extra bread. You can eat it while we walk. He's a mite impatient. For the rest of you lot—" he said to the room, and threw several smaller loaves onto the middle of the floor.

The door slammed shut and the other women dove at the bread, pushing and biting to get to it. Arista watched with distaste. Bones used to do things like that when they were children. He said it helped them develop a fighting edge. Arista refused to fight for her food. She would *never* use her body, either.

"I got you a piece. It ain't much, but we don't get much." The young girl handed her a piece of bread the size of her thumb.

Arista shook her head. "You eat it. I'm not hungry." The thin girl shoved it into her mouth without argument. Neither mentioned the truth that hung in the air between them. Arista would hang very soon. No use wasting bread on the dead.

"So, why are you here? I like the colors in your skirt—is it yours? I'm Grace, by the way." The girl smiled rather shyly. "It's okay, I don't mean to pry."

"I didn't steal it, it's mine. They think I killed someone, but I didn't." Grace's eyes went round and she moved away just a bit. "I promise I didn't," Arista said. The girl's nervousness made her uncomfortable, and she tried to put the girl at ease. "Why are you here, Grace?" she asked.

"My father owed a debt he couldn't pay. He gave me in exchange." Her gaze lowered to the floor.

A knot formed in Arista's stomach. "How long have you been here?"

"Two days." She raised her head and tears glistened in her eyes. "I thought he would come back for me by now."

It was a surprise that Grace had been here that long and had not been harmed—or worse, been led out of the cell to service the inmates who could barter or pay for female companionship. It wouldn't be much longer before that happened, though. The girl was too pretty to go untouched if no one came to claim her.

There wasn't anything she could do to help her. Arista looked around. How many of the women were here because of something frivolous? How many here were innocent?

In the cell, the women sat in groups of two or three. Some played games with bits of stone and straw, others chatted quietly. The one Arista had knocked out earlier lay on the ground, unmoving. They sat in silence, groans echoing in the stone walls all around them. One might go crazy from listening to that for too long.

The sudden sound of keys turning in the lock caught Arista's attention. All the women stopped what they were doing and looked up.

"You—come with me." The man pointed at Arista.

She stayed where she was. Grace gripped her arm tight with both her hands. "Why? I won't whore myself out for a piece of bread."

The jailer growled and stepped into the cell. "You're needed for other purposes. It's time to go. Now, I can drag you, or you can walk—it don't much matter to me, girl."

She glanced at Grace, who stood trembling with fear. While the girl watched with wide eyes, Arista reached under the collar of her dress and pulled the silk scarf free. The one she wore always for strength.

"It's okay," Arista whispered, even though it wasn't. She wrapped the scarf around the girl's shoulders and tied it under her chin.

"Don't give up. There is a big world out there, just waiting for you. Someone very special gave this to me and now I'm giving it to you."

Tears fell down Grace's cheeks. "Thank you, miss."

Arista fought back her own tears. This had all happened much faster than she'd expected. Was it dawn already? Arista lifted her chin and glared at their jailer.

"I can walk on my own."

The guard muttered something and slammed the door shut behind her. He started down a different hallway than Wild had exited from.

Arista's throat tightened as she followed the jailer. The hallway grew darker, and the lantern the guard held threw little light. Arista used the wall to steady her balance, and cringed at the slimy feel of the stone. The air in the tunnel grew chillier, and still they walked on. The moans and screams faded behind them, and the stale air took on an earthier quality.

"Where are we going?" she asked his back, but the man only grunted. "Am I to be hanged before dawn? With no say to my own innocence? That is not justice."

She might as well have been speaking to the stone walls for all the reaction she got from him. Finally he stopped and pulled the keys from his belt. The door opened soundlessly, and the jailer lifted the lantern high over his head. "Go." His one-word command propelled her forward, but she came up short outside the prison.

A hooded figure stepped from the shadows and handed the man a bag of coins. The jailer grabbed it and slammed the door closed behind her.

"Come quickly," the figure said. "They are not the most trustworthy sort."

Arista looked back. Whoever this was, they were saving her

from Newgate, but for what? Had Wild concocted an even worse punishment for her? "Who are you?"

"You will see in a moment, miss, but we have to hurry." The figure started across the yard. After a moment's hesitation, she followed. Wherever he was leading her, it was away from the prison.

A carriage awaited on the next corner, and when the hooded figure rapped twice on the door, it swung open. She slowed to a stop. Had Wild bought her freedom, just so he could kill her himself? Or did he plan to torture her first? She prepared herself to run.

"Where is she?" a familiar voice asked. The figure pointed at her and then lifted the hood from his head. Tomas.

And there, leaning from the carriage window, was Grae.

CHAPTER 20

*A*rista sat in the cabin of Grae's ship, fighting the rolling in her stomach that was not caused by the ship, but by the cold fury in Grae's eyes. She sat on his bed, arms wrapped around her middle. For twenty minutes, she'd been trying not to spill the contents of her stomach onto the polished wood floor. They had sat in silence for so long that she was ready to crawl out of her own skin. It didn't help that Grae had not stopped pacing back and forth in the small cabin since they'd arrived.

"How did you find me?" she finally asked.

He dragged his fingers through his hair and sat down next to her on the bunk.

"My mother sent for me when she found Father in his study. He was . . . not in a good place, but he told me what had happened. I went to your room but you were gone. I found the note you left your maid, and when I confronted her, she begged me to find you. Said that something went wrong. It wasn't until a note came to the house, addressed to Becky, that we knew where you were." He glanced at her face but didn't look her in the eye. "I couldn't leave you there. But that doesn't mean I can forgive you."

His words felt like a dagger in her heart. "I promise, Grae—I didn't know, not until tonight. I tried to fix everything . . . but nothing's changed. Everything is still so messed up. I'm so sorry." She dropped her face into her hands.

"So you didn't know my father would be asked to transport human cargo?" His voice was raw with emotion.

"No! I promise I didn't know what Wild planned to do." It was time to tell him the truth. "I knew your father owed Wild a debt, because otherwise I would never have been admitted to your home. I was supposed to go out, collect money and secrets like I did before, only this time, Wild promised me half the cut. That was my ticket to freedom. I've never had the chance to earn enough money to get Becky and myself away from London. I accepted his offer because I had nowhere else to go. I didn't know his plans, or that Lord Raffer planned to blackmail your father. He used me as well. If I had known . . ."

Wild had made sure that she remained in the dark about her role in the extortion plan. Every move he made had been calculated— from reeling Nic in, to saving her life, to setting her up in the Sinclair household. He'd played the game with the precision of a chess master.

Arista had paid with her freedom, and Grae's family was still under Wild's thumb.

"It was all for nothing. I'm so sorry." Her shoulders shook and tears dripped out from between her fingers.

"What were you trying to do tonight?" he asked.

"I was offering to give someone control over their own secret, in return for a Parliamentary investigation of Raffer. To bring his activities to light and discredit him so he couldn't make accusations against your father."

Grae sighed. He sounded so tired. "So, now what?"

"I failed. I couldn't save your family." She might as well go back to Newgate. She was as much a prisoner now as she had been then.

"There has to be something we can do. Is there anyone else you can contact?" His warm hand rested on her shoulder, and that tiny bit of comfort gave her the clarity she needed. Arista stopped and lifted her head.

"The note that said I was in Newgate—do you have it?"

Grae released her hand and reached into his pocket. The note was a crumpled-up ball of paper now. Arista pried it from his fingers and smoothed it open. She only had to glance at the writing to know who'd sent it. Nic.

"Do you recognize it?" Grae asked.

She immediately shook her head. The vile taste of guilt sat on her tongue. Why didn't she tell him about Nic?

Because then she would have to tell him everything—and somehow she knew that if he found out Nic had set her up for murder, he would be less than understanding.

She still didn't quite understand. Nic had vowed that he would never let anyone hurt her, yet he'd let Wild manhandle her. But all the while he'd known that Grae was on his way to save her. Was he just keeping up an act for Wild? Or was all of this just an act to trick her?

"We could leave London. All of us. My father is willing to move the family someplace safe," Grae said. "The ship is bound for India. Mother and Sophia have always wanted to go there."

"And what would happen to his business? To his ships? He built this for you and Sophia. So that you would have a future. There is no life in hiding, in looking over your shoulder every single day. Trust me, I know it all too well."

He sighed and leaned into her hand. The rough stubble on his cheek scratched against her fingertips. It was a sensation she wanted to feel every day for a lifetime.

"You make it hard to deny you anything." He turned his face and pressed his lips against her palm. "You asked me to trust you once, and I want to. I really do. No more secrets between us. Tell me everything and we'll figure this out together. Promise me."

Arista swallowed. How could she look him in the eye and lie to him? If she did, there would be no going back. Tears burned her eyes and she spun away.

"Don't. Please don't turn away from me again, Arista." She crossed her arms and hugged herself.

"I can't make that promise," she said softly.

Grae sighed. His eyes were watery. "Why not?"

She had to take several steps away from him to suppress the urge to throw herself into his arms and promise him anything he wanted. "My entire life is based on secrets and lies. I've done horrible things that I never want to say out loud. Isn't the fact that I stayed—that I'm trying to help you—enough?"

"No." He crossed the cabin and pulled her into his arms, against the hard planes of his chest. "And what you've done to survive doesn't matter—not to me." He shook her gently by the shoulders, then slid his hands around to cup her face in both his hands. His gaze was hard, intense, but filled with something that took her breath away. "Damn it, Arista, the fact that you've not only stayed alive, but retained your integrity—it proves how strong you are. No one deserves to be happy more than you."

Nic had told her the same thing. She wanted to believe it more than she'd wanted anything in her life.

"*No one* deserves it more than you," he said again, holding her head still so she could not look away.

"Why are you doing this?" Her voice came out scratchy and raw. He kept coming back. He kept saving her. But why? Why did he care what happened to her?

"Because I have to."

Her spine straightened. He thought she was some kind of charity case, then? She tried to pull away, but he wrapped his arms around her waist, holding her against his body.

"I have to because I'm in love with you, and the more I know about you, the more certain I am that it's real. I would never have asked you to marry me if I distrusted you."

Marriage. She still had not gotten used to the idea that Grae truly wanted her for his wife. Her stomach churned and her throat grew tight. "You only feel sorry for me. You want to help some poor little beggar girl." The words were punctuated by huge sobs ripping from her chest. He couldn't really want her or love her. She was nothing. An orphan girl with no past.

She had nothing to offer anyone. She didn't deserve happiness— isn't that what Bones had drilled into all their heads, year after year? That they were all unwanted from the beginning.

Arista twisted furiously in his arms, but he wouldn't relent. He just held her there, solid and warm and strong.

"What I see is the bravest person I know. You're kind and compassionate. You care about my family, one you've only known for a short time, but you cared enough to risk your life to help. You could have run, but you chose to stay and fight. That is not what a selfish, undeserving person would do. You have a good heart inside you. *You* are good. You still feel, Arista—I know you do. And that's why I love you."

The pressure in her chest cut off her ability to breathe. He was saying words she had longed to hear all her life. The ones she kept locked deep inside her mind.

"Please stop," she begged through her tears.

"I will tell you the same thing every day for the rest of your life until you believe it."

Her shoulders shook and she tried to pry his arms from around her. She opened her mouth to drag air into her lungs, but a deep sob escaped. More followed, until her entire body shook violently.

Her legs crumpled and Grae held her upright. Something inside her let go. She clung to him as if her life depended on it. Dug her nails into the back of his jacket while he whispered words she couldn't understand through her grief. The years of bottled-up feelings burst free in huge waves. She'd fought against feeling anything for so long that the rush of emotions was overwhelming.

As the sobs grew weaker, her limbs felt as if they were weighted down with stone. As if he knew, Grae carefully lifted her into his arms and walked across to the bunk, where he deposited her carefully. He brushed his lips over her forehead and pulled a quilt up over her body. Before she could protest, he sat in the chair closest to the bed. "Rest. I'll be here when you wake. I promise."

She wanted to talk more, but heaviness pushed down against her eyelids, forcing them closed. She would be no good to anyone if she were too exhausted to move. Maybe a short rest, before she had to do what she still planned on doing . . .

"Captain, I've got a message. . . ." The knock and the man's voice came at the same time. Arista pulled away and ducked her head.

"Begging your pardon, sir, I didn't know you had a guest. This came from your father's house, and the lad said it were urgent." The man handed Grae a note and backed out of the room. The door clicked shut behind him.

"Sorry about that," Grae said. She could hear the smile in his voice. "My men aren't used to their captain entertaining women aboard the ship." His confession produced a most pleasing feeling of contentment in her chest.

"I should see what it is, though. Father never sends me messages about urgent matters. He comes himself." Grae slid his thumb under the wax and broke the seal. After a few quick seconds, his expression changed.

Grae handed the letter to her. "I believe this is for you."

Her hand shook as she took the letter.

> *Gypsy ~*
>> *I've got what you asked for. Meet at our spot at dusk.*
>> *~N*

"Who is it from?" Grae asked.

"A friend," she whispered.

Arista stared at the crudely written words. She'd taught Nic to write years ago, after Becky had taught her, but he'd never managed to get past the basic steps. The letters were uneven and jagged.

Grae took the note and read it. "Who's N? Where is this spot?"

"I . . ." The words died on her lips. She'd told Nic she needed something on Wild. Did this mean he had it?

"How well do you know this person?" Grae asked.

Once, Arista might have said she trusted him with her life. Now? She wasn't sure. He had saved her by sending the note to Becky, but he was also the one who'd set her up for murder. Still, he'd warned her about Wild, and he'd given her Bones's secrets. That must mean he did still care what happened to her.

It really didn't matter, though, because if he had something that could free Grae's father from Raffer's grasp, she'd do anything. Take any risk to get it.

"I know him well enough." She watched his jaw flex.

"You want to meet him? How do you know it's not a trap?"

She didn't. That was the biggest unknown in all this. Something in his eyes at Newgate gave her hope that he didn't really want her to die. *Next time I say run, you run,* he'd told her.

Nic had been working for Wild. He must have something she could use to blackmail the Thief Taker into calling off Raffer. She just needed *one* secret. Something irrefutable that could be used if needed. Something that would scare Wild.

But Grae would never understand. She watched as he paced the length of the cabin like a caged tiger. Frustration rolled off him like the waves lapping at the ship's hull.

"What about your safety? If you leave the ship, you'll be arrested immediately. They know who you are now. Everyone has seen your face under the mask. It's too risky."

Arista stood on wobbly legs and walked across the room to him. "Grae." Her hand shook as she raised it to his face. When she touched his cheek, he froze. Neither of them dared to breathe.

"I appreciate everything, more than you'll ever know," she said softly. "But for the first time in my life, I can control something. I can keep people I care about from getting hurt. I wasn't always able to do that, and it will haunt me until I die. This is a small way to make amends."

"I'll go instead." He stopped pacing and stood with his arms crossed over his chest. A surge of love filled her, so sweet and overwhelming that it brought tears to her eyes. This had to work. If Grae's family fell apart because of her, she would never forgive herself.

"We can go together," she finally conceded. "But I need Becky. Tell her to bring me the traveling bag that's in the back of the wardrobe. It has everything we'll need. I can't leave London without it or her."

"I'll take care of it myself. You can stay here on the ship. It's safe and you can rest. My men won't let anyone on. I'll be back very soon and we can finish this business and then . . ." He leaned closer. His kiss was soft, gentle. "We can set sail and start our lives together."

Grae meant it to be a brief, parting kiss, but she realized it might be the last time, and her hand snaked up his arm and held the back of his neck. She tangled her fingers into his hair. When he started to pull back, she moved closer and deepened the kiss. Desire and sorrow twisted together inside her, fueling the burning need to be as close as possible to him. Just one last time, in case things went bad.

"Arista," he murmured against her lips. Her tears threatened to spill over, so she closed her eyes. They sat like that for a few precious minutes. When he finally tore himself away, his chest rose and fell with his rapid breaths. There was a soft look in his eyes. She could see the love in them.

"I love you." His lips curled up in a tender smile that almost undid her resolve. He did. She could see it clearly. He really did love her.

It took all her strength to smile back. Her lips trembled with the effort. When the door closed behind him, the tears finally slipped free. She brushed them aside.

This was not the end.

In Grae's wardrobe, she found several jackets hanging neatly side by side. She took the one that looked most well-worn. Grae's familiar scent of cedar and exotic spices enveloped her. She slid her arms into the sleeves and turned the collar up. The sleeves hung well past her fingertips, and the shoulders hit halfway down her arms, but it would have to do.

She couldn't help burying her nose in the fabric and inhaling deeply before she reached for the smallest-looking set of trousers. She paused at the sound of movement near the cabin door. She pressed her back against the wall and waited. After only a minute, whoever-it-was left, and Arista heard steps going back up to the deck. The air whooshed out between her teeth.

Arista walked around the cabin, running her fingers along the shiny wood surfaces, committing every detail to memory. Everything was neat and orderly—the heavy wood furniture built into the walls and secured to the floor to prevent movement when the ship was at sea. The spicy scent of cedar and salty sea air filled the space. Grae smelled exactly the same.

She would never forget the combination.

He'd sat in that chair. Worked at that desk. Slept in that bed. A shiver of excitement danced over her skin at the thought. She ran her hand over the quilt they had both laid on. Her pulse quickened, and she removed her hand hastily. She could spend all day simply touching things that belonged to him. But that would not solve her problem.

With one more quick check to make sure the door was locked,

she unlaced the corset and threw it onto the bed, then pulled her stained shirt free from the waistband of the skirt.

A noise outside the door had her scrambling into the stolen clothes. She waited, her heart in her throat, but no one tried to enter the cabin. Arista gathered her gypsy disguise and tucked it under the mattress. Carefully, she slid the lock free and opened the door. The hall remained empty. She started out, then realized that she had not remembered to take a cap. Anyone with eyes could see she was a girl. Grae had to have one somewhere.

She checked the cupboards and the built-in wardrobe, and found nothing except more clothing. A smaller chest sat at the foot of the bed. It was the only place that she hadn't checked, because it was locked. But people were predictable, and she went to the desk to check for the key. Sure enough, in the second smallest drawer, she found the key that fit the lock.

Before she opened it, Arista hesitated. No one kept their hats under lock and key. What if she found something inside that changed her opinion of Grae—that proved he wasn't as sincere as she thought? What if his darkest secrets were inside this chest? Her hands shook as she lifted the top.

On top of a stack of papers, the first thing Arista saw was a black raven feather. It was the one she'd lost from her mask the night they met. Becky had fussed mightily over it, too. The feather was still sleek and soft, and she ran her fingers over it. A smile teased her lips. Grae had kept this as a memento of her.

She ran the feather across her lips, and then set it aside. There was nothing else but papers, maps marked up with ink, coordinates that made no sense to her. After replacing the feather, she closed the lid and turned the key.

She'd have to go back below deck, where the crew would most

certainly have many caps. Hopefully her luck would hold. She crept back to the stairs and quietly went down into the dark room.

Every member of the crew should have a cap in their belongings. The first trunk had none, nor the second. She moved to another, farther away from the porthole. She fumbled with the trunk's clasp.

"You there—what are you doing down here?" The voice boomed across the room and Arista froze. "All hands on deck."

"Right there, sir," Arista mumbled. She'd slipped back into the rough tones of the street and kept her voice low. "Forgot my cap, sir."

The man grunted. "Git yer arse back on deck."

Arista threw up the trunk's lid and hoped with all her might that this one had a cap.

"Time's up. If you don't move now, boy, I'll whip yer backside."

She swallowed back the sob of frustration. There had to be one. She dug her fingers through the fabric, searching for the familiar feel of wool. Boots stomped behind her, getting closer. If he got her in the light, he'd know the truth. Grae would be summoned, and she'd have to explain what she was doing. Her plan would fall apart.

"Got it!" She pulled the cap free, slammed the trunk and slipped it over her head. Using the dark to hide her face, she darted past the man.

"I'll just get back to work, sir," she said.

She didn't see his hand, but a sharp burst of pain bit into her ear. "Next time, when I tell ye to do something, boy—do it."

"Yes, sir." Arista ran up the stairs, down the hall, and above deck before he could do worse. The sunlight blinded her for a moment and she stumbled to a stop. Men were busy everywhere. Some were rolling barrels toward the open hatch on the far side of the deck. Others climbed through the rigging, each with a coil of rope slung through one arm, to repair any signs of wear. None paid her any attention.

Except the man coming up the steps behind her.

"You waitin' for an invite, guvnor? Get yer arse to work." As soon as she heard him, Arista bolted across the deck. So much for slipping away unnoticed. By the time he realized she meant to cross over the gangplank, he was too late to stop her. A shout came from behind her and a hand reached out, but she ducked and spun away, barely escaping the grasp of a great, burly man. In one leap she was on the narrow plank connecting the ship to the wharf.

Don't look down.

If she fell, she was dead. She would sink to the bottom of the Thames and never resurface. The board jerked and Arista shrieked. She windmilled her arms to keep her balance, and barely kept herself upright. She raced across the last few feet and jumped onto the solid wood of the wharf.

When she looked back, no one was giving chase, but the man who had clobbered her upside the head stood with his arms crossed over his chest.

"Don't ye be showing yer face back here, boy, or I'll beat you and throw you to the fish."

Arista didn't wait to hear any more. Her boots skidded on the damp wood as she ran toward Fleet Street. She would meet with Nic, beg him to help her—but the first thing she had to do was find a weapon.

Because the most important lesson Nic had ever taught her was not to trust anyone.

CHAPTER 21

*I*t had been too easy to steal the wicked-looking knife from the butcher's stall at the market. Concealing it, on the other hand, proved to be a challenge, and she ended up taking another, smaller knife instead. It wasn't intimidating to look at, but she could still wield it with precision. It was carefully tucked in her waistband now.

She kept her head low as she moved among the crowd of shoppers. Blending in was effortless, and soon she was past the people and skirting the riverbank. The stench of the water was thick in the air. Children in rags ran along the edge, pulling out anything that looked like it could be sold. It was something she had done as a child, too.

Her time away from this part of London, where squalor lurked in every crevice, made her realize how bad it really was. Had she truly lived there all her life? She walked with her forearm over her nose to try and keep some of the noxious smell out of her lungs. Cool air battered her face, bringing the stench even closer. How could she have forgotten the smell?

Only a few more blocks and she'd be at the small dock where

she'd spent so many nights wishing for a different life. A few men passed, pulling heavy carts filled with coal. Their skin was covered in soot, their clothes stained with black smudges. She gave them a wide berth, as much for their smell as to avoid attracting notice.

The closer she got to the warehouse, the fewer people she passed.

The old warehouse that sat back from their small dock would be the perfect place to hide and make sure Nic came alone. She hoped he did. If not, it meant that he really had changed—had become the person she dreaded he would.

Someone had boarded up the doorway, but the wood was rotted through, and the boards came away easily enough. After a quick glance around, she slipped inside. The air inside smelled musty with age. Light filtered in from the side of the building that had burned, so she picked her way over to where the cargo would have been loaded into the warehouse. Where the doors met, there was an opening the width of her hand. Perfect. She could watch the waterfront and remain unseen.

She took a roll from her pocket, one she had actually paid a half pence for, and bit into it. As she chewed, the noises around her became clearer. Rats scratched through the debris somewhere behind her. The low horn of a freight barge made the wood under her feet vibrate. The huge vessel came into view to her right, and she watched its lazy progress.

A lone figure moved into her line of sight. He was dressed in a black coat and had a wool cap pulled down low. It could be Nic, or it could be a random worker. Or it could be Wild. Arista stayed hidden.

The person stopped and looked out over the river. He thrust his hands into his pockets, a move so very familiar that her heart ached. It was Nic. But was he alone?

She waited. Several long minutes passed, but he didn't step away from the riverbank. The first move, it seemed, would have to be hers. She got up and walked out, carefully scanning the shadows around the building for movement. She waited again, behind the pile of broken crates, before stepping out into the open.

She must have made a sound, because Nic turned and their eyes met. She closed the distance between them until they only stood a foot apart and she had to look up to see the expression on his face. "I wasn't sure if you'd come," he said.

"Is this another trick? Will I be framed for another murder today?"

Nic cringed and would not meet her eyes. "No. You don't understand. I tried to tell you to leave—that Wild knew what you were doing—but you came back."

"Why didn't he just kill me instead of setting me up for murder?"

"Wild needed a scapegoat. By taking down Lady A, he would solidify his place as Thief Taker. Things have gotten . . . bad, gypsy. People are accusing him of working both sides. He needed this in order to keep his position untarnished."

"How long has he been planning this?" A sick feeling turned in her stomach. When Nic didn't answer, she took a step closer, forcing him to acknowledge her. "How long, Nic?"

"Months," he finally said.

"So all of this—everything that's happened—was all to get to this point. To set me up so he could save himself. And you went along with it? You dragged me into it, knowing what would happen? I thought we were friends. I *trusted* you. Did you know that Bones almost killed me that night? Did you know that he beat Becky so badly, she probably won't be able to use her right eye again? Do you even care?"

Instead of being contrite, Nic's eyes narrowed. "It was hard for all of us. We were nearing the end of our usefulness, gypsy. Did you think we'd just be able to walk away when Bones was done? Live like *normal* people? I was trying to save us both." He paced back and forth in front of her.

"Is Wild waiting around the corner to kill me himself?" she asked.

"Christ, no! I had no idea that when Wild approached me, he had this planned out. It wasn't until the Luckettes' party that I knew everything, and by then, it was too late. If I'd crossed him, he would have done worse than kill me."

"So you framed me for murder?"

Nic drew his fingers through his hair and exhaled sharply. "I thought I could get you out. The jailers there are known for their greed, and I still have the money I took from Bones. But Wild kept me right by his side afterward. The only thing I could do was send that note to Becky, and hope that the man I've seen you with cared enough to go get you."

Her stomach twisted into knots. So much could have gone wrong.

"You were never alone, gypsy. I promised to always look out for you, and I did."

"By betraying me? By lying? By handing me to Wild on a silver platter?" Arista made a fist and slammed it into his gut. His sudden exhalation did little to quell her anger, and she turned away before he could see the tears in her eyes.

"All you've ever wanted was freedom, gypsy. Yet just when you could have taken it, you chose to stay and help a family of strangers. The girl I knew would never have sacrificed herself for anyone."

Arista clenched her hands at her sides. "I am not that girl anymore."

"I know." Nic stared at her, as if memorizing every feature. He tilted his head. "You *are* different. Softer. Even dressed as a boy I can see it. Are you happy, gypsy? Really happy?"

She thought of Grae, of Sophia, of Grae's parents, and nodded. "I feel like I belong. There are people who care about me. Who want me."

He lifted his hand and cupped her cheek. "You were always wanted, gypsy. But even a blind man could see you were never cut out for this life."

He dropped his hand to his pocket and pulled out a stack of papers that had been rolled and tied together.

"This is what you need to blackmail Wild." He hesitated, and when he looked at her, regret shone from his eyes. "I'm sorry for everything, gypsy. I never meant for you to get hurt." He took her hand and gently placed the packet in it. His thumb stroked her fingers.

"I had hoped that one day, we could go away together—maybe we still can?"

She sucked in a shallow breath. How long she had wanted, needed, to hear those words from him. If he had told her this on the night of the fire, she would have gone with him without hesitation. But everything had changed in a matter of weeks. She shook her head and pulled her hand from his grasp.

Instead of being angry at her withdrawal, a sad smile curved his lips up. "I knew the answer already. I've seen you with him. And I know you almost better than you know yourself." He gripped both of her shoulders so she would have to look at him. "You do deserve to be happy, gypsy, despite what you've been told your whole life. Give him a chance. Only one of us is worthy of a second chance, and it's most definitely not me."

Her lower lip trembled, and she swallowed the sob that was building in her throat. "This"—she lifted the packet—"if I use it, he will know that you betrayed him."

Nic shrugged, as if his life were not in danger now. "It was worth it. Maybe this one good deed will make up for a lifetime of mistakes."

"I'll make sure he doesn't hurt you," she said, clutching the packet to her chest. "But you should leave London, too." She wasn't asking him to come with her. Disappointment flashed over his face before he quickly hid it.

"Don't worry about me. I'll be okay."

It was time to go. It was harder than she thought it would be to say goodbye.

"I just want to . . ." Three figures stepped from the shadow of the warehouse. Her blood ran cold. Two were great burly men, and the one between them was covered by a long cloak.

"You lied," she gasped.

Nic spun around, and before she could pull her knife free, he had pushed her behind him. "Run, gypsy." The fear in his voice was real. He didn't know these men.

"No, I'm not leaving you alone."

Nic growled low in his throat. "Gypsy, please."

"There's no way I'm . . ." The words faded. She knew the two men standing a few feet away. They were the same ones that had beaten her before the fire. Then the man in the middle pushed his hood back. Shock sent the words into hiding. "You're alive," she gasped.

Bones sneered at her. The burnt flesh that clung to his face in black patches made him look more monstrous than he ever had before. Huge, gaping wounds covered his neck, and his hands were blackened and misshapen. Bile raced up her throat.

He leaned heavily on his cane and when he breathed, the wheezing noise sent chills through her body.

"No thanks to you, girl," he snarled. "And you," he pointed a blackened finger at Nic, "you stole from me, boy. You know the punishment for stealing, don't ya?"

"I'm not afraid of you anymore," Nic spat.

Bones took a step forward and laughed. "You'll pay for your treachery, boy. I know what you did—turned on me to work with the Thief Taker. I've been watching you all this time. Did you think I was stupid, boy? I knew it was just a matter of time before I'd get you alone. Didn't expect I'd have the chance to take care of that one too, though. Shoulda put you both down when you were young. More trouble than you both were worth."

Arista watched the two men draw closer. She had her knife out and ready, as did Nic. The men split off, and came at them from opposite sides. Arista lunged for the same man who had driven his fists into her stomach over and over on the night of the fire.

He twisted, moving far more gracefully than she'd expected for someone of his size, and knocked her wrist with the thick piece of wood she had missed. It immediately went numb and the knife fell into the dirt at her feet. He kicked it away and she heard a splash. From behind her she heard grunts and the sound of fists hitting flesh.

"Tell me where those papers are, and I'll let you go," Bones wheezed.

"Never," Nic gasped. Blood dripped from one cut on his lip and another over his eye. Already the blows on his jaw were making his face swell, and she saw the way he winced every time he took a breath in.

"Very well then." Bones nodded and the man holding Nic

yanked his arms behind his back so hard that Nic groaned. Then the other man started pounding his fists into Nic's stomach.

"*Stop!*" Her pleas fell on deaf ears. The man continued to pummel Nic. Nic's eyes were now fluttering open and closed.

"All right!" Arista shouted. "Here." She thrust the rolled-up papers at Bones and he took them from her. The man stopped his assault and Nic hung limp between them.

"Let him go," Bones said. His smile turned malicious as his gaze moved to the river.

"No!" Arista started beating her fists against the closest man's arm, but he backhanded her as if she were nothing but an annoying insect. She caught herself before her face hit the ground and stayed there for several seconds, fighting back the wave of sickness that washed over her.

It was the splash that brought clarity to her fuzzy mind. They had thrown Nic in the river. In his current state, he would surely drown—she had to save him—

But she couldn't swim.

Without thinking, Arista pushed off the ground and launched herself at Bones. His lackeys were at the river's edge, so it gave her time to push Bones to the ground and plant her boot in his gut over and over. He curled in on himself and grunted each time her boot made contact.

She knew there were only precious seconds before the two men saw her, so she grabbed the papers out of Bones's hand and threw them as far as she could toward the warehouse. Stumbling toward the river, she screamed for help, and heard an answering shout in the distance. Out of the corner of her eye, she saw the lackeys take off.

Nic had floated too far for her to reach from the end of the small dock. She ran to the riverbank and waded into the water, but it was up to her waist before she could reach him.

"Help me." She splashed out farther and the cold water rose over her chest; she couldn't breathe through the panic clouding her head. Tears streamed down her face and her voice grew hoarse. The water lapped at her chin, and the acrid taste of the river coated her tongue every time she shouted. The current tugged at her feet, making it nearly impossible to stand up. If she didn't go back, she would be swept deeper into the river.

But she had to save Nic.

One summer, Nic had been determined to teach Arista how to swim. He'd showed her over and over again how to kick with her legs and paddle with her arms, and it had done no good. She'd never learned. But now she had no choice.

With her eyes on Nic's body, Arista shoved off the river bottom and plunged toward him. She kicked and paddled with every ounce of strength she had, trying to keep her face above water.

When the river closed over her head, she panicked, thrashing her way to the surface just long enough to suck in a breath before she went under. The next time she pulled herself above the water, she'd lost sight of Nic, but it didn't matter because she sank yet again.

Her muscles screamed in protest. Cramps were seizing her legs, making it impossible to keep kicking. She had no strength left to try and fight her way to the surface again. Water clogged her nose and mouth. She fought the urge to draw it into her lungs, and they burned. An eerie silence filled her head.

Slowly, she began to sink.

Then, suddenly, her jacket tightened around her chest and water rushed past her body. An explosion of sound and light erupted around her and she instinctively sucked in choking breaths of air. An arm wrapped around her middle and she was pulled against a solid body.

"I've got you." The familiar timbre of Grae's voice unleashed the torrent of fear bottled inside her. She grabbed his arm and sobbed. When she felt ground under her feet, her legs were useless. Grae picked her up and carried her to the riverbank as she wrapped her arms around his neck. Her entire body shook uncontrollably.

"I told you I would save you if you ever fell in the water," he said, setting Arista tenderly on the ground before he lowered himself to sit next to her. Then Becky was there, her face wet with tears, putting Grae's jacket around Arista's shoulders.

She threw it off and struggled to stand. Nic. She had to save Nic. "I have to . . ." Her gaze was drawn to three men swimming to where he'd drifted, almost at the middle of the river. They began pulling him toward the riverbank and Arista struggled to get to him. Grae wrapped his arms around her from behind and held her tight.

"They've got him," he said.

She frantically searched for any sign of life as the men carefully pulled him from the water and lay him on the riverbank. They were talking in hushed voices, but from their tone, she knew.

"I couldn't get to him," Arista sobbed. "I tried, but I just couldn't."

Grae pulled her into his arms and held her face against his chest as she cried.

"It's over," she whispered, looking up at Grae. Then her glance slid to Becky. "It was Bones. He did that to Nic." She looked past her friend to the spot where she'd last seen Bones, but of course he wasn't there. The packet? Had he taken it with him?

"Bones is alive?" Becky gasped.

Of course there was no sign of her tormentor or his lackeys. But . . . "The secrets." Arista tried to free herself, but Grae kept her in his grasp.

"You need to be still. You inhaled half the Thames," he said.

"Becky—there, by the warehouse. I threw the packet that Nic gave me. Will you see if it's there?" If it was, then this had not all been for nothing.

Becky hurried away, searching the ground as she went.

"I'm sorry," Arista said to Grae. "For lying to you again."

"Nothing else matters, except that you're alive. When we got back to the ship and you were missing, I wanted to tear the thing apart. My first mate remembered a boy running from the ship. Becky knew the place that the note mentioned, and we were able to get to you in time." His entire body shuddered against hers. "I came so close to losing you. If we had been only a few seconds longer . . ."

She laid her face against his wet shirt. "But you weren't. You saved me. Again."

"Miss!" Becky's excited shout rose above Grae's heartbeat in her ear. "I've got it."

This time Grae allowed her to stand as Becky came rushing over. The papers, still rolled tightly, were right there.

"What is it?" Grae asked.

Arista shook her head. "I have no idea. But Nic gave his life to get it to me." Grae gently touched her arm. He watched the river and, from the expression on his face, Arista knew what he saw. Becky took the papers from Arista's numb fingers.

Arista stared at the spot where the men had left Nic's body on the riverbank. She had to be sure. As she stood and started toward them, Grae fell into step beside her. She stopped and looked up at him. "I need to do this alone. I hope you can understand that."

"Of course. I'm here when you need me." Grae pressed his lips to her forehead.

"Thank you," she whispered.

It was the hardest thing she'd ever done, taking that short walk. The way the men stood, so solemnly, told her that it was too late. That Nic was gone. They moved aside as she stepped closer.

"I'm sorry, lad. He were gone before we got to him." The closest man dragged his cap off his head and hugged it to his chest.

Arista stared down at Nic's body. He looked peaceful, as if he were only sleeping. He'd not been in the river long enough to look like any of the bloated corpses she'd seen dragged out of it. Her knees weakened and she sank down next to him. His flesh was cool as she took his hand.

"I'm sorry. I'm so sorry." Her head fell forward and she pressed her lips to the back of his hand. His hair was matted to his forehead, and she gently pushed it away from his face. The gash Bones's men had left on his temple remained, but only a small trickle of blood ran from it now.

Great sobs erupted from her chest. He couldn't be gone. Not Nic. She draped herself over his chest, willing him to take a breath, but he remained still.

"Lad, they've brought a cart to carry the body. Is there someplace we can take it?" the man asked.

Grae helped Arista to her feet and wrapped one arm around her shoulders, pulling her against his chest. She clung to the sound of his heartbeat, so strong and sure and alive under her ear.

"I'll take care of the arrangements," Grae said. "Please have the body taken to the coroner, and give him my name, Graeden

Sinclair. I will be there to take care of everything in the morning."
Grae gave each of the men a shilling and their eyes went wide.

"Aye, Mr. Sinclair, I'll take care of it myself," the man said.
"Don't you worry about a thing."

"He's really gone, isn't he?" Arista whispered.

"I'm afraid so," Grae said, pressing his lips to her temple.

Arista lifted her head to look at Grae. "He saved me. All my life
he looked out for me, made sure no one ever harmed me. And in
the end, I couldn't help him. He died protecting me."

"Anyone who knows you would do the same." Grae stared
intently into her eyes. She saw everything there. The relief; the fear;
the love.

"I want to learn to swim. When we get to India, will you teach
me?"

"Anything you want is yours." Grae led her past the warehouse,
where Becky was standing next to the carriage. Tomas was pacing
next to her, and when they got close enough he yanked off his cap.
"Are you okay, miss?"

"I'm okay, Tomas." Grae gently lifted her and set her in the carriage, then climbed up beside her. Becky sat across from them, her
fingers wrapped tightly around the roll of papers.

Tomas grabbed the reins and looked over his shoulder. "Are we
set, then?" he asked. Grae and Becky both looked at Arista.

After one last glance toward the river, where the men were loading Nic's covered body onto a cart, she nodded. "Yes, Tomas. Let's
go home."

CHAPTER 22

wo days later, Arista and Grae sat at a corner table at Lloyd's Coffeehouse. Arista had dressed in some of Tomas's clothes, disguised as a boy, as she was still a wanted criminal.

When Wild walked in, he didn't see them at first. It gave Arista the opportunity to study him. He looked wary, and the loss of confidence made him seem almost like a different man. And, just as she had specified in her note, Wild had come alone.

Grae turned and waved at him. Wild's glance immediately slid to her, and she met his stare head-on. There would be no cowering before him today. "Sit," she said, her voice still hoarse from the water in her lungs.

When he didn't move, she looked up at him with one raised eyebrow. "You're here on my terms this time. I'd suggest you make yourself comfortable, because I have a lot to say to you, and you will listen to it all very carefully."

Wild growled low in his throat. A tic began at the corner of his eye. Once he realized that she would not be intimidated, he pulled out a chair and sat down.

"This is what will happen," Arista began. "First, you will 'find' a witness to Lord Huntington's stabbing who will swear that it was a man he saw that night—and you will drop all allegations against me. Second, you will tell Raffer that he may never contact the Sinclairs again."

Wild actually snorted. "How do you expect me to do that, exactly? He paid handsomely for that information."

Arista waved her hand in the air. "You're creative. You'll figure something out. All I care about is that Grae's family will be freed from his blackmail. If he tries to collect in any way, I *will* take you down. Weigh that consequence for motivation." Her words came out coldly. In truth, she cared nothing for Wild. All her years watching Bones deal unemotionally with people had taught her the skills she needed now. "Do we have a deal?"

Wild clenched his fingers into a fist and glared at her. He did not like being the one who was told what to do. "How do I know you even have anything to use against me? You're bluffing."

Arista smiled. She knew he'd ask—would have been disappointed if he had not. Men like him always wanted proof. She reached into the inside pocket of her jacket and took out a folded piece of parchment.

Wild immediately snatched it from her grasp, and she noticed how his face turned a shade paler. It should. The list of names and addresses and items, printed clearly in neat rows, detailed exactly what Wild had stolen from each house. And how much the owners had paid to get it all back—in reward money, of course.

"Very nice of you to keep such meticulous records of your crimes," Grae said. Arista tried not to laugh. Wild crumpled the paper in his fist and glared at her.

"I have the rest of the ledger somewhere safe," she said. "Now, what do you have for me?" He reached into his jacket and pulled out a thin stack of papers, tied together with butcher's string. The rest of the secrets that Nic had stolen from Bones.

They would meet the same fate as the ones had Nic left for her, and be returned to their owners. Arista took the packet from Wild and pushed her chair back. "I expect the other terms of this deal to be implemented without delay. I'll wait for word that everything is in order." The sum she demanded was more than they needed, but Wild had the money, and she wanted to make sure that he paid for the pain and suffering he'd caused.

Wild glared at her, and she had no doubt he was contemplating sticking a dagger through her heart right there in the coffeehouse. But he wouldn't dare. Without the upper hand, he was a coward.

"If you think to double-cross me, don't," she said. "The information I have is in very capable hands, and if anything happens to me, it will be posted on the front page of the *Spectator.* Are we clear?" Wild didn't answer, but his clenched fists and hard jaw said it all. He would cooperate. He knew he had no choice.

"It's been a pleasure doing business," Arista said with a big smile. She closed her eyes for a brief moment. *Thank you, Nic. You did set me free, after all.*

Wild stood and pushed back the chair so hard, it almost tipped over. He left without a second glance. Only then did Arista dare to exhale. "We did it."

"I would love to show you how happy that makes me," Grae said, "but we may raise a few eyebrows, even in this tolerant atmosphere." Laughter danced in his eyes.

Arista smiled back—a real smile. A happy smile.

"So, are you ready for this?" Grae asked.

Arista took a deep breath and nodded. "Yes."

They stood and went outside to where Tomas waited with the carriage. "All set, miss?" He already knew where to go. Arista gripped Grae's hand and nodded again. He squeezed it back, and she took some of the strength he offered. It was strange to rely on someone else, yet at the same time, she couldn't imagine him not being there.

Tomas guided the horse through the crowded streets with precision and skill, and soon they were back at Grae's home. Arista changed quickly, and soon they were off again. It was not long after that that Tomas slowed the carriage to a stop in front of an iron gate. The sign read CROSSING ROADS CEMETERY.

Grae got out first and helped her down. She still had to be careful until Wild cleared her of murder, but not many people knew that she had escaped from Newgate. The ones who did would not turn her in—either out of love or fear.

"Would you wait here?" she asked Grae, half expecting him to argue. He had barely let her out of his sight to sleep.

"Of course." He crossed his arms and leaned back against the carriage. "Take all the time you need."

She couldn't thank him enough, for this and for making sure that Nic wasn't thrown into an unmarked pauper's grave. He'd made sure that Nic had a proper spot, with a simple stone to mark it.

"Here are the flowers you asked for, miss." Tomas handed her a large bouquet of daisies.

"Thank you, Tomas."

A groundskeeper directed her to where Nic had been buried. The mound of fresh dirt made the tears flow again. She'd cried more in the past few days than she had in her whole life. She ran her fingers over the three letters carved on the stone:

NIC

That was all she had known him as. None of them had ever had a last name.

Tears dripped off her chin and fell into the dirt below as she laid the flowers down. Nic would have hated getting flowers. She thought of the face he would have made, and smiled. "Thank you, Nic."

She took out the letter that she'd found wrapped in the papers Nic had stolen from Wild. She smoothed the paper and stared down at the crudely written words.

> *Gypsy,*
>
> *This weren't how it were supposed to go. You and me, that were always the plan, but you wanted out—I saw it in your eyes that night. I'm not good like you. My soul were blackened a long time ago. You're right, I took the letters and money that night and left you behind. I did let you suffer and I will never forgive myself for that.*
>
> *I didn't kill Huntington. I did take your knife, but I gave it to Wild. I didn't know what he had planned. I hope you used what I gave you, and got everything you ~~want~~ deserve. I've always wanted you to be happy.*
>
> *You always thought you were nobody because you didn't have a future, but you do, gypsy. Everyone does. Find yours. Find it so you can finally be free.*
>
> *Live happy, gypsy. Out of all of us, you deserve it the most.*
>
> *Nic*

She brushed the tears from her cheeks and took a ragged breath. "There was a girl in Newgate that reminded me of myself. Except she didn't have anyone to watch out for her, like I had you. Her name is Grace, and I paid for her freedom. She's with the Sinclairs as a kitchen helper. She won't ever have to live the kind of life we did. I know she's just one of too many, but maybe I can give her a chance. Like the one you gave me."

She hesitated, then kissed her fingertips and pressed them to the stone letters of his name.

Finally, she stood. A slight breeze wafted across the cemetery, lifting the ribbons of her bonnet to dance along her shoulders. The day dress in a matching shade of blue had been a traveling gift from Sophia; Becky's skilled needlework made it fit to perfection in only one afternoon.

To anyone watching, she was just a normal girl. But, for the first time in her life, she *felt* normal as well. Nic had given her this opportunity for a better life.

Strangely enough, Wild had given her a family.

And Grae: he had given her unconditional love.

Arista glanced toward the carriage. Grae stood with his arms crossed over his chest, watching her. They were meeting the family at the docks in an hour to say goodbye. Marguerite had been overjoyed by the news of the engagement, and had insisted that Grae give Arista a ring that belonged to his grandmother.

She glanced down at her finger. The beautiful sapphire glistened in the sun. The Sinclairs had welcomed her and Becky into their home; their family.

She would finally see India with Grae, and could not imagine sharing it with anyone else.

The thought filled her with excitement, but she felt she could find happiness anywhere now.

With Grae by her side, she would always be home.

ACKNOWLEDGMENTS

First, I would like to thank the team at Hyperion for everything. I could not have asked for better editors; from the immediate enthusiasm of Emily Meehan to the kick-butt feedback of Laura Schreiber. With Laura's help, *Tangled Webs* is a thousand times better than when I started and something I am so proud to share. Anna Leuchtenberger was the most amazing copy editor, and as for the cover—can you say LOVE!? Whitney Manger did such an incredible job capturing the story in just an image.

Next, I need to give props to Mandy Hubbard. When it comes to agents, she is a superstar, hands down. I would not be where I am without her guidance and support. She keeps me grounded, but encourages the crazy ideas I send her at midnight on a Sunday. And if all that wasn't enough, she has cows. For real.

I have such an amazing crit partner and friend in Joy George. You rock, BÉBÉ! I could not keep my head on straight if not for you. Keep on kicking my butt, and I will do the same for you! We got this!

Writing is such a solitary endeavor most days, and having a great support group makes all the difference. Everyone should have friends like the girls at YA Highway, if only to remind you that you aren't alone. I am surrounded by such talented, amazing women: Kris, Kaits, Kate, KrJr, Sarah, Vee, Amy, Kir, Leila, Deb, Steph, and Sumayyah, I love you guys!!

Todd and the boys. My family is amazing enough to give me time to do this thing I love, and not complain when I forget to make dinner sometimes. I could not do this without their support, and I love you guys so much. The rest of you guys; my mom and step-father, sister, niece, cousins, and co-workers who read what I write, it is so humbling, and it means the world to me.

Finally, my readers. You all are the real superstars. I do this for you and still can't quite believe people are reading my words. Thank you all so much!

Y Bro
Bross, Lee,
Tangled webs /